THE ACCARDI TWINS BOOK ONE

COLD KING
of *New York*

SIOBHAN DAVIS

ISBN-13: 978-1-916651-07-4

Edited by Kelly Hartigan (XterraWeb) editing.xterraweb.com
Proofread by Final Polish Proofreading
Research and critique by The Critical Touch
Cover design by Robin Harper of Wicked By Design
Cover imagery © depositphotos.com
Formatted by Ciara Turley using Vellum

BOOK DESCRIPTION

Seducing the enemy was the goal—not falling for my mafia boss.

As a rookie spy, my first mission is to seduce the Irish mafia boss's brother and prove he is behind the threat to the *mafioso* in The Big Apple.

It's a dream job.

Except my new boss is sucking all the joy from my life. Don Joshua Accardi seems way too invested in my personal safety, and he's constantly scolding me for taking too many risks.

Gone is the friendly older guy I knew growing up. His ex's betrayal changed him. Now, Joshua is a cold, controlling man living his life by a rigid set of self-imposed rules.

He thinks he can push me around and I'll do his bidding like every other woman in the city.

But I enjoy pushing back and seeing him lose his cool is the ultimate high.

Sparks constantly fly, and it's not long before we cave to our insane chemistry.

Joshua has wormed his way into my heart, but the downside of loving a powerful man is getting noticed by his enemies.

Now, I'm a target and my mission just got a lot more dangerous.

Note From the Author

This is a spin-off interconnected duet set in my *Mazzone Mafia* world. While you do not need to read the existing books to enjoy *The Accardi Twins Duet*, it is highly recommended. Each book in the duet features a different twin and his love interest, and the mafia plot carries forward between both books.

If you have read the *Mazzone Mafia Series*, and/or *Vengeance of a Mafia Queen*, note this book starts two years after the epilogue in VOAMQ.

Mazzone Mafia World Reading Order

Condemned to Love
Forbidden to Love
Scared to Love
Vengeance of a Mafia Queen
The Accardi Twins Duet

This is a dark mafia romance, and it contains mature themes and content that is consistent with this genre. For a full list of triggers, refer to my website. Please note this page contains spoilers.

Mafia Glossary

- Barone – Made men from New Jersey who are hired by other made men for jobs and contract killings.
- Bastardi – Bastards.
- Bastardo – Bastard.
- Bratva – The Russian mafia in the US.
- Capo – Italian for captain. A member of a crime family who heads/leads a crew of soldiers.
- Consigliere – Italian for adviser/counselor. A member of a crime family who advises the boss and mediates disputes.
- Consiglieri – Plural of consigliere.
- Cosa Nostra – A criminal organization, operating within the US, comprising Italian American crime families.
- Don/Boss – The male head of an Italian crime family.
- Famiglia– Italian for family.
- Famiglie – Italian for families.
- Five Families – Five crime families who rule in New York, each headed by a don.
- Made man – A member of the mafia who has been officially initiated/inducted into a crime family.
- Mafioso/Mafiosi – An official member of the mafia or a reference to the mafia in general.
- Principessa – Italian for princess.
- RICO laws – The Racketeer-Influenced and Corrupt Organizations Act, a federal statute

enacted in 1970. It allows prosecutors to seek tougher penalties if they can prove someone is a member of the mafia.

- Soldati – Italian for soldiers.
- Soldato – Italian for soldier.
- Soldier – A low-ranking member of the mafia who reports to an assigned Capo.
- The Commission – The governing/ruling body of Cosa Nostra, which sits in New York, the organized crime capital of the US.
- Tesoro – Italian for treasure.
- Triad – Chinese crime syndicate.
- Underboss – The second-in-command within a crime family and an initiated mafia member who works closely with and reports directly to the boss.

FIVE NEW YORK FAMILIES

GRECO	MAZZONE	DIPIETRO	ACCARDI	MALTESE
Massimo Greco Don & Commission President	**Bennett Mazzone** Current don	**Cristian DiPietro** Current don	**Caleb & Joshua Accardi** Current dons	**Fiero Maltese** Current don
Sons	Sons	Brother		
Cassio Greco	Rowan Mazzone	Cruz DiPietro Las Vegas don		
Armis Greco	Rhys Mazzone			
Rocco Greco				

ACCARDI FAMILY

Natalia Messina (Nee Mazzone)

Gino Accardi (Deceased) — **Married** — **Juliet Accardi** (Deceased)

Married

Caleb Accardi — **Twins** — **Joshua Accardi**

Leo Messina

Step-siblings

Children

Rosa Messina

Leif Messina

MAZZONE FAMILY

Bennett Mazzone (Ben) --- Siblings --- **Natalia Messina (Nee Mazzone)**

Married

Married

Sierra Mazzone (Nee Lawson) — Sisters — **Serena Salerno (Nee Lawson)**

Leo Messina

Children

Rowan Mazzone

Joshua & Caleb Accardi (Stepsons)

Raven Mazzone

Rosa Messina

Rhys Mazzone

Leif Messina

DIPIETRO FAMILY

Josef Di Pietro (Retired) — Married — Beatrice DiPietro

Cruz DiPietro
Current don

Cristian DiPietro
Current don

Sabina DiPietro

Married

Cousins

Anais DiPietro
(nee Salerno)

Alesso Salerno

Half-sisters

Catarina Greco
nee Conti

GRECO FAMILY

Maximo Greco (Deceased) — Married — Eleanora Greco

- Carlo Greco (Deceased)
- Primo Greco (Deceased)
- Gabriele Greco
- Massimo Greco
  Current don

  Married

  Catarina Greco
  nee Conti

  Children

  - Cassio Greco
  - Armis Greco
  - Bella Greco
  - Rocco Greco

MALTESE FAMILY

Roberto Maltese (Retired) — Married — **Ingrid Maltese**

Fiero Maltese Current don

Zumo Maltese

Sofia Maltese

Tullia Maltese

SALERNO FAMILY

Anais Salerno
(now DiPetrio)

Cousin

Alesso Salerno

Married

ex-lovers

Caleb Accardi

Married

Cruz DiPetrio

Serena Salerno
(Nee Lawson)

Children

Elisa Salerno

Romeo Salerno

Will Salerno

Aria Salerno

THE ACCARDI TWINS BOOK ONE

COLD KING

of *New York*

Chapter One
Joshua

My cell phone vibrates across the top of the bedside table again as the woman between my legs looks up at me. "Don't stop." Fisting handfuls of her dark hair, I push her mouth back down on my dick as I grab my cell and answer it. If Fiero is calling this late, something must be up. "Don Maltese," I say. "This better be important."

"You need to get to Staten Island ASAP."

I stifle a groan as my balls lift and a tingle builds at the base of my spine. "I'll be there as quick as I can," I say, stroking Sorella's hair as she works me faster.

Fiero hangs up, and I tug on my regular fuck buddy's hair, forcefully shoving her face down as I thrust up inside her warm skillful mouth. Pleasure zips along my spine as I fill her up with salty cum, ignoring her muffled protests when I keep her face locked in position until I'm fully done. "Thanks, babe," I say thirty seconds later, releasing my firm grip on her hair. Hauling her up the bed, I slam my lips against hers in a quick kiss. "I need to go."

"I understand." She softly drags her nails through the dark-

1

blond strands of my hair. "It's not like you ever stay the night anyway."

Sorella is *mafioso*. Her father, like his father and grandfather before him, is one of our *soldati*, and she's the second youngest of seven sisters. The poor bastard kept on trying for an heir, but it never happened.

Sorella is on my list of reliable fuck buddies because she understands the score, she is discreet, and she knows not to expect anything but mind-blowing sex. The instant I sense she wants more, I'm out. I have always been up front with the women I screw. It is sex and nothing else. Kissing and hugging is kept to a minimum. I don't shower them with gifts or take them on dates. I have never taken any woman to the penthouse I call home, preferring to rail them in hotels or their apartments, so the message is received loud and clear.

Attachments are not my thing.

Love will never be something I indulge in again.

Bettina drilled that point home in the most devastating way.

"And I never will." I spear her with a sharp look. "If our arrangement no longer suits, say the word, and it ends now." I slide out from under her, swinging my legs over the edge of the bed.

"I wasn't complaining," she says as I stand, buck naked, and walk to the chair where my clothes are neatly folded. "Just stating a fact."

"A fact that won't ever change," I remind her, glancing over one shoulder as I tug my boxers up my legs and reach for my pants.

"I'm aware, and I'm fine with our arrangement." She glides out of bed and grabs her red silk robe, wrapping it around her tempting body. "How can I help?" She stands in front of me as I pull my black pants on. "Coffee for the road maybe?"

"That would be good."

She leans down, as if to kiss me, before straightening up. "Coming right up."

I finish getting dressed and walk out to the kitchen, snatching my keys and wallet from the island unit where I left them.

"Black with no sugar," she confirms, handing me a silver travel mug.

"Thanks, sweetheart." I squeeze her ass before walking toward the exit. "I'll be in touch."

"I'm at your disposal." She smiles, and despite the impending shitstorm I suspect I'm facing, I have a smug grin on my face as I close the door behind me.

After a quick stop at my place to change out of my suit and switch my Maserati for my Land Rover, I'm on my way. At least there isn't too much traffic on the roads at four a.m. on a Thursday morning, but it still takes me forty minutes to reach the large shipping hub Don Maltese and Don Greco own.

Fiero and his buddy Massimo—the man presiding over all Italian American *mafioso* in the US—own this building on Staten Island and a Colombian manufacturing plant in Cali. They're into all kinds of shit, but their real estate and property development business is the most visible and a legit front to hide their illegal drug production and shipping empire.

Fiero and I currently manage the supply and distribution of drugs to the five families in New York and our Irish partners, and we oversee the street trade on behalf of the other dons in The Big Apple. They washed their hands of the street business years ago, preferring to supply VIP clients who frequent our various bars, clubs, restaurants, and casinos. It's safer, and that's where the real money is made. But someone has to supervise the street trade so other parties don't invade our turf. I offered to help six months after my twin and I finally took our rightful places on the board of The Commission. Fiero and I have worked closely ever since, and we work well together.

My partner in crime is waiting in the parking lot when I pull into my assigned space, leaning against the wall in what might appear to be a casual stance. But I can read his body language, and he's seriously pissed.

"What's happened?" I ask after I exit the car and stride toward him.

"We've got a big fucking problem."

"Tell me."

"I'd rather show you." Instead of heading back inside the building, he moves toward the side door that leads portside where one of the Accardi cruise liners is currently docked.

We walk in strained silence toward the large ship, tipping our heads at one of the men who stands guard at the gangway. Stepping onto the ship, I follow Fiero to the elevator that takes us to the lowest level where the secret stowage area is housed.

When Caleb and I inherited our family business, after our cousin Luca handed it over when we turned twenty-one, the shipping part of the Accardi Company empire was vastly undervalued and underdeveloped. Given what Fiero and Massimo had set in motion, it made sense to use our ships to ferry the narcotics from Colombia to the city. In the almost six years since we've been at the helm of the company, I have largely focused my interests on developing the shipping business, moving from commercial freight transporters to luxury cruise liners, legitimizing the business and using it as a front to move huge quantities of drugs on a regular basis. We also ship supplies to dons in other states, and it's the most lucrative aspect of all our businesses.

It has always run smoothly. Until now.

Fiero punches in the code to the main container area, and I grind my teeth to the molars at the scene awaiting us inside.

"Fuck." I scrub a hand along my smooth jawline as I inspect the empty cargo holder, the pile of dead bodies, and the river of blood staining the floor. I step to the side to avoid ruining my shoes.

"That's putting it mildly." Fiero pounds his fist into the wall.

"Is everything gone?" I ask, lifting my eyes to the wall-mounted cameras.

"They took the lot, and this is going to cause major issues with O'Hara."

Diarmuid O'Hara is head of the Irish mafia and a man we have worked closely with for years. "It's O'Hara's inability to control his operation that's caused this in the first place."

"We don't know that for a fact." Fiero cleaves a hand through his jet-black hair. For years the dude dyed it white-blond, and he was notorious among *mafioso* circles. The day he became the new Maltese don he went back to his roots.

"We know the Irish are involved even if our spies couldn't conclusively confirm it." I shake my head as I walk toward the body spiked to the wall. "How are they one step ahead all the time?" A muscle clenches in my jaw as I inspect the barely recognizable face of the latest informant we had implanted into the rank and file of the Irish a mere five weeks ago.

"It seems obvious now." Fiero walks to my side, and we both stare at Aldo's garish remains.

"We have a rat," I surmise, shoving my hands in the pockets of my black cargo pants.

"And possibly spies," Fiero adds.

"We need a new plan." I turn around and head toward the door. There is nothing else to see here.

"I have already called Massimo. He's convening an emergency session of the board. This can't wait."

We step into the hallway, and the air barely seems less suffocating out here. "Someone wants a war."

Fiero levels me with a lethal look. "If they keep this up, they'll get it."

Chapter Two
Joshua

"Can I grab a ride with you?" Fiero asks when we reach the parking lot, swiping wet hair off his brow. The heavens decided to open, battering us with torrential rain and bristling winds on the walk back from the dock. "I don't fancy taking the chopper in this weather." Fiero and Massimo both have pilot licenses, and they regularly travel here via helicopter from their homes in Long Island and the city.

"Sure. We can head to the meeting together, but I need a coffee refill first." I stop at my car to grab the travel mug Sorella gave me.

"Always so organized." Fiero's lips tip up as we head inside the vast building.

"Not me this time." I waggle my brows and grin.

"I thought I might have disturbed something earlier." Fiero smirks as we step into the elevator, and he presses the button for the third floor.

"Don't feel bad. I made sure she finished me off before I left."

7

Fiero throws back his head and laughs. "Man, I miss being young."

"Dude, you're only forty-two. That's hardly over the hill. And you're a don. No pussy would ever reject you." Fiero's a handsome man for his age. I often wonder why he never settled down; maybe he has history that means family life no longer holds any appeal, like me.

"I get plenty of pussy if I want it, but that playboy lifestyle gets old after you've been doing it so long." The elevator stops, and the door pings as it glides open. We exit together. "I had a good time in my twenties and thirties, but it's just not doing it for me any longer."

"Then get hitched. I'm sure you have no shortage of offers."

Forced marriages are rare these days because Don Mazzone changed a lot of the traditions when he reestablished The Commission fourteen years ago. It's still proposed for political strengthening at higher levels, but most arranged marriages are consensual. Not like how it was for my mom when she was forced to marry our widowed dad.

"I haven't found anyone I want to marry," he admits, walking into the empty staff cafeteria. "I'm not even sure marriage is for me." He shrugs as we fix our coffees side by side. "And I don't necessarily need an heir."

"Because Zumo can take over, and he'll most likely have kids," I supply. Zumo Maltese is one of our good friends, and he likes being in a committed relationship. He and Cristian—another good friend and the don of the DiPietro *famiglia* in New York—have that in common while the rest of us are happy to remain unattached.

"Exactly." He puts the lid on his takeout coffee before rubbing at his eyes. "It's entirely too early to be discussing this shit."

I snort out a laugh as I grab my coffee and we walk off.

8

"Trust me, I'm more than happy to leave the subject of marriage behind. We've got way more pressing issues."

"Do you really think O'Hara's involved?" Fiero asks as we head toward the city for the early-morning Commission meeting in Manhattan.

"I didn't before, but now I don't know what to think," I truthfully reply. "I've always found him honorable, and it didn't seem like he was lying when we put him on the spot, but who's to say he isn't working an angle with his brother? Maybe they've decided they want it all now."

"They hate one another," Fiero reminds me as I swing around the corner onto a main road.

"Fucking hell!" Fiero stares out the window, tipping his head up and chuckling. "They used to say Massimo and I were the poster boys for the *mafioso* in the city, but we never had our faces splashed all over Times Square."

I glance out the window at the massive billboard, grinning at the image of Caleb and me looking like two smug pricks in expensive clothing from the winter catalog. "You should be used to it by now. It's not the first time our faces have appeared on advertising campaigns."

I graduated NYU early with an honors business degree and went straight into working for the Accardi Company. Caleb shunned college to pursue other things, but he joined me in the family business at the same time. My twin channeled his energies on building our clothing brand into a leading-edge design house that is now most sought after among fashion-conscious men across the globe. Years ago, our father had attempted to expand the clothing division by acquiring Kennedy Apparel from Alex Kennedy, but Gino Accardi lacked vision, and he had no creative flare.

Caleb loves fashion almost as much as he loves the notoriety and fame that comes from being the face of our brand. We both like to look good, and Caleb has used that to grow our brand and triple the profits. Ironically, one of our biggest competitors is Keanu Kennedy's brand, but it's friendly rivalry. The market is big enough for both brands, and we have hired models through his modeling agency to prove there's no bad blood.

"If Massimo and I had thought of the idea, we'd probably have started our own fashion line too. You have the pick of pussy in the city I'm guessing."

"I don't indulge much." I prefer the short list of girls I call on when I need to fuck. They've all been carefully vetted and signed NDAs, and they submit to regular testing. I know what I'm getting, and the risk is low.

"Unlike your twin." Fiero grins. "He must be a walking STD by now."

"No more than you would have been back in the day."

"Truth, and I'm a judgment-free zone."

His grin expands as I take a right at the junction, driving in the direction of the impressive glass building in the near distance that is our destination.

"At least he's not fucking Anais anymore, and that's a win," I say.

Well, not much. She's in Vegas most of the time and the separation has been good for my twin. Caleb's loyalty knows no bounds, and I couldn't love him more for it. But she's a toxic bitch and bad news. Anais feeds that cruel streak inside Caleb, and I don't like who he is when he's with her. I want her as far away from him as possible. Caleb has delivered the message and continuing to fuck with Cruz is playing with fire.

That narcissistic asshole is unpredictable and power-hungry, and he's set his sights on Caleb. My brother can hold his own, but he needs additional shit like a hole in the head. I'd rather Caleb completely cut ties with Cruz's wife so we can draw a line under the whole sorry affair.

"That was not a good scenario." Fiero drums his fingers on his knee as I turn into the underground parking lot of Commission Central.

Caltimore Holdings own the building, but Don Mazzone leases it at cost to The Commission. Every *famiglia* in the US pays a monthly stipend to The Commission, which covers the costs of running a governing body and pays for the variety of support services provided to members.

"Cruz is a vindictive prick," Fiero adds as I drive into my designated parking space and kill the engine. "He won't forget what Caleb's done." His blue eyes stab mine. "Caleb needs to always watch his back. Don't let him get complacent. I know your brother is lethal, and if he went one-on-one with Cruz, he'd nail that shithead to the wall. But Cruz also knows that, which is why he won't come for him head on."

"Caleb can handle Cruz."

"In theory." Fiero turns in his seat to face me. "Caleb is prone to bouts of recklessness, and he displays a worrying lack of regard for his safety at times. That's when Cruz will strike. He'll hit him when he least expects it. When he's vulnerable."

"Only if we let it come to that." The unspoken sentiment behind those words goes unsaid. To articulate it is tantamount to treason.

"My allegiance is with you and your brother. I hate that self-righteous bastard, but I'd hate to see either of you lose your life over him. Make smart choices, Joshua, and ensure your twin does too."

I'm still mulling over Fiero's words as I stand in front of the mirror in the men's locker room after my shower. We all keep clothing and supplies here because we're often called in on short notice. Massimo runs The Commission professionally as his predecessor, Don Mazzone, did. No one is permitted to show up unless they are well groomed and dressed the part.

We go to extremes to protect the criminal elements of our businesses and our darker reputations. In public, we always present as successful entrepreneurs. Mazzone's IT companies control the stuff that goes out on the web, and there are dedicated teams who work twenty-four-seven to remove any incriminating evidence.

After I'm dressed in a custom-fit charcoal-gray suit and I've styled my hair back off my face, I exit the locker room and head toward the conference center on the top floor.

"Bro." Caleb emerges from the elevator as I walk by, clamping his hand down hard on my shoulder. "What the fuck's going on?" he asks, stifling a yawn.

Whiskey fumes drift over my face, and a muscle ticks in my jaw. "You reek," I hiss. "Go clean up."

"Fuck off. You're not my father."

More like babysitter. I think it but don't say it. Keeping my brother in check is occupying more of my time these days. "You can't show up hungover." This is the one place my brother cannot get away with breaking rules or appearing disinterested.

"I've got it under control, and you need to get laid more often. You've been even more uptight these past few months."

"I get laid plenty, and you know why I've been stressed."

Caleb's expression turns serious as he pumps minty spray into his mouth. "This is about the Irish threat."

"It's accelerating," I confirm, watching as he pulls a bottle of cologne out of his pocket and douses himself in it. "War seems inevitable at this point."

"Good." He circles his arm around my shoulders and flashes me a devilish grin. "Things have been too quiet for years. I'm itching to gut a few fuckers."

"Keep those kinds of comments to yourself in there." We round the corner and reach the double doors to the main conference room. "This is a time for shrewd thinking not blood-thirsty proclamations."

"Violence and death are the normal way of life, J. No matter how 'peaceful' things have been since The Commission was reformed, there is no getting away from the basics. We're lucky we've enjoyed relative stability since we took control, but it could change in the blink of an eye. We saw enough of it growing up to know that's our reality."

He's not wrong, but is it wrong to want peace instead of bloodshed? "I saw the reality with my own eyes this morning, and it wasn't pretty. I sense something big brewing." I stop outside the doors and turn to my brother, Fiero's warning still ringing in my ears. "This fight might look external, but I have a feeling we're waging a war on two fronts, and you especially need to watch your back."

Chapter Three
Joshua

"I don't trust O'Hara," Don Mazzone states sometime later after Fiero and I have brought the board up to speed. "He knows this threat has come from within his organization, and he still hasn't found any proof or done anything to stop it."

I wonder if it's hard for Ben not being in charge. No one was surprised when Massimo replaced him as president because Ben had been grooming him for the position. All the old dons are either dead or retired now, and we have a younger, more dynamic commission.

When Massimo's ten-year tenure expires in seven years, there will be competition for the presidency for the first time. I wouldn't mind a shot at it myself, but if the plans to expand the board of The Commission go ahead, it will only add to the list of contenders.

"He failed to protect our informants too," Cristian says, forcing me to focus.

"What is more concerning is the breach within our own

ranks," Caleb says. "We need to find out who and why and eliminate the threat before it grows."

"All are valid concerns," President Greco says, "but let's deal with them one at a time." His gaze swings to me. "Tell me everything you know of O'Hara and your thoughts on his loyalty."

"O'Hara is the result of an affair, and his parents were never married. He lived with his mom in Ireland until he was thirteen, when his father came for him after being thrust into the leadership role. Sean McDermott's true heir, Liam, was only five then. Heart problems run in the family, so Sean chose to groom his bastard for succession. A smart move considering he died of a massive coronary when Diarmuid was twenty-two."

"How prophetic," Caleb drawls, bouncing his leg.

Ignoring him, I continue. "Diarmuid faced a lot of opposition and dealt with constant threats to his rule the first few years. But things have settled especially after he made the deal with us six years ago. The Irish operation has been more profitable under O'Hara's reign than at any other time in their history. That should be enough to keep everyone happy."

"Except Liam is a greedy fuck with a chip on his shoulder," Fiero adds.

I nod. "Diarmuid and Liam have been at loggerheads since Liam turned twenty-one and felt he had a God-given right to the throne. For the past ten years, he has tried to sow seeds of discontent, but he's always been shot down."

"Until now," Cristian says.

"What's changed?" Massimo asks, his brow puckering. "Why is he making a move now?"

"An alleged move." I quirk a brow and look around the table. "We still have no proof Liam is behind the missing supplies, stolen goods, and trail of dead bodies. Neither of our undercover informants were able to find anything before they were killed."

"Because neither of them could get close enough to McDermott." Caleb swivels in his chair. "Liam is no dumbass. He's every bit as intelligent and savvy as O'Hara. He knows Diarmuid is on to him. He knows we have a strong working partnership, which means he more than likely knows we're infiltrating his ranks in the hopes he'll out himself."

"Caleb is right. It's all too obvious." I scrub a hand over my smooth jaw. "We now know that Liam has someone on the inside. Someone inside our *famiglia* is helping him. It's got to be someone with beef."

"Everyone has beef over something." Mazzone taps his pen on the table. "Just because we're all united under The Commission and we've had relative peace and prosperity for years doesn't mean everyone is happy."

"We need to stop allowing non-Italian Americans to join our *soldati*," Caleb says. "They're not as invested as we are. It would be easy to turn them. I bet the traitor is one of them."

"Only five percent are outsiders, and we only use them in certain circumstances. Most are kept on the fringes, and I dispute your loyalty contention. All are carefully vetted before initiation. We don't let loose cannons into the fold." Ben straightens his spine as he turns a blistering look on my brother. Ben's security company hires staff for legitimate clientele and to bolster our ranks when needed. Most of our *soldati* do time with the security firm as part of their training as it invokes discipline.

"You're forgetting I know these men too." Caleb narrows his eyes at our uncle. "I train them, and I know them better than you. I agree most are commendable and trustworthy, but not all. I've already raised objections with our president."

"We're getting sidetracked," Massimo says. "There is merit

in discussing your concerns, Caleb, but this isn't the time. The traitor in our ranks couldn't have come from the *soldati* corp. Only a *capo* or a higher-level *mafioso* has the authority to access the container rooms and tap into the security systems to disable the camera feeds. Whoever this person or persons is, they are technologically savvy because the detection warnings were also disabled, and that's not something we train any of our *capos* to do. It requires knowledge of programming to achieve."

"He could have hired someone," Cristian suggests, and heads bob around the table.

"The immediate issue is the missing shipment." Fiero stands and stretches his arms over his head. "We can't meet our deliveries. O'Hara will be up shit creek too."

"Unless he's the one who stole from us," Mazzone says.

"I really don't think he is." I take a sip of my water before continuing. I voiced similar concerns to Fiero earlier, and I've been thinking about this ever since. It doesn't make sense he was involved. I believe he's innocent and telling us the truth. "Loyalty matters to O'Hara. He has proven it repeatedly over the years. He is the last person who would risk the wrath of the entire Italian American *mafioso*. I think it's Liam. He wants to usurp his brother. He is working with a traitor, or traitors, within our organization and possibly others outside it too. He wants us to point the finger at Diarmuid so we do his dirty work for him."

"That is a plausible scenario and reason we need to tread carefully," Ben says. "I trust your instincts, but I'd still like to meet with O'Hara and have him say it to our faces."

"I agree," Massimo says, eyeballing his best friend. "Set up a meet for tomorrow."

"Consider it done." Fiero pulls out his phone.

"Could we use the chip-tracking software to find our rat?" I direct the question to Ben. One of his IT companies developed the technology. "If we ran a report on location and time status, we could pinpoint who was on the ship earlier this morning. I've already emailed you the roster for men who were assigned on this run. Logic would dictate it's one of them, but it would be unwise to assume."

"We can run that report for sure." Ben removes his suit jacket and hangs it on the back of his chair. "But only sixty percent of all New York *mafioso* have a chip. Most *famiglie* don't insist on them, leaving it a voluntary choice."

"Even if the perp did have a chip, I'm guessing he removed it," Cristian says. "This all points to someone who is tech savvy. They wouldn't be that stupid."

"Valid point," Massimo says, "but it's worth looking into it. As is looking at who wasn't in the area during the crucial time. It could help us to eliminate those people."

"We don't know if this is an individual or a group. I don't think we can discount anyone," Fiero says. "And we still haven't resolved the current supply issue."

"We have some backup supplies," Massimo says. "Use those and contact Juan Pablo at the plant to determine how much stock is on hand. Tell him to hire more workers to produce double our next shipment." The president turns to look at me. "How fast can you get a ship to Buenaventura?"

"Our regular schedule is operational, but it'll be six days before the next liner docks in Colombia." We have ships sailing all the time because it's a seven-day trip each way, and it's the only option to ensure we receive biweekly deliveries. "We'll have to look at other transportation options."

"Vegas has their own airline now," Cristian says, but it's not news to anyone sitting at this table.

Massimo shakes his head. "I don't want Cruz anywhere near this."

No one contests his assertion. None of us trust Cristian's

older brother—the residing don in Vegas—and our suspicion is warranted. Cristian is a good man, but the same cannot be said of Cruz DiPietro.

"Leave it with me," I say. "I'll see if I can come up with some transport options."

"Let's put that issue aside for now. We are back to square one with the main issue, and we need to find evidence to pin this on Liam so Diarmuid can deal with him officially."

"I say we just take him out." Caleb shrugs while inspecting his nails. "I'll do it. You need to keep your hands clean," my twin tells our ex-gun-for-hire president.

"We can't take action without evidence, and it's not our responsibility to handle." I turn in my chair to face my brother. "It's O'Hara's. If we step on his toes, it could ruin the relationship we've spent years cultivating and fuel the entire Irish operation to act against us."

"Let them. We outnumber them in all areas. It would be their funeral." My brother is the only man around this table who will celebrate if we end up at war.

"We're not assassinating McDermott," Massimo says. "At least not yet."

"I have another idea. One I think has a greater chance of success." Every pair of eyes in the room settles on me. "We send in a female informant this time. Liam is a known ladies' man. Let's send someone to seduce him into giving up his secrets."

"I think it could work," Mazzone agrees.

Fiero's brows knit together. "You cannot be thinking who I'm thinking."

"You know any other woman more capable?"

There are more opportunities for women within *mafioso* circles these days, but most opt for roles in our businesses rather than being initiated. But there are exceptions.

Caleb slams his hands down on the table and grins. "She is fucking perfect. She's got the looks, the body, the smarts, and the skills to protect herself."

"You're forgetting one vital thing," Fiero supplies. "My *consigliere* will never allow it."

"He won't have a choice," Massimo says, grimacing a little in understanding. I'm sure he's thinking of his daughter and empathizing with Rico as a father. But that can't play a part in this decision. "Rico knew what was involved when she agreed to become one of our informants. This is why we allowed women into the program."

"We can't talk about equality and then balk at the first real test," Cristian says.

"Shit." Fiero slumps in his chair. "You're right."

"She'll want to do this." If I have gauged her personality correctly, she will be champing at the bit for this assignment. There will be no greater opportunity to prove her worth. She won't turn it down.

"Elisa will have your balls," Mazzone says, his lips twitching.

"That is the least of my concerns." I have very little to do with his niece or her friend.

"Caleb can take one for the team if she throws a hissy fit," Cristian jokes.

Caleb narrows his eyes as Ben jabs his finger in my twin's direction. "Do not even think about it. I will riddle you with bullets if you as much as touch a hair on her head. Elisa is far too good for you."

I fix Ben with a sharp look. He knows how my brother operates, so why would he throw down the gauntlet so blatantly?

"Wow, look at that," Caleb says, leaning back in his chair and smirking at our uncle. "We finally agree on something."

"Enough snarking like bitches," Massimo snaps, shooting Ben and Caleb a warning look. "Do I need to remind anyone of the seriousness of the situation? Enemies are snapping at our heels, and we're wasting time. Fiero, call Rico and set up a second meeting for tomorrow. Let's put the proposal to Gia Bianchi and see what she says."

Chapter Four
Gia

"Y ou don't have to do this," Mom says, hovering in the doorway of my bedroom, chewing on her lip and practically exuding worries from her pores. "I don't want you to do this. It's too dangerous."

"I'm not sure what to wear." I ignore her on purpose. We've had this same conversation, repeatedly, since yesterday when Dad slammed the phone down on his boss—a disrespect that would be punishable in the past or with any current don who is not Fiero Maltese—and told us I've been summoned to Commission HQ to attend a meeting with the board about a high-profile, field-based informant assignment.

I hold up a fitted black dress. "Should I wear a sexy dress?" Snatching the red pants suit from the bed, I ask, "Or a power suit? Or should I go in my combat gear? Or an understated undercover look?" If I knew exactly what the assignment was it might help me to dress appropriately, but it's all hush-hush for now. I think Dad knows but he's not permitted to say.

"Don't go." Mom rushes across the room, and I drop the

clothes on my bed. She grabs my cheeks. "I have a bad feeling about this, and you know I always trust my instincts."

"Mom, she can't turn it down," Antonio says, materializing behind her.

I'm glad my brother is here. He is generally the voice of reason among my siblings even though that probably should be my role as the eldest. But I've got too much of Mom in me. Antonio takes after Dad, and he's hoping to fill his shoes as the official Maltese *consigliere* when Dad retires. Which won't be for a while, because papa is only forty-nine, and there are plenty of years left in him yet. It also gives Antonio time to hone his skill and experience, because there is more to being a *consigliere* than being reasonable and calm. Confidants to the dons, the most powerful men in our world, *consiglieri* need to advise and strategize, and that only comes with maturity and time. Something my brother doesn't have in spades yet since he's only twenty. "This is what she signed up for when she applied to join the first informant's program."

Increasingly, the way we do things is evolving. In the past, the *mafioso* ruled with an iron fist, and violence was the normal way of handling things. The organization has moved with the times, and information is the key currency these days. It's why the leadership rubs shoulders with and greases the hands of authority figures. Politicians, judges, cops, lawyers, and even the police commissioner now work for us.

Don Greco is keen to make his mark as president, and the informant's program was his idea. I love it. For years, the FBI has been using informants to rat on their mafia bosses. Now, we're turning the tables. Developing our own network of spies to protect our interests and serve our aims.

I had just graduated early with my computer science degree from NYU when the program was announced. I applied without telling my parents because I knew they wouldn't approve. I didn't even tell my best friend Elisa because she'd try to talk me out of it. The only person I told was Antonio, and he encouraged me to go for it.

There was a huge number of applications, and only fifty were chosen for the initial training. Now, we're a team of twenty, and I'm the sole female representative. I only returned from Nepal a month ago, and I've been on desk duty while waiting to be assigned a mission.

The very last thing I'll be doing is turning it down.

"Antonio is right, Mom." I pull her into a hug because she's genuinely worried. "This is my job now. Sometimes, I'll be working behind a computer gathering intel, and other times I'll be out in the field."

"I want to support you, Gia." Mom clasps my cheeks. "I'm so proud of you, and I want you to be happy, but this is not the life I would've chosen for you."

"Frankie, it's done now." Dad steps into the room, trying to mask the concern from his handsome face. "There's no point making her nervous before the meeting."

"Don't bullshit a bullshitter, Rico." Mom turns and glares at her husband. "You hate this every bit as much as me."

"Yes, my love." Dad reels Mom into his arms. "But the difference is I've accepted it." He brushes her long blonde hair back off her face.

"We never should have let her take those Krav Maga lessons as a kid. I bet that's where it started."

I roll my eyes as Antonio grins, and Dad hugs Mom to his chest, smiling adoringly at her. "It's in her blood, darling."

"If you want to blame anyone, blame yourself," I tease. "You're the one who married a *mafioso*."

"And I'd do it all over again because your father makes me incredibly happy, and he's given me the best life." Mom beams at Dad as he swoops in and kisses her deeply and passionately.

My heart swells behind my chest as I watch my parents. The way they love one another is couple goals for sure. Growing up, we were always surrounded by love. The one they share for each other and us. I want that too. To be the center of someone's universe and for our family life to be filled with laughter and love and happy times. I had the best childhood, with the best support system, and I know I'm luckier than most.

"Ahem." Antonio clears his throat. "Your children are in the room, and it's far too early for all this mushy touchy-feely stuff."

Our parents break their lip-lock but not their embrace. "Our children are grown-up and doing all the things we do and more." Mom waggles her brows at Antonio, and I wonder if she's remembering the time she busted him nailing Sorella Caprese in the ass.

Mom freaked out, not just at the act, because Antonio was only sixteen at the time and Sorella was twenty-one. I went to school with her younger sister, and she's every bit the bitch her older sister is rumored to be. Both women should have awards for bedding made men. I'm not throwing shade, just stating facts. Apparently, Sorella is limiting her fuck buddies to one these days in the hopes Joshua will propose to her.

What a dumb bitch.

No made man worth his salt hitches himself to a woman who has fucked her way through *mafioso* circles. Especially not a don. And especially not this don. Joshua is as anti-love and anti-marriage as Caleb is now. That bitch Bettina really did a number on him.

I was fourteen when it all went down, and I remember how broken Joshua was. Until he reinvented himself as a cold, emotionless bastard whose only commitment to women is fucking them like they're a dying breed.

I can't say I really blame him, but it's sad. It's no way to live your life.

I know Joshua mostly because our moms are best friends, but he works closely with Fiero now, so we sometimes see him at Maltese events. But I can't say I know him or his twin well. We have only ever spoken in passing. In the past, it was because of the age gap, but in recent years, I'm not sure why. He probably still thinks of me as a kid the same way Caleb thinks of Elisa.

"Let's not go there, Mom. I'm pretty sure Dad would make me wear a chastity belt if he knew the stuff I got up to at college." And in Nepal, but I'm not mentioning what went down while I was training with a bunch of stupidly hot yet irritating made men.

What happened in Nepal stays in Nepal is my mantra these days.

"Gia Maria Estella Bianchi! That had better be a joke!" There is no trace of humor on Dad's face, and I probably shouldn't add to his stress when he's already worried about my assignment.

"Relax, Papa. I was exaggerating. You make it too easy to wind you up."

"You will give me gray hairs, *tesoro*."

"Hate to break it to you, old man, but you've already got some." Dad and Antonio share the same dark-brown locks but not the gray strands that have recently appeared in Dad's hair.

Mom glides her hand up Dad's chest. "I like the silver streaks. You look like a distinguished gentleman."

"You've still got it, Dad," I joke, waggling my brows before I spot the time on my cell and screech. "Everyone out. I need to get ready!" I start running around the room in a fluster as the others leave.

"Wear the pants suit," Antonio says, poking his head

through the door. "Casual or combat isn't appropriate, and the dress will only draw attention to your tits. You want them to see you as a professional, so dress the part."

Nerves fire at me from all angles as I sit outside the conference room at Commission Central, waiting to be called. Discreetly, I wipe my clammy palms down the front of my red pants, hoping it doesn't leave a mark. I managed to pull myself together in record time, and I made it here with seconds to spare. My red pants suit conveys business in a sexily understated way. My makeup is on point. Enough to make the best of my features but not so much I look caked in the stuff.

My cell vibrates in my purse, and I take it out, blowing air out of my mouth when I see it's my bestie. She is probably calling to wish me luck. While Elisa didn't want me to sign up for the program, as soon as I committed to it, she was fully supportive. She might worry, but she wants me to be happy. And like me, she enjoys the fact I'm one of the women steering a new path within our world and opening previously closed doors.

"Hey," I say quietly when I answer her call. "I'm waiting to be called in so I may have to hang up."

"That's okay. I just wanted to wish you good luck. I'm dying to know what it's about."

"Me too. It's exciting, but I'm nervous also."

"That's only natural, but you wouldn't be there if they didn't think you could do it."

"Thanks. I needed to hear that. Mom has me on edge because she's so freaking worried."

"She's your mom. It's her job to worry."

"I know, but she needs to find a way to deal with it because this is the career I have chosen, and there will always be dangerous assignments. Like, would she worry this much if it was Antonio?"

"I think she would but not to the same extent."

"And there you have it. Things will never be truly equal unless we can shift those traditional mindsets."

"I agree, but if anyone can change minds, it's my best friend."

"Love you. We should hang out this weekend. We still have tons of catching up to do."

"I have an assignment for art history class due Monday, but I'll try to finish it Friday night so we can go out on Saturday night."

"Yes, definitely. Hopefully, we'll have something to celebrate!"

"Sneak me a photo of Caleb," she asks, and I bite back my retort.

"I'm not sure it'll be possible in the middle of a meeting of the most powerful dons in the US."

"At least commit what he looks like to memory so you can tell me every minute detail."

"Jesus, you've got it bad." This isn't even the hundredth time I've said this. If I counted it up over the years, it would probably run into the thousands because she's just that obsessed.

She can do better. So much better. But try telling her that. Elisa is one of the most stubborn people I've ever met. She is also one of the kindest and sweetest, which is why Caleb Accardi will never be good enough for her.

The door starts opening, and butterflies swoop into my chest. "I've got to go," I whisper as a man steps out of the room.

"You've got this, babe. Go show them how it's done."

Powering off my cell, I slip it into my purse and stand,

straightening my spine and lifting my head. A smile plays across my lips as the familiar dark-haired green-eyed hottie approaches.

"Hello, Gia." Cristian extends his hand. "Long time no see."

"It's been a while." I place my hand against his warm, callused palm.

"We're ready for you," he adds, letting me go after our handshake.

"Okay." I smile as adrenaline courses through my veins. "Let's do this."

Chapter Five
Joshua

W hile Cristian makes introductions, I subtly rake my gaze over Gia Bianchi. I haven't previously paid her much attention because she was always just a kid, but there's no denying she's all grown-up now. Gia has matured into a stunning woman who strongly resembles her mother. Frankie has been best friends with our mom since they were little kids, and they remain super close.

Fiery shivers shoot up my arm when we shake hands, and what the fuck is up with that? "It's good to see you, Don Accardi," she says, whipping her hand back like I've just electrocuted her.

"Wow, Gia. When did you get so hot?"

Caleb just has to go there. I honestly think he can't help himself. It's an inbuilt reaction, as natural to him as breathing. "Caleb," I snap under my breath. "Don't."

Gia narrows her eyes at my twin before remembering where she is. A fake smile ghosts over her mouth. "Don Accardi." She grips his hand in a firm but brief handshake, ignoring his unprofessional remark.

"Please take a seat," Cristian says, holding out a chair for her. We're all lined up on one side of the table, and she's in the firing line on the other, yet she looks poised and unruffled as she sits.

My eyes soak up every delicious inch of her body as she lowers herself into the chair. Her suit is good quality and a perfect fit, hugging her figure in all the right places. She is tall and slender with shapely hips and big tits, and my dick is stirring in my pants, which is annoying. Her long golden-blonde hair is swept up in a high ponytail that emphasizes her high cheekbones and exquisite face. Ruby-red-painted lips pull into a pleasant smile as she pins me with striking ocean-blue eyes.

She will have Liam McDermott drowning in a pool of his own drool in no time.

"Now who's being a dick, brother?" Caleb says under his breath so only I can hear him. "You are obvious in the extreme."

Massimo clears his throat and pins us with a warning look.

We zip our lips and let our president open the meeting.

"Thank you for meeting us on such short notice, Ms. Bianchi."

"You can call me Gia, Don Greco, and it's no problem. I'm happy to be here." There's a slight tremble to her voice, indicating nerves, which isn't surprising. She's only twenty-two and sitting across from a group of formidable men who are about to grill her. It's only natural.

Massimo's warm smile attempts to put her at ease. "We have a proposal to put to you. Before I outline the situation and the assignment, I want to make it clear this is highly confidential, and it cannot be discussed with anyone outside of this room."

"Apart from your father," Fiero clarifies, fiddling with the cuffs of his suit jacket. "He is privy to the details."

Gia nods while wetting her lips. My eyes follow the motion

like they have a mind of their own. "I understand, and I won't discuss it with anyone."

"That includes your best friend," Caleb adds. "You cannot mention anything to Elisa."

Heat flares in Gia's eyes, but she hides it fast as she looks at my twin. "I don't think I was unclear, and using your personal knowledge of me like some kind of weapon is not welcome or professional."

Cristian fights a smile as does Ben. Gia is ballsy, and she's only going up in my estimation.

"Let's stick to the agenda, Don Accardi," Massimo says, leveling Caleb with another warning look.

"I'm ensuring our informant understands the severity of the situation. Clarifying the need for confidentiality is important."

"Now we've confirmed that, let me outline the situation," Massimo says, redirecting his gaze from my twin to Gia. "For the past ten weeks, someone has been stealing narcotics from under our noses. Several delivery vans have been hijacked on the roads in slick operations. Two nights ago, our entire shipment was stolen from an Accardi cruise liner docked at our shipping port."

Her eyes pop wide. "How is that even possible? Our security is the best in the business."

"It is, but someone has found a way to infiltrate it. Knowledge of deliveries is restricted to us, our Irish partners, and the local dons we supply product to across the US. Don DiPietro's freight company handles all distribution in and out of New York. By a process of elimination, we determined someone within the Irish mafia was double-crossing us."

Lines crease her brow. "I thought Diarmuid O'Hara was a trusted partner?"

"He is," I interject. "We believe it's his brother and he's

trying to frame him so we take O'Hara out, paving the way for Liam to assume control."

"Is that the only motive?" Her big blue eyes stare straight into mine. "Or does he plan on replacing us as the main supplier of narcotics in The Big Apple?"

I smooth a hand down my tie. "That's a smart question. It's one we have considered, but we don't have an answer to it."

"Yet." Fiero leans forward in his seat. "Which is where you come in."

"You want me to infiltrate the Irish and find evidence pointing to Liam." Her gaze bounces around the room, and there's no mistaking the sheen of excitement in her eyes.

She wants this, just like I thought.

"Two of your colleagues have already tried and failed," Ben says, gripping the arms of his chair tight.

Her face pales, in stark contrast to her vibrant lips. "You're talking about Aldo and Pisano?"

"Yes. Both are dead," Massimo says, his tone grave.

Fear spikes in her eyes, quickly replaced with sadness. "I trained with them. They were friends as well as colleagues and highly skilled made men."

"They were, but the stakes were high. *Are* high," Massimo corrects.

"You'll be entering enemy territory alone," I explain. "Surrounded by hot-blooded highly trained men. They'll be expecting us to send more spies."

"But they won't be expecting us to send in a woman," Caleb adds, leaning his elbows on the table. "It was Joshua's idea, and it's genius. They won't see you coming."

"How exactly will I be infiltrating their ranks? It's not like I can sign up as a foot soldier. They'd instantly smell a rat."

"Your task is to seduce Diarmuid's brother Liam. To get close to him so he trusts you and you can uncover evidence of his treachery," Fiero confirms, running a finger along his collar. The guy hates wearing suits, feeling more at home in his bike leathers.

I didn't think it was possible, but she turns even paler. "How do you know it's Liam who is behind this?"

"We don't." Cristian links his fingers together on top of the table. "But whoever is doing this is sophisticated, controlled, and intelligent. They also have the right contacts and resources to pull this off. We spoke extensively with O'Hara this morning, and he is adamant his brother is the only one capable of running this kind of operation."

"As you're aware, the Irish HQ is in Boston, but they've held a smaller operation in The Big Apple since we partnered with them a few years ago," Ben says. "Liam has been pushing his brother to take control of the New York business for some time. Diarmuid has always resisted because he doesn't trust him, but today he'll be confirming Liam as head of their business here."

"You want to give him enough rope to hang himself," she says.

"There is more chance of discovering what he's up to if he's right under our nose. We also believe there is someone on the inside helping him. There is no other way to explain how he stole a whole cargo out from under us and bypassed our security systems," Massimo says.

Before Gia came in, we discussed whether to mention the possibility of a potential rat. We need to contain that intel for several reasons. But everyone immediately agreed she needed to be fully informed so she's not going in blind.

"You will need to be extremely careful," Cristian adds. "Aldo and Pisano may've been identified by our rat. They could do the same to you."

"Which is why you'll need to go undercover in disguise."

Massimo slides an envelope across the desk. "That contains ID in a fake name, a fake résumé, and family history. Memorize it. If Liam checks, what he finds online will corroborate that backstory."

"You'll need to dye your hair, wear contacts, and dress a certain way," Ben says.

"What exactly am I expected to do?" She shifts uneasily in her chair.

"Whatever is necessary to get him to trust you." I drill her with a look.

"You want me to *fuck him* to get intel?" Her nostrils flare.

"Don't act so horrified," Caleb says. "You're not a virgin, and from what I've heard, you have no issue spreading your legs to achieve a goal."

Her mouth pulls into a thin line as she glowers at Caleb. If Gia was armed, she'd probably shoot or stab him for those words. I'm not sure I'd blame her. It's lucky for my twin all visitors must leave their weapons at the armory downstairs.

"Unless what I've been told about Nepal isn't true?" Caleb asks, leaning back in his chair and smirking.

I work hard to keep a neutral expression on my face as my brother spews that horseshit. I have no clue what he's talking about, and from the furious looks the others cast his way, it's clear they are in the dark too.

"I don't know what you think you know, but you're wrong. I'm not a *whore*, Don Accardi." She hisses the word. "I'm an educated, trained informant, and I wrongly thought I was being treated as an equal when I was hired to this program." She turns her rage in Massimo's direction. "Is this why you allowed women to apply? To be whores masquerading as spies? Has everything I've worked so hard for this past year all been for show? Was this your plan all along?"

"No. Absolutely not," Massimo says, and it's hard to doubt

his sincerity when it's written all over his face. Massimo trains a vicious gaze on Caleb. "Apologize to Ms. Bianchi. You are way out of line."

"I'm not apologizing for speaking the truth, and it seems we were wrong about Gia. If she's not prepared to do what is necessary, she doesn't belong in the program."

"I belong as much as every man I trained with. My objection is using my sexuality instead of my intelligence and skill."

"I hear you're pretty skilled in the sack, so that's a moot point."

"Out." Fiero's chair slams to the floor as he abruptly stands. He jabs his finger at Caleb. "Get the fuck out now."

"I'm not leaving. I have every right to raise these concerns."

Massimo forces Fiero back into his chair. "Don Accardi, please refrain from saying anything unless it's conducive to the conversation, and you still need to apologize to Gia. I'm your president, and I demand it."

Caleb clenches his jaw as he eyeballs the woman across the table. "I apologize, Gia. Sorry if the truth hurts."

I briefly close my eyes. Why must my twin continuously do this? It's like he has a self-destruct button he can't help flipping.

"If you'll excuse Don Accardi and me for a few moments, please," Ben says, standing up and stalking toward Caleb. Caleb makes no move to get up until Ben whispers something in his ear, and then the two of them walk out, taking most of the tension with them.

"I apologize, Gia," Massimo says. "What Caleb said is not what we think."

She lifts her chin defiantly. "You shouldn't apologize for him. He's the one who said it, not you. I'm well aware of the trainwreck that is Caleb Accardi. I've watched that shit show going down for years."

"Watch your mouth," I snap, unwilling to sit by and let

anyone talk shit about my brother when he's not here to defend himself.

"I thought we were speaking openly, but my bad if I misconstrued the situation," she calmly replies as our eyes go into battle.

"Everyone needs to calm down," Cristian says, claiming Gia's attention.

I rotate my neck, attempting to loosen the knots in my shoulders.

"Caleb was harsh and misguided in his delivery. Yes, your role is to seduce Liam, but you also need to utilize all your skills to investigate every aspect of his life and the Irish operation while you are on the inside," Massimo says.

"We will equip you with the relevant tools so you can scan documents, take photos, and capture every piece of intel," I say.

"And no one is saying you must fuck him. There are creative ways to avoid that if you're smart enough, and I know you are."

Cristian, Massimo, and I stare at Fiero like he's grown an extra head. How do you avoid having sex with someone when your role is to seduce them? Liam doesn't do virgins, so we can't take that approach.

"Liam likes confident ballsy redheads," I say, sliding a few photos across the desk to her. "These are some of his exes and most recent conquests. The ones who lasted the longest were those who challenged him. He doesn't want a mousy broad. He likes his women sexy and smart."

"This role was made for you, Gia." Cristian and Gia exchange a meaningful look, and I sit up straighter in my chair. What the hell was that? "And it's so much more than sex."

"Keeping your wits about you while you gather evidence requires balls of steel, cunning, and street smarts," Massimo says. "If we wanted someone purely to spread their legs, we would not be talking to you. We need someone who is the full package, and that someone is you. I understand aspects of this will be unpleasant, but that is the nature of the informant role. There will always be things you have to do you won't like, but you signed up for this."

"My father knows this?"

Fiero nods. "If it helps, he threatened to kill me at first until he calmed down."

"Well, shit." Gia knits her hands together on her lap.

"We wouldn't be asking this if the situation wasn't serious and urgent," I supply.

"We will do our utmost to ensure you are protected and you get out alive. O'Hara has promised to provide protection from the inside. We can't tell you one hundred percent you will come out of this unscathed, but we will do everything we can to keep you safe," Massimo adds as Ben and Caleb reenter the room.

Air expels from her mouth. She waits until everyone is seated before nodding. "Okay. I'll do it. I understand the risks and what's expected of me, and I'll do everything I can to get the intel we need." She drills Caleb with a look. "Including spreading my legs if that's what it takes."

Chapter Six
Gia

"Nice car," I say, admiring the custom leather interiors as Joshua reverses his Maserati out of the parking space.

"Do you have history with Cristian?" he asks, out of nowhere, completely ignoring my comment. He didn't say a single word to me from the time we left the meeting, rode the elevator, collected my stuff at the armory, and got into his car in the underground parking lot of Commission HQ. He just stared straight ahead, exuding irritation. It's not my fault he's been assigned as my handler or that he had to reschedule his entire day to assist with my transformation. I could easily have managed it myself, but time is of the essence, and Joshua will apparently be able to pull strings to get shit done quicker than me.

It's not like I can disagree anyway. I know I crossed the line a few times upstairs when I let anger get the better of me. I was so freaking mad at first until it was explained more clearly. Can't say I'm happy I might have to fuck that Irish prick, but I'll do it if it comes down to it. I just don't want the board to see me as some femme fatale they can roll out when the need arises. I didn't sign up to be Mata Hari. I want the assignments the guys get too.

"Answer me," Joshua commands, yanking me from my inner monologue.

Joshua used to be sweet and kind, but there is no trace of that boy in the man he is today. It's sad really, but this life can do that to a person. I've seen it more times than I can count. I glance out the window as he drives into lunchtime traffic. "I know Cristian because of the circles we mix in. You were at most of the same parties, events, and family gatherings." I'm fudging my answer on purpose because fuck him. He doesn't get to ask me personal shit and snap at me like I'm some kind of performing animal.

"Unlike you, Cristian actually acknowledges me and takes the time to speak with me. We know one another." I'm feeling particularly mean-spirited because his twin really pushed my buttons, and Joshua's cold treatment of me thus far hasn't endeared me to him either, so I blurt the next part knowing it will hurt him. "You were always too busy fawning over Bettina and sucking face with her to notice anything or anyone else."

I jerk forward in my seat as he slams his foot down on the brake and flicks the hazards on. Horns blare around us, and it's a miracle the car behind didn't rearend us. Joshua's hand is wrapped around my throat before I've had time to process him unbuckling his seat belt and lunging at me. "Do not mention that fucking bitch in my presence ever again unless you have a death wish." Vitriol drips from his lips and spews from his eyes.

I grab his wrist, scratching at his skin as he tightens his grip and squeezes my throat. Panic surges through my veins as I struggle to breathe. Joshua is like the devil incarnate as he glowers at me with visible hatred. I'm not even sure he's fully with it.

Someone bangs on the driver's side window, and Joshua snaps out of it. My hands gently clasp my sore neck as I gasp loudly, trying to drag enough air into my lungs so I can breathe. Joshua grabs his gun from the glove pocket and lowers the window.

"What the—woah, buddy, put that thing away." I move my hand toward my leg while watching the interaction with the poor sucker who thought he could challenge Joshua for stopping in the middle of traffic like the freaking lunatic he is. Joshua prods the man's chest with the muzzle of his gun as I stealthily unsheathe the dagger strapped to my lower leg.

"I'm in a real shitty mood, and I don't need much incentive to pull the trigger, so get the fuck out of my face," he snaps at the terrified man.

He's in a shitty mood? He wasn't the one almost strangled. Asshole.

"Fucking psycho," the man shouts as he tears off before Joshua can put a bullet in his skull.

I always thought Caleb was the unhinged twin, but I'm reassessing my beliefs now. "Was that really necessary?" I rasp, hiding my dagger under my right thigh.

"It's your fault," he says in a detached tone, shutting the window and putting his gun away.

"Real mature, asshole. How old are you again?"

"Shut. Up." He starts the engine, and I make my move.

Joshua turns rigid in his seat as steel presses against his crotch. Horns blare behind us again as he lowers his gaze to where I'm holding my dagger snug against his dick. I glare at him, pouring every ounce of hatred I currently feel into the look as I push against him with my blade. "If you try anything like that ever again, I'll chop your dick off and stuff it down your throat. I don't care you're a don and I might lose my life. I'll do it."

How fucking dare he put his hands on me without permission.

He could have strangled me!

Fucking psycho prick.

A muscle pops in his jaw as he levels me with a lethal look. "Point made." His eyes bore into mine as we face off for a few tense seconds.

"Good. Don't forget it," I say, retracting my dagger and re-sheathing it as he finally resumes driving.

Silence descends as we both stew for the rest of the journey. I take the opportunity to read the paperwork in the envelope Massimo gave me. Emma Brown is my new name. Boring but inconspicuous. Brown is the third most common last name in the city, so it's a good choice. My pic on the ID has been doctored to show me with red hair and green eyes, and it's how I'm going to look by the end of the day.

"Where are we?" I blurt, unconsciously breaking the silence twenty minutes later when he signals to turn into an underground parking lot. I look up at the tall modern building facing onto Central Park with curiosity.

The jerk ignores me, so I decide not to speak to him again.

I follow him out of the car and into the mirrored elevator, watching as he punches a code into the mounted keypad. I inspect my throat in the mirror, hoping it's not going to bruise. It's still tender, but I don't think there is any permanent damage.

We get out on the highest level, entering a small square lobby with painted black walls. A plush gold carpet is soft underfoot, leading to two glossy black doors, one on either side of the space. A fancy table housing a bunch of white roses is propped against the wall in front of us. A framed work of modern art is mounted above the table, looking like it probably cost a small fortune. Overhead spotlights provide adequate illumination as I trail Joshua to the door on the left.

He presses his thumb to the digital panel on the door, and it opens with a subtle click. Joshua steps aside to let me enter first. This hallway is wider and longer than the one outside, decorated in cool grays, whites, and blues. My eyes are out on stalks when I reach the main room, widening as I drink in my surroundings. To my right is a decent-sized kitchen with marble counters and expensive appliances. Four stools rest against one side of the island unit. Apart from a fruit bowl and a complicated-looking coffee machine, there is nothing else out on the counters. Almost like it's not lived in.

"Keep up," the asshole says, striding past the kitchen and me. I flip him the bird behind his back. Childish but hugely satisfactory.

A long wooden table and ten sleek chairs with gray velvet backs rest alongside the first floor-to-ceiling window. Light floods the space from all angles, and I wish I could stop to admire the view of the park, but the dickhead is powering through the living area, heading for the winding staircase at the rear.

I rush past the L-shaped beige leather couch positioned in front of an electric fire. On the other side of the large room is a small library and reading area with rows of shelving and comfy tub chairs. Colorful throws, cushions, rugs, and artwork lift the otherwise stark space, elevating it into something classy but homey.

This can't be where Joshua lives, but it was my initial assumption when he first opened the door.

"Gia. Get up here!" Annoyance threads through his tone as he shouts down to me from the next level. His arms are resting on a glass half-wall that peers down on the floor below. A firm scowl is etched on his face, but it still doesn't detract from his hotness.

Unfortunately.

I hate to admit it, but Joshua Accardi is a beautiful bastard. I always thought so as a young girl, but he's really grown into his skin now he's older. He takes care with his appearance, and it shows. Unlike his twin, he doesn't usually sport facial hair, preferring a smooth jawline, which I happen to love. His big blue eyes can be equally smoldering and as glacial as the Ice Caves at Sam's Point. Where Caleb wears his dark-blond hair in a stylishly messy fashion, Joshua's thick hair is always slicked back off his face.

He's consistently immaculately groomed and always dressed to impress, favoring expensive suits that highlight every gorgeous inch of his toned body. The confident vibe he emits is that of a man who is always in control. In fact, everything about him screams control, and I sense that's on purpose.

I trudge up the spiral staircase hating that I'm attracted to the jerk.

But who doesn't drool over a hot guy in a suit?

It doesn't mean *anything*.

When I reach the second level, Joshua has his arms folded across his chest as he leans against the far wall. His impatience bleeds into the air, and I'm glad I'm annoying him.

His eyes lower to my throat for a second, and some of the harshness leaves his face. He drops his arms. "Come."

I follow him down the hallway, passing copious doors, until we reach a large bathroom.

"Sit." He jerks his head at the closed toilet seat as we enter the room.

What the fuck? Keep up. Get up here. Come. Sit. Natalia didn't raise her sons to be such mannerless dicks. Holding my ground, I plant my hands on my hips and shoot daggers at him. "I am not a dog. I do not obey your every command. I'm a person, with feelings, and I deserve a certain level of respect." Anger pitches inside me. I jab him in his chest, and it's like trying to poke a wall. Ugh. He frustrates me to no end. "That includes not trying to strangle me because I mentioned *she who should not be named.*" I was tempted to say it again, but I value breathing, and I know how to pick my battles.

Differing emotions flit over his face before settling on remorse. I arch a brow as I eyeball him. His tongue darts out, wetting his plump lips. "I apologize, Gia. That was unforgivable. It's my issue, and I had no right to take it out on you."

I stare at him in shock. Did the cold and mighty Joshua Accardi just show emotion and say sorry? I could continue to bust his balls, but I've got to work with him for the foreseeable future. Massimo assigned Joshua as my main contact on the undercover op. It's better to try to reset things from the outset, and I won't need the additional stress, so I decide to be magnanimous.

"Apology accepted, and I'm sorry for bringing her up. I'm aware of what she did and how you must feel about her." That's true, but I honestly thought he was over it by now. Apparently not if it's still such a touchy subject.

A muscle pops in his jaw, and he's holding himself rigidly still.

"For what it's worth, she is a fool. Elisa and I used to watch you two together and dream of having a boyfriend who treated us so well. You worshipped the ground she walked on, and she was a complete bitch to throw that back in your face."

"I don't want to talk about it," he says in a clipped tone, opening the bathroom cupboard and retrieving a medical kit.

"I just wanted you to know it was nothing you did, and if you ask me, you had a lucky escape."

"Gia," he growls, narrowing his eyes as he sets the kit down on the counter.

"Shutting up now." I drag my finger along my lips in a zipping motion.

He points at the toilet again. "Please take a seat so I can examine your neck."

I move quickly, depositing my butt on the closed lid. His brows climb to his hairline, and I answer his unspoken question as I smile up at him. "You asked nicely. It's as simple as that, Joshua."

Chapter Seven
Joshua

I probe her neck with a soft touch, careful not to inflict any more damage. I lost it in the car. I zoned out, and for a few seconds, it wasn't Gia's smooth skin under my fingertips, it was Ina's. I'm usually more successful at blocking out thoughts of my ex—and no one talks about her anymore—so Gia caught me off guard, but it's no excuse for the way I treated her.

"I don't think it'll bruise, but I'll put this on anyway," I say, reaching for the arnica cream. I'm embarrassed I reacted like that. Disgusted I attacked her so viciously when she's done nothing to deserve it.

Mom would be furious with me and not just because Gia is Frankie's daughter. She has raised us to always treat women with respect and to never raise a hand in anger to any female, no matter the circumstances. We have both failed, and she'd be so disappointed if she knew. I hate upsetting Mom because she means everything to me. She sacrificed a lot for Caleb and me, and she's been the one true constant in our lives. Disappointing her is something I try to avoid, so this kills me.

"I can do it." Gia reaches for the tube.

"Let me." I circle my hand around her wrist, purposely gentling my touch. "It's the least I can do."

Her brows climb to her hairline, and I feel like a piece of shit all over again. I don't know if I got out of the wrong side of bed today or if it's all this shit with the Irish and the traitor in our midst, but I'm not feeling in control, and I'm on edge. I don't overreact to situations. I don't react with anger or violence, yet I've done both today, and it unsettles me.

"Joshua. Are you okay?"

I realize I've just been staring into space. Releasing Gia's hand, I squeeze some ointment onto my fingers. "I'm fine. It's been a tense couple of days, and I haven't gotten much sleep."

What the actual fuck, Joshua? Why on earth did I blurt that shit? Maybe it's her. Maybe Gia is the one messing with my mind.

Shoving those thoughts aside, I concentrate on applying anti-bruising cream to her skin. Her flesh is warm and silky smooth as I massage it in, taking my time to ensure I'm covering both sides of her neck where my fingers gripped her. A fresh wave of shame washes over me before I'm distracted by the slight hitch in her throat and the faint blush crawling up her neck and onto her cheeks.

I'm suddenly aware of how intimate this is with me bending down over her within the confines of my bathroom. Our faces and bodies are close enough to touch, and tingles spread over my hand and up my arm as I caress her soft skin.

"I think that's enough," she whispers. Her chest heaves, and air trickles from her full lips. Her warm breath fans across the side of my face, scorching my skin every place it touches. Our eyes connect, and I should look away, but I can't. We stare at one another as electricity crackles in the small space between us, and it's as if there's a string connecting our bodies and I'm being tugged into her orbit.

She's fucking beautiful. How have I never noticed before?

Her big blue eyes convey so much, and I know I'm not the only one feeling this weird chemistry between us. The thought is enough to break the spell, and I jerk back and straighten up, needing distance. My heart is pounding against my rib cage, and my goddamn hands are still tingling. Must be the arnica, I lie to myself.

She clears her throat and stands as I turn on the faucet and apply soap to my hands. "Thank you."

"Don't thank me. Not for that," I say, irritated all over again. I lather my hands and rinse them under the flowing water while I avoid looking at her. I'm drying my hands when a security system alert pings on my cell phone. I glance at the screen before repocketing the phone. "The hairdresser is here." I fold the towel and place it on the heated radiator before walking out of the bathroom after Gia. "I'll get you settled and then let him in." I lead her to my private spa and open the door.

"Holy shit." She steps inside with a dreamlike expression on her face. "I can't believe you have all this at home." Her brow puckers, and she loses the childlike wonder in her gaze. "I didn't realize you had a girlfriend."

"I don't." I lean against the doorway, fighting amusement.

"Oh. *Oh.*" Her fingers dance across the massage table as her eyes flit over the hair station, freestanding tub, and rainforest shower, drinking it all in. The shelving unit tucked into the corner holds various toiletries and towels. "This is for your wh —lady friends."

A laugh bursts from my lips of its own volition. "That's one way of putting it."

She narrows her eyes and plants her hands on her hips.

"I'm trying to be polite, out of respect for the women you sleep with, not you," she adds, shooting fire from her eyes.

"I don't bring women here. Only the female staff and my mom have been at my penthouse."

She blinks repeatedly. "You don't take your fuck buddies home?"

I arch a brow. "What happened to respect?"

"I'm done being polite. Let's call a spade a spade unless you're telling me I'm wrong?"

"You're not wrong, and we're not doing this. Who I fuck is none of your business." I step into the room. "My home is my haven, and I like privacy. It's why I pay a masseuse, a beauty therapist, and a hairdresser to come once a month to attend to my needs."

Her face contorts, and she looks like she just sucked on a lemon. I fight the urge to laugh again. "Get your mind out of the gutter, Gia. It's all strictly professional."

"Actually, that's not what I was thinking. At all. I was trying to decide if I was jealous or horrified that any man could be so vain to have all this in his private residence."

"You call it vanity. I call it self-care."

"At least it explains all this." She waves her hands up and down my body.

I can't fight my grin this time. "Liking what you see?"

She scoffs before rolling her eyes. "As if. I'm just stating the facts. You know you look good. You had a freaking spa built at your home for fuck's sake."

My cell pings again letting me know Alexander has arrived at the front door. "My hairdresser is here, and Rosemary, my beauty therapist, will arrive in a couple of hours. I'm having your new wardrobe delivered later. By the time you're done tonight, I'll have a new apartment and car lined up."

"Wow, you're a fast worker."

"We don't have time to waste."

Her expression turns more sober. "No, we don't."

I leave Gia in Alexander's expert hands while I retreat to my office on the upper level to make a few calls. I'm turned around in my chair, looking out the window at the view of Central Park when the call I'm waiting on comes through. "Kennedy," I answer the second I press the speaker button on my desktop phone to accept Keanu's call.

"Accardi." There's a brief pause. "I spoke with Rachel, and we made it happen. I have a driver on the way to you. He should be there within the hour."

"Thank you. I appreciate you pulling out all the stops. Send me the invoice directly, and I'll pay it immediately. Please pass my regards and gratitude to Rachel."

"Consider it done."

"Hit me up anytime I can return the favor."

"I'm still intrigued. I didn't think you dated let alone date a woman who refuses to wear the Accardi brand." He chuckles. "Your girlfriend must be someone special if you're going to all this trouble."

Movement behind me lifts all the hairs on the back of my neck. I swivel in my chair, eyeballing the stunning redhead standing in my doorway. "She deserves to look a million dollars, so no trouble is too much trouble."

"Cagey as ever, Accardi." Keanu chuckles.

"I owe you one."

"Happy to help. Say hi to Caleb," he says before hanging up.

"Who was that?" Gia asks, stepping into my office.

"Have you ever heard of knocking?" I cross my feet at the ankles and lean back in my leather chair as she walks toward me.

"I planned to, but then I heard you speaking, and I didn't want to interrupt your call."

"You'd just rather eavesdrop."

She shrugs, like it's no biggie, as she flops into the chair in front of me. "Is it eavesdropping if it concerns me? And I'm an informant. Spying is second nature."

"Glad to hear it. To answer your question, that was Keanu Kennedy."

"No way!" She sits up straighter in her chair. "He's gorgeous. All those Kennedy men are."

"If you're into old dudes."

She bursts out laughing. "I can appreciate a good-looking man of any age, and youthful genes clearly runs in their family. Besides, Hewson Kennedy isn't an old man. He's a freshman at Harvard."

"Stalker much?"

More laughter spills from her mouth. "If you weren't such a cold fish, I'd say you were jealous. But we're getting off topic. What's going on, and why does he think I'm your girlfriend?"

"You need a new wardrobe, and we can't dress you from our label because there can't be any hint of an Italian connection. We want to keep this on the down-low, so I called Keanu. He understands the need for discretion, and I knew he could get his hands on what we needed ASAP. Rachel McConaughey is practically his family, and she has a large store near Sak's Fifth Avenue. She's sending over your new wardrobe now."

"Oh my God. I freaking love Rachel's brand!" She's close to bouncing in her chair, and amusement tickles the corners of my lips. "It feels like I'm having my own *Pretty Woman* moment."

"I don't recall there being a gun-toting Irish mafia prick Julia Roberts had to seduce in that movie?"

"You've watched *Pretty Woman?*" Her tone drips with disbelief.

All good humor fades. Why does my ex keeping cropping up? Fuck this day. Can it seriously be over already? "Change the subject," I grit out.

She drills me with a pensive look, like she's trying to dig a hole in my head and extract my innermost thoughts. Her features soften a little, and I'm guessing she's worked it out. I'm grateful she doesn't articulate it. "How did you know what size to buy?"

"I called my mom, and she called yours."

"You could have just asked me!" Her voice elevates a few notches. "I'm a grown-ass woman and a professional. You didn't have to involve either of our mothers."

"You were busy with Alexander, and it seemed easier to call Mom."

The muscles in her face relax. "Okay, fine. I suppose that makes sense. But, in the future, I'd prefer you keep our families out of work-related matters."

"Sure."

She tosses her hair over her shoulders, and waves of glossy reddish-brown hair cascade down her back. Blonde highlights glint under the stark overhead lighting adding an extra dimension.

"Your hair is stunning. That color really suits you, and it looks very natural."

A genuine smile ghosts over her mouth, transforming her beauty into something ethereal. "Thank you. Alexander was thrilled with my 'virgin' hair." She makes little quote marks with her fingers. "He said the fact I haven't ever dyed my hair made his job easier." She shrugs. "Anyway, he sent me up here to check you were okay with it before he left." The smile fades as she purses her lips. "I thought about stabbing him when he said that, but he's too nice and too skilled to deprive the world of his talent."

"Unlike *someone* I could mention, he knows how to conduct himself appropriately and do what he's paid to do."

"I know how to act appropriately." Her lips jut out in a pout. "The overly misogynistic commentary today is playing havoc with my professionalism. Every time a man says something disgustingly sexist, I have this crazy urge to cut their tongues from their mouths so they can't utter anything so heinous ever again."

"You'll need to control those urges because you're about to seduce a senior member of the Irish mafia, and you can bet the environment will be sexist."

"I'm well aware and capable of dealing with it. It's a job. What I don't expect is to receive that treatment from my own kind."

"Everything we are doing is for your protection."

"I don't see how *you* having to rubberstamp *my* new hairstyle has anything to do with protection."

I get up and walk around my desk, stopping behind her. "You're tasked with seducing a powerful man, so a man's perspective is all-important."

"This is such bullshit, but whatever," she says, tipping her head back to look up at me.

I reach for her hair, stopping at the last second. "Can I touch you?" Her eyes startle, and a chuckle rips from my lips. "Your hair, Gia. Can I touch your hair?"

"Why?"

"Humor me."

She mutters something under her breath before conceding. "Fine."

Threading my fingers through the silky-soft strands, I marvel at how luxurious her hair feels to the touch. Alexander cut some layers, and it looks thicker and glossier, and it feels amazing.

"Well?" she asks in a slightly breathless voice. "Do I pass inspection?"

My eyes lower to her chest for the first time, and I stop breathing. I was so entranced with her hair I didn't even realize she'd ditched her red suit jacket and she's only wearing a white silk camisole top over her red pants. From this angle, I have a decent view of her chest, and it's possible I might be frothing at the mouth. Her breasts rest high on her chest, held together by a white silk bra with a lace overlay. They are fucking huge, and I'm practically drooling now. Visions of burying my face in her ample flesh accost me without warning, and I jerk back to put distance between us, removing my hands from her hair. I'm praying she doesn't spot the semi growing in my pants.

"I meant my hair, you pig." Her nostrils flare as she folds her arms protectively against her chest and storms past me.

Shit.

"Gia!" I call out after her.

"Fuck off," she hollers before disappearing through my door.

I sigh as I reclaim my chair and spin around to look out the window. Is this what my life will be like over the coming weeks and months or however long it takes for us to shake down McDermott and identify the rat in our ranks? And why is there a fissure of excitement racing through my veins at the thought of spending more time with the fiery Gia Bianchi?

Chapter Eight
Gia

I knock back a shot of vodka for liquid courage as I stand in front of the full-length mirror and inspect my reflection. I look as out of place as I feel in this new Brooklyn apartment. Joshua drove me here last night and someone—probably Mom—boxed up my things, and they were waiting in the large open-plan living space when we arrived.

The apartment isn't huge. Just an open-plan living space with a modest living room, modern kitchen, compact laundry room, and a small dining area. The other side houses a main bathroom and a large en suite bedroom with a walk-in closet. It's brand-new and clearly catering to young professionals. The design is minimalist with a mix of cool gray and white walls and plain furniture. There's the odd splash of color, but it's quite austere. It's not something I'd choose for myself, but it fits the profile.

Instead of spending the day making my goodbyes to my family and my best friend, I've been holed up here, memorizing every minuscule detail of my fake background.

Elements of my own history are embedded in my fake ID.

Joshua said it's easier to base the lies on some truth so I'm not caught off guard. Emma Brown is the oldest of four siblings; her parents have been happily married for twenty-four years; her father is a financial adviser in the city, and her mom is a stay-at-home mom. She, I, graduated early from NYU with a computer science degree, and I now work as a freelance project manager for a small portfolio of niche clients, mainly start-ups.

My personal cell rings, and I smile when I see my friend's gorgeous face on the screen. I swipe to answer Elisa's call. "Hey, babe. Did you get my text?"

"I did. Sorry I'm so late calling. I've been locked away in the library all day."

"It's cool. I'm sorry for bailing tonight."

"How come? What's up? And what happened at the meeting yesterday? I tried calling you last night."

"I know. I didn't have time to call you back. I was too busy moving into my new apartment." I walk toward the window in my bare feet and lounge on the window seat as I stare at the dark New York skyline.

"What's going on?"

"I wish I could tell you, but I can't. It's highly confidential and not safe for anyone to know. I couldn't even tell Mom. I'm not going to be around for a while."

"How long is a while?"

I shrug even though she can't see me. "It could be weeks or months. I don't know."

"You're going undercover, aren't you?"

"Yes, but you didn't hear that from me." I figure I'm safe telling her that much. I'm sure the rents are all aware, and someone was bound to mention it at some point.

"Is it dangerous?" Worry threads through her tone.

"Yes, but I'll be fine. I've got skills, and they've given me a ton of high-tech tools to help with the mission. I'll be okay."

"I'm really going to miss you. I'd just gotten used to having you back."

"I'll miss you too, but you've got your college friends, and maybe you should give that guy a chance. The one who keeps asking you out on a date. He can distract you if you're missing me too much."

Elisa and I are super close, and we usually talk every day on the phone and hang out at least a few times a week. It's been harder in recent months 'cause I was in Nepal undergoing training, but when we were both at NYU studying, we spent tons of time together.

"Seb is nice, but he's not my type."

I snort out a laugh. "You don't have a type, Lise. There's only one man you've ever crushed on, ever noticed, and I hate to break it to you, babe, but Caleb Accardi is an arrogant sexist pig. If I was determined to help you get over him before, it's nothing on how determined I am now."

"Why? Did something happen at the meeting?"

"He was rude and disrespectful to me. Ben even had to pull him aside to talk to him. Honestly, babe, I don't know what you see in him. I know he's hot. Both twins are, but Caleb is a pig, and you deserve better."

"He's always nice to me."

I'm not surprised she's defending him because she always does. Her statement isn't untrue either. Caleb is considerate with Elisa in a way he's not with most other women—his mom, my mom, and aunts excluded. I'm guessing it's because he knows Elisa much better than me. They even spent time living together in Ben and Sierra's house as kids, and he's got to be aware of how she feels about him.

She was always following him around, drawing him pictures, baking goodies for him, and offering to help with anything he needed growing up. Elisa literally worships the ground he walks on, and I honestly don't get it. While I know he cares for her, he has never given any indication he sees her as more than a casual friend. "I know, and it's his only redeeming factor. But trust me when I say he makes an exception for you because he was disgusting."

"I will talk to him when I see him next. Tell him he's got to be nice to you too."

I love Elisa to bits, but man, she's so sheltered. And so blind when it comes to that man.

"I've got to go, babe. I'm sorry for ditching you tonight. You should go out and party. No point in wasting what's left of your college experience. And if I was you, I'd be climbing Seb like a spider monkey and taking a bounce on his dick."

"You're incorrigible."

"And you're wasting all that college dick holding out for a guy who is not worthy of you." I want to say more, but Elisa gets testy when it comes to Caleb. He's the only thing we have ever argued about.

"I want Caleb to be my first, and I'm prepared to wait for him."

"Let's not fight," I say, counting to ten in my head. "Have fun and don't call me. I'll call you whenever I can."

"Be safe. Love you, Gigi."

"Love you too, Lise."

"You look good," Joshua says an hour later when I arrive at the warehouse where we're meeting Liam's brother Diarmuid. Joshua hired a guy to act as my taxi driver for the night, and he's waiting outside to take me to the club where Liam is celebrating his promotion. I'm guessing the driver is trustworthy, or he wouldn't be here.

Joshua's gaze crawls over my fitted black and gold knee-length dress and matching stilettos. He doesn't linger on my chest, but I'm sure he wants to. Or maybe he got a good enough look yesterday when he ogled me like it was the first time he'd ever seen a pair of tits.

I hate having big tits. I hate the attention it garners from the opposite sex. I developed early and had to endure lewd propositions and disgusting comments from guys at school while fielding jealous looks from most of the girls. Constant back strain is another reason I'm considering having a breast reduction. I normally dress carefully to avoid drawing attention to my large cleavage, but there's no hiding the girls with this neckline. It highlights enough to clarify I'm well-endowed without showing the goods. Liam likes his women young, busty, and confident, apparently, but he prefers them to look elegant, not trashy.

"Come around the back," Joshua says, glancing around before we walk off.

The ground is uneven, and I stumble a little in my heels. Joshua's arm darts out, and he slides it along my lower back, helping to keep me steady. In my heels, I'm only a few inches shorter than him, yet his presence looms over mine as he commands the air around us. Heat seeps through the sleeve of his suit jacket and my dress, warming me all over as my heart thumps faster and the vein in my neck pulses. Spicy citrusy notes of his cologne tickle my nostrils, and I hate I'm so aware of him.

"What is Diarmuid like?" I ask, needing to engage in conversation to distract me.

"He's a good man. You'll like him."

Joshua ushers me into the warehouse where a couple of armed Accardi *soldati* are waiting. "Diarmuid is en route. I wanted to talk to you first to ensure you're ready."

"I'm as ready as I'll ever be. I'm wearing my contacts. I've memorized my background, got my new cell with built-in dagger, and I'm wearing the watch." I didn't bother bringing the camera pen with me tonight as I won't need that yet. I hold up my wrist, showcasing the specialist watch he had delivered to me today.

"Good." Joshua taps the small button on the left of the watch face. "If it's an emergency, press that one to alert Diarmuid." His finger moves to the second button on the other side. "And this one to alert me." He removes something shiny from his pocket. "May I put these on?" he asks, peering deep into my eyes as he holds two pretty circular diamond earrings in his palm. He gains brownie points for asking. I think his remorse yesterday was genuine, and warmth blossoms in my chest at the thought he's trying for me.

I nod to signal my consent.

"They match the bracelet you're wearing, but these aren't just for show," he says, gently clasping my left ear. "Once worn, if you press in on them, they will activate the audio recording." He makes quick work removing my stud and replacing it with the diamond. His touch is precise and careful, and I'm feeling it all the way to the tips of my toes. He presses in on the earring twice. "Press on it a second time to switch the audio off, but I suggest you always wear them when you're with him. It's safer that way. Lie and say they were your dead grandmother's and you never remove them."

He turns his attention to my other ear, and his fingers brush against the side of my neck as he replaces that earring. Delicious tremors skate over my skin, and lust coils low in my belly. Heat swamps my cheeks, and I'm feeling out of my depth as he stares at me. "Did Aldo and Pisano have access to the same tech?" I ask, needing to keep him talking before I do something stupid like jump him.

"They did. We ensure all our informants have as much support as we can give them. The issue your friends faced was inability to get close enough to McDermott. The rank and file don't know anything, or if they do, they didn't share that intel with our men."

Joshua's fingers dance against the top of my chest as he picks up the sapphire necklace I'm wearing. I barely contain a moan as fire scorches my skin from his touch. "Is this what I think it is?"

I nod. "Your mom had one made for my mom years ago. It was with my things at the new apartment."

He carefully pries it open, exposing the two hidden vials within. "This is a replica of the necklace that saved Serena Salerno's life."

"I'm aware. It's why Natalia had one made for my mom."

"What's in it?" He squints as he examines the clear liquid in both vials.

"A sleep aid in one and poison in the other." My lips twitch. "Fiero said I could get creative, and I intend to."

"Be careful." His hands rest lightly on my shoulders as he peers deep into my eyes. It's like being sucker punched in the crotch because I feel the intensity of his look and his touch in my most intimate place. "I mean it. Liam is manipulative. Don't underestimate him, and make sure you cover your tracks. If you sense something is amiss or you're in danger, use the watch. Or say the codeword. We have a dedicated four-person team listening to the audio and scanning your location on the chip-tracking system twenty-four-seven. If you need help, they'll know, and we'll move in fast. Do not take unnecessary risks."

"Careful, Accardi. You're starting to sound like you care," I tease to deflect the rising tension and my growing anxiety. The closer I get to doing this, the more real it becomes. I'm excited to be doing something useful and so important. This is what

I've trained for. This is why I wanted this job so badly. But I'd be lying if I said I wasn't scared shitless.

"Of course, I care. You're one of us, Gia, and if anything happens to you, your father will riddle the board with bullets. We've already lost two good men; we don't want to lose anyone else."

"I can handle myself. They put us through the wringer in Nepal. It's why so many dropped out or failed to make the cut. I'm a survivor, and no Irish prick is taking me down."

"Good to know," an unfamiliar man says from behind me. The lilting accent gives his identity away, and my eyes pop wide as I realize who I've just insulted.

Chapter Nine
Gia

I turn around and face Diarmuid O'Hara as he approaches. "Although I was not referring to you, my comment was unprofessional, and I apologize, Mr. O'Hara." This isn't the kind of first impression I wanted to make. Diarmuid will be my only ally on the inside, and I want him to like me so he fights to ensure I make it out alive.

I've seen photos of him and his brother—they were in the file I received—and both are good-looking dudes, but Diarmuid's picture has not done him justice. His blue eyes are a deep navy with vast swirling depths, and his thick hair is darker in real life. If it was sunny, I'd no doubt see the evidence of reddish undertones. He's tall and broad but not quite as tall or broad as Joshua.

"There is no need to apologize, Ms. Bianchi. Calling my brother a prick is a kindness he doesn't deserve."

"Wow. I really can't wait to meet him now," I joke, extending my hand. "And please call me Gia."

"Only if you call me Diarmuid." He lifts my hand to his mouth, pressing a kiss on my skin. Out of the corner of my eye,

I notice Joshua clenching his jaw. "You are very beautiful, Gia," Diarmuid says in that singsong voice, smiling as he casts a quick respectful glance over me. "My brother will be tripping over himself to get to you."

"That's the plan," Joshua says in a voice devoid of warmth and emotion. "We're all set to go on our side."

"As are we." O'Hara sends a curious gaze Joshua's way.

"You can let go of her hand now."

Diarmuid's eyes widen as he releases me. "Apologies, Gia. I didn't realize I was still holding your hand."

"It's fine. I didn't mind." I flash him a flirty grin.

What the hell, Gia?

"So, um, how will the introduction work?" I ask, my gaze bouncing between both men as they appear to size one another up. I thought they were friends as much as work partners, so I don't understand where this masculine bullshit is coming from.

"You're to act as the date of one of my men," Diarmuid explains. "He's a regular at the club Liam is attending tonight. You'll dance and flirt in front of my brother. He won't be able to resist when he sees you on the arm of one of my guys. He'll enjoy stealing you from him."

"I read your report in the files I was given. How does this strategy fit the play-hard-to-get suggestion?"

"Liam's ego exists on its own planet. He'll expect you to be attracted to him and to be unable to resist ditching your date for him. Once he knows you're into it, then you keep him dangling. If you give in too easily, he'll lose interest fast. He loves the chase."

"We don't have time to let this play out long-term," Joshua says. "Gia needs to gain his trust quickly."

"I didn't say the chase had to be long. Just don't give in the first few times he asks you out, and make him wait to bed you. The more worked up you can get him, the more he might slip up and give something away. Liam is thirty-one in a few weeks, and he's been talking about finding a bride. Show him you're marriage material, and you'll have him eating out of the palm of your hand."

"Okay. I can do that."

"I have a couple guys watching out for you. They are close with some of Liam's men. I won't introduce you because it's better you don't know. But they'll be keeping their eyes and ears to the ground and protecting you as best they can."

"I appreciate it. Don't worry about me. I'm trained and resourceful."

"I've seen your credentials. You're a very impressive young woman, Gia, and no one is taking you down on my watch."

"Call me when you're on your way home," Joshua says as we linger by the taxi. "And we expect regular reports, as long as it's safe to submit them."

"I know the score, Joshua. And I'm a computer science major. I'll leave no trace."

"We have faith in you. Watch your back." He walks off, and I admire the view of his broad shoulders, trim waist, and toned ass before I get a grip and climb into the back seat where my fake date is waiting.

Owen is a nice guy, and we chat casually on the way to the club, and it helps to keep my nerves at bay.

Owen helps me out of the car when we arrive, keeping a firm hold of my hand as we bypass the long line and head straight toward the VIP entrance. He gives our names to the beefcake at the door, and we're escorted inside.

The club is bustling as you'd expect from one of the most popular hangouts in The Big Apple. It's been on Elisa's list and mine to check out and a pang of sadness slaps me in the face that I'm not experiencing it with my bestie.

Owen gets us drinks. A virgin mojito for me and a beer for him. He steers me toward the VIP entrance with one hand on my lower back. "Stick by my side at all times until you've snared Liam," he says into my ear as we climb the stairs to the upper level.

"Got it."

He stops at the top, turning to face me. "We'll have to get a bit handsy, maybe kiss a bit. That okay with you?"

Owen is cute, so flirting with him won't be a chore. I grin as I plant my hand on his chest. "Not a problem, Owen. We've both got jobs to do, and this isn't the hard part." I brush my lips against his mouth. "We should both act how we would on a real date."

He chuckles. "I don't date. I fuck." He waggles his brows, and I roll my eyes. "But I can pretend."

What is it with made men being complete and utter sluts? I think the Italians and the Irish are more alike than they'd care to admit.

Finding two empty stools at a high table close to the bar, we settle down to enjoy our drinks. Conversation flows easily as we scan our surroundings. It's busy up here too. All the booths at the back are occupied, and a heaving crowd throws shapes on the large dance floor. Beats thump through speakers from the DJ area downstairs.

It doesn't take long for us to locate Liam. His crew of ten commandeers two large booths tucked into the corner. Girls have gravitated to the area like flies on shit, and the Irish are lapping up the attention. Buckets with beer, cider, and bottles of whiskey sit on the tables as servers work fast to remove empties and replace glasses.

"I'm going to go to the bathroom," Owen says after taking a

swig from his beer. "Look around like you're bored. See if you can capture his eye."

I nod, and he walks off. Licking my lips, I raise my glass to my mouth and toss my hair back as I subtly look around. I angle my body in the stool, sitting up straighter and ensuring he has a good view of my side profile.

I feel him watching me, but I don't look over at first, casting my gaze around the room. Then I purposely turn in his direction, locking eyes. I dart my tongue out, wetting my lips, before I take a slow drink of my mojito. I look away and look back, deliberately fighting a smile and ensuring he sees it before I break eye contact again. We play this game for another few minutes, and I know I have his attention now. It's an effort not to squirm at the way his gaze lingers on my chest, but I remind myself I'm just acting. My normal insecurities about my chest have to take a hike for this mission.

The blonde perched on his lap shoots daggers my way. Her big tits are practically shoved in his face as she attempts to reclaim his attention, but I already know she's just someone he's picked to screw. She doesn't fit the profile, so she's only a temporary distraction.

When Owen returns, I plaster a big smile on my face, giving him my full attention. "It worked," he says, leaning in to kiss me.

"Like a charm," I agree, grabbing the back of his head before he can pull away. Our lips collide in a firm kiss, and I angle my head and thrust my chest out as I wind my arms around his neck. Owen is a good kisser, and if this was a normal date, I'd probably screw him later.

"Wow. You're really going for it," he says a few minutes later, tugging on my earlobe with his teeth.

"Go big or go home is my motto tonight. I can't afford to fuck this up."

"Come on then." His hands land on my hips as he helps me down from the stool. "By the way, you are fucking gorgeous. I should have said that already."

"You don't need to charm me, Owen, but I appreciate the compliment."

"It's no lie." He smirks at Liam as we walk by his table, and I fake big doe eyes when I quickly look in his direction. Liam's nostrils are flaring, and he's gripping the edge of the table. I'd say we've definitely ignited his competitive spirit.

Owen and I put on the show of a lifetime on the dance floor. I'm conscious not to overdo it. Liam is looking for a lady, not a woman who gives it away to others on the regular, so it's natural that I slap Owen's hands away when he gets a bit too amorous.

"He's watching us like a hawk, and he's not happy," Owen says, pulling me into his chest and squeezing my ass. "It's time to force him to make a move. Are you ready?"

"Born ready," I quip. I palm his face. "I was pretty nervous coming out tonight, but you've helped to put me at ease. Thank you."

"I got to kiss a pretty girl, and hanging out with you was fun. Trust me when I say no thanks are necessary." He presses a hard kiss to my mouth. "Maybe some time, when this is all over, we can go on a date for real."

"I thought you didn't date?" I lift a brow as we grind against one another, swaying to the music.

"I'd make an exception for you."

A genuine smile spreads across my mouth. "Rain check then?"

"Yes please." He moves his mouth to my ear. "He's probably going to get me thrown out, but I can wait outside to ensure you make it home safely."

I press my mouth to his ear as I shimmy my hips, conscious

Liam is watching. "Don't. He may want to escort me home, and I don't want him trying anything with you if he sees you outside."

"Are you sure?"

"One hundred percent."

"Okay. Let's do this." He waggles his brows before turning me around so Liam is getting a front-row view. "I apologize in advance." Owen's left hand digs into my hip as he grinds against me from behind. He's hard, and I'm a little turned on too. When he roughly grabs my boob with his free hand and fondles me in front of everyone, I don't have to act when I stomp down hard on his foot and dig my elbow into his stomach. He releases me with an oomph as I let the full force of my anger through. I spin around and slam my palms into his chest, knowing Liam is on his way over here without having it confirmed.

"How dare you touch me without permission! I'm not some whore you can feel up in public. I've got more respect for myself. We're done, and I never want to see you again."

Heat warms me from behind, and all the fine hairs on the back of my neck lift.

"Let me handle this, miss," a man with a deep voice says, and shivers skate over my skin. They're not the good kind though. His voice exudes arrogance and possessiveness that isn't even slightly attractive.

I briefly glance over my shoulder and lock eyes with Liam, forcing a little shock on my face before I compose myself. "I appreciate the offer, but I can handle myself." I hope my apology is written on my face as I lift my leg and knee Owen in the balls.

He curses, bending over and cupping his crotch.

"I can see that." Liam's amusement underscores his tone. He sounds nothing like his brother, but I wasn't expecting him to. Diarmuid lived in Ireland for thirteen years, yet Liam has lived his entire life in New York. There is no hint of an Irish accent in his voice.

"Ouch," another unfamiliar man says, coming up alongside Liam. I turn to look at him, instantly recognizing him from the file. He's Rian Murray, Liam's best friend and reported unofficial number two. "I wouldn't want to be on the receiving end of that."

"Get rid of him," Liam instructs, circling his arm around my waist uninvited.

"I don't like to be touched without permission," I calmly say, stepping out of his reach.

"I'm just keeping you safe, baby," he confirms, reaching for me again.

I fold my arms around myself, knowing it'll push my tits up. "Like I said, I appreciate it, but I can take care of me." Liam's eyes lower to my chest, and his pupils darken.

If he continues being this predictable, this should be a cakewalk.

"What's your name, beautiful?" he asks as Rian and a couple of other guys haul Owen up and drag him toward the stairway.

"I'm no one," I say, moving to push past him.

"You're most definitely someone." He falls into step alongside me. "I saw you looking at me earlier."

"You were looking at me first." I fling my hair over my shoulders.

"I'm not denying it." His fingers run through my hair because consent clearly means nothing to this guy. I let it go though, content to reel him in and push him away as we start to play this push-pull charade. "You have the most beautiful hair. You're fucking gorgeous, and I'm smitten."

I stop at my table and turn to face him. "You don't even

know me. It's impossible to be smitten with someone you've only just met."

"I beg to differ, gorgeous." He takes my hand and kisses it. Unlike the courteous way his brother did it, he presses his smarmy mouth to my skin, lingering as he sucks on it like it's his God-given right.

I yank my hand back. "I thought we already discussed this. I don't like to be touched unless it's consensual."

"Trust me, it will be." He flashes me a grin, dazzling me with a bright white smile. There is no denying he's a good-looking guy. He's got a couple inches in height on his older brother, but he has a similar build, and the same brownish-red hair. His eyes are green to Diarmuid's blue, but I'd still identify them as brothers in a lineup.

"Wow. I can't decide if you're arrogant or confident."

"Truthfully, it's a mix of both."

I grab my purse.

"Let me buy you a drink."

"I've already got one, and I'm not staying."

"What do I have to do to get you to stay and have a drink with me? I'll buy you the finest champagne. The most expensive bottle they have." He lifts his hand and snaps his fingers, and a guy gets up from one of their tables.

"I don't drink alcohol," I lie. Diarmuid mentioned Liam doesn't like women who drink too much and act inebriated. It's such sexist bullshit, especially since their tables are dripping with alcohol. His eyes automatically dart to the half-finished mojito on the table.

"It's a virgin. I prefer to stick to nonalcoholic beverages unless it's a special occasion. I'm concentrating on building my business, and I don't like losing time to hangovers when I could be out there growing my empire."

"Smart as well as beautiful? Now I'm intrigued. And this

definitely *is* a special occasion." He lifts his hand and touches my face. The guy truly has no respect for boundaries. "It's the night we met. We're going to remember this moment and tell our kids and grandkids all about it."

I blink repeatedly, and I don't even have to act shocked. "How many times have you used that line, and don't tell me it actually works?"

He throws back his head and laughs. "Never. It's not a line. I swear."

Liar.

He takes my hand again, rubbing his slobbery lips all over my knuckles. The guy is aesthetically pleasing to the eye, but he just creeps me out. If I manage to pull this off, it will be the greatest test of my willpower.

"I can't stay late. I have a project to work on tomorrow."

"I'll ensure you're home at a reasonable hour. I promise."

I pretend to think about it.

"Say yes, gorgeous. You won't regret it."

"Okay." I drill him with a look. "One drink, and no touching."

He offers me his arm and a smug grin. "Whatever you say."

Chapter Ten
Joshua

"**A**t least we've stopped the hijacking of our vans," I remind Fiero as he paces the length of my office, almost wearing a line in the carpet. "Using the security staff from Mazzone's firm to accompany all deliveries is working. We foiled another attempted robbery last night."

"It helps, but it's not enough."

I located an airline company willing to do business with us two weeks ago when our entire cargo was stolen. Fiero and Massimo's manager at their Colombia plant procured two-thirds of what we needed, and we had it on the streets three days later. But it was already too late. McDermott had used our supplies to undercut us.

The average joe on the street doesn't give a shit about loyalty when he's offered the same quality drugs for less. Now a large chunk of our street trade is being supplied by someone other than us, and it's a big issue. We can't concede and save face, and we don't want other outfits returning to the city. We drove the Triad, the Colombians, the Russians, and the

Paraguayans away five years ago, and I'm fucked if they're gaining new footing on my watch.

"More foreign supply has come in through Canada," Fiero confirms, "and we're losing customers every day. We need to catch McDermott in the act, and we need to do it the fuck now."

"We have men following him every time he goes out, but they are getting jack shit. Either McDermott has made the guys, or he's getting someone else to do his dirty work for him." I drum my fingers on top of my desk, puzzled as to how he's evading us so effectively. It doesn't make sense.

"I'm guessing it's the latter. He doesn't want his hands anywhere near this so O'Hara can't pin anything on him."

"He's got help." I lean back in my chair as I smooth a hand down my tie. "There's no way he could be avoiding detection unless he has a big backer."

We have a lot of manpower on this. Both online and on foot, and it's yielding no leads so far. The chip-tracking reports didn't give us much to go on either. Apart from a list of men who weren't in the vicinity during the time of the robbery. But there are still hundreds not accounted for 'cause they don't have a tracker. It's pretty much a dead end unless we can identify some criteria to narrow down the list. In the meantime, we have all agreed to manually peruse the chip-tracking lists and reports in case anything stands out. But it's a "needle in a haystack" task that is unlikely to deliver results.

"Or backers." Fiero drops into the seat in front of my desk with a weary sigh. "Is Gia gaining any traction yet?"

"It's still early days, but Liam is definitely on the hook. He's calling her twice daily, sending her regular flower and chocolate deliveries, and constantly asking her out on dates." He's so predictably cliché. The guy irritates me to no end.

"She needs to say yes." Fiero stabs me with a solemn look. "We need to move this along before we have no business left to protect."

"Any updates?" I ask one of the team working out of the basement of my building. Ben sent his tech specialists here so they were readily available to me. I decided to stop by before I head home early. There's a good chance my twin has forgotten our family dinner date, and I'm planning to swing by our apartment building to grab him before heading to Greenwich.

"Gia has agreed to a date with Liam tomorrow night."

"Good. Send the details to my secure cell and tell whichever *soldato* is shadowing McDermott to ensure he isn't spotted. I want regular updates throughout the night." Gia would bust my balls for keeping such a close watch over her, but I can't let anything happen to her. Liam is not trustworthy. He could pull any kind of shit.

"I'm heading home early today. Call if there is anything significant to relay," I add.

"Will do, boss."

I've just reached my car when my temp PA, Lavinia, comes rushing toward me. "Sorry to bother you, Joshua, but I need your signature on this paperwork."

"It's Mr. Accardi," I correct her, *again*, wishing my normal personal assistant would hurry up and return from maternity leave. Ruthie hired Lavinia through an agency, and she underwent thorough vetting by HR and our IT security team. Apparently, she has good credentials. I've yet to notice because she seems to spend most of her time attempting to flirt with me, and I'm low on patience.

She bats her eyelashes as she hands the paper folder over. "Sorry, Mr. Accardi. It's just we're so close in age it seems silly to stand on such formality."

"This is a professional workplace, and I expect all my employees to conduct themselves accordingly. If you can't address me properly or stop acting so familiar, it may be time to call the agency to seek a replacement."

Her face pales. "That won't be necessary, sir. I'm really sorry. It won't happen again."

I work my way through the folder, carefully checking each document before I sign it, wondering why it couldn't have waited until Monday.

"So, um, will you be back in the office this afternoon?"

I scrawl my signature on the last page and hand the folder over, drilling her with a sharp look. "Did I not ask you to keep this Friday afternoon free on my calendar?"

"You did." She flashes me a smile as she runs her hands through her long dark hair.

"Then you have your answer."

"Going anywhere nice?" she asks as I open the driver's side door to my Maserati.

I draw a calming breath before I turn to face her, crossing my arms and fixing her in place with a lethal look. "What did I just say?"

Heat swamps her cheeks, and her lower lip wobbles. "I was just making conversation. You work so hard all the time; I was hoping you were doing something nice."

"Goodbye, Lavinia."

Her cheeks stain fire-engine red as she clutches the folder to her chest and runs off.

I get behind the wheel, remove my tie, and toss it on the passenger seat before opening the top two buttons of my dress shirt. Choosing some soothing classical music, I drive out of the building heading toward home.

I decide to drop by Caleb's adjoining penthouse apartment first, letting myself in when he doesn't answer. Loud music blares throughout the apartment, but there's no sign of my brother in the main living space.

The place is a mess. As usual.

Half-drank champagne bottles reside beside empty vodka, scotch, and beer bottles, all fighting for floor and table space in the living room. A stack of pizza boxes litters the island unit. On the dining table, half-eaten bowls of nachos, wings, fries, and garlic bread lie uncovered, congealed with a dry layer on top, and it turns my stomach. Pungent smells crawl up my nostrils, and I pinch the bridge of my nose to block the scent. I'm stepping over a trail of clothing on the floor just as a loud scream emits from somewhere upstairs.

Bile travels up my throat when I spot the white powder remnants on the coffee table. I tap out a message to the cleaning service we both use, asking the owner to send a team here to clean up the place, before I dispose of the drug evidence.

I walk upstairs as more moaning and screaming filters out through Caleb's bedroom door.

I don't bother knocking, entering my twin's room without announcing myself. I'd like to say I'm shocked by the scene in front of me, but I'm not. A woman with a black pixie crop is riding my brother, cowgirl style, while a blonde sits on his face, and he has his fingers in the redhead lying upside down on her back groping the dark-haired woman's tits while she bounces on Caleb's cock.

They are all lost to lust and oblivious to my presence. Striding around the bed, I yank Caleb's phone from the sound system, muting the heavy metal as my ears offer up silent thanks.

"Oh look," the blonde says, smiling as she reaches for me. "It's your clone." She rakes her gaze over me from head to toe and licks her lips. "Come join us. You can fuck my ass while your brother eats me out."

"Don't fucking touch me," I snarl, stepping back. "I wouldn't fuck you if you paid me." I glower at Caleb as he locks eyes on me. I imagine he's sporting a smirk, but I can't tell cause his lips are devouring the blonde's pussy while she fondles her tits and writhes on top of him. I point my finger at Caleb. "Finish this now. We're due in Greenwich by six, and I want to leave in an hour to avoid getting stuck in traffic."

Traffic in the city is a shit show most days, but it'll be worse this evening with the usual mass exodus for the weekend. "I'll be back in ten minutes. If you're not done, I don't care. I'm throwing them out on their asses."

I stomp out of his room, sick of this shit. I love my brother. We've been through hell together, and I would stand in front of a bullet for him, but some days, he really tests my sanity. I'm not sure what's up with Caleb, but he's more reckless than usual lately.

Heading back downstairs, I move around my brother's penthouse picking up empties and other trash, trying to ignore the moans wafting down the stairs. I need to get laid. I haven't fucked anyone since Sorella, because I've been pulling all-nighters at work, and I need a release. Pulling up my contacts list, I send a message to Elizabeth to see if she wants to hook up tomorrow night.

"You're no fun," the redhead says, materializing in front of me as I pocket my cell.

"The door is that way." I point to my right as she slips her high heels on.

"Spoilsport," the blonde says, pouting as she flips me the bird before trotting after her friend.

The pixie-haired beauty levels me with a poisonous look as she fixes her dress into place.

"What, no insults?" I ask as she walks past me.

"I wouldn't waste my breath."

"Don't let the door hit you on the way out," I call after them, pulling up the lobby cameras on my phone to ensure they exit without incident.

Caleb appears at the top of the stairs as I watch the girls enter the elevator and leave our lives. My twin rarely fucks the same girl twice, so I'm pretty sure that's the last we've seen of those three.

My brother saunters down the stairs in his boxers, yawning as he attempts to tame the bird's nest on his head.

"Really, Caleb? A foursome at two fucking p.m.?"

"We were still partying from last night." He waggles his brows and grins as he bypasses me, heading straight for the refrigerator.

"You look like shit. Mom will throw a hissy fit if you show up like this."

"Relax, bro. I'll shower, drink a bottle of mouthwash, and smother myself in cologne, and she'll be none the wiser." Caleb throws me a bottle of ice-cold water before popping the cap on his own bottle.

"Weren't you supposed to be at the office today?" I ask before taking a drink.

He shakes his head and leans back against the refrigerator. "I booked the day off weeks ago when Mom said she was throwing a small party for Leo's fiftieth."

As much as I bust my brother's balls, he doesn't shirk his responsibilities. To family or the business. He's the only man I know who survives on four hours sleep a night and still functions effectively. I need a solid eight, or I'm a grumpy mother-fucker making mistakes left and right.

"Okay. I'm going home to get showered and changed. I'll drive. Meet me in the lobby at three."

Chapter Eleven
Joshua

"**S**hould I be worried about your drug use?" I ask, glancing at Caleb as I drive us out of the city.

"Nah." He moves his seat back, stretching his legs in front of him. "I've got it under control."

"You'd tell me if you didn't, right?"

He levels me with a sober expression, and tension bleeds into the air for a few beats. "I wouldn't keep it from you."

"Is that the truth? You were pissed that time I told Mom and the others what was going on."

"That was years ago, and we were kids. I was pissed at you for a long time. It felt like a betrayal, but I see it now for what it was. You were protecting me. I might have died in Mott Haven that night if you hadn't intervened."

Caleb got in with a bad crowd when we were teens. It coincided with shit going down at home. He went off the rails, and I had to rescue him from a drug house. I'd given Mom scant details, but she knew where I was going, and she'd called in the cavalry. I'd never been happier to see Ben, Leo, and Alesso when they showed up. "You were completely out of it when I found you, and I was terrified. I decided in that moment to tell them everything. I couldn't say nothing and let you die. I did it to save you because I couldn't see you stopping."

"I don't think I would have. You did the right thing, brother."

"I worry when I see you doing cocaine." Cocaine and ketamine were his drug of choice at fourteen.

"It's only recreational, and I'm not addicted. I learned my lesson young." He clamps a hand on my shoulder. "Don't worry about me. I'm not going down that path again."

"Do you ever think about him?" I ask as I continue onto Pelham Parkway South. I can't think about that night without thinking about our father because it was his secret partnership with Don Maximo Greco that led Caleb down that path. He was deliberately targeted by the drug dealers, on Greco's command, making it too hard for him to resist.

A muscle pops in his jaw. "Not if I can help it."

"I still have nightmares sometimes," I admit. "I see the moment the bullet entered his skull. I remember the light dying in his eyes, and I wake up in a cold sweat." Our father was gunned down in front of us not too long after that night in Mott Haven.

"I should have shot him when I had the chance and saved you the pain." Caleb's voice holds no warmth, like usual when he talks about Dad.

"I'm glad you didn't. I wouldn't want that on your conscience." I keep left to stay on Bronx and Pelham Parkway.

"He doesn't deserve to occupy any of your headspace, J," Caleb says, popping a piece of gum. "Awake or sleeping."

"He was still our father."

"He was a shit father, and we both know it. As far as I'm concerned, Leo is my father. He's the one who showed up for me, who continues to show up for me. I don't waste any energy thinking about Gino Accardi, and you shouldn't either. Don't forget what he did to Mom."

"I never forget how he treated her. I still feel guilty we didn't do anything to stop it."

"Me too, but we were kids. We weren't aware of everything."

"I'm glad Mom has Leo. She's a different person since she married him." I head onto Shore Road, glad the traffic is moving and not at a standstill.

"He's good for her." Caleb glances out the window while his foot taps on the floor.

"What's up with you? You've been especially restless lately."

My brother turns to look at me, brushing strands of dark-blond hair out of his eyes. "Honestly, I'm sick of my life. I'm bored, and nothing interests me. It feels like I'm just coasting through life, and I'm slowly going insane."

"Coasting through life is not something I'd ever say about you. You live your life at warp speed, Caleb. You don't *coast* through anything."

"It's hard to explain. I just know I'm not happy."

"You sure looked happy an hour ago," I quip, trying to lift my brother's melancholy mood.

"Sex is great in the moment, but I'm even sick of that. I'm sick of women. I'm sick of me. I'm sick of everything."

"You don't feel fulfilled," I surmise. "Even with everything you do and your busy life, you're not satisfied."

"I'm not. I go through the motions at work, but I've lost my passion for it. I'm not like you. You live and breathe the business, but my heart isn't in it. It never really has been."

It explains why he's been lashing out so much lately. "You should have talked to me."

"I'm not even sure what this shit in my head is, J, and I'm talking to you now."

"I'd suggest we go overseas. Take a mini vacay. Head to Europe maybe, but the timing sucks."

"I'm not sure that'd even help. I need to be doing something...active, proactive." He shrugs. "I don't know."

"You should call Massimo. Ask him if you can do something in the field for The Commission. I know you're itching for some action. I'll look after the brand. Maybe we should give the senior management team more responsibility and free up some of your time."

Caleb spent time training in Nepal, and he's a skilled warrior and marksman. I've often thought it's a shame he's wasting that talent, but having a don actively out on the streets engaged in violence is not encouraged or even welcome. There are safety concerns, and it undermines the image that's been cultivated of a legit businessman. However, if that's what my brother needs to feel more content, I'll make it happen for him.

"He'd probably say no just to spite me." Caleb kicks his feet up on the dash, and I level him with a sharp look.

He chuckles, facing off with me before finally removing his offending appendages. "I swear you have legit OCD. No one could be this anal and not have it."

"It's called being organized and in control. Appreciating the things I have, and not wanting someone's dirty shoes messing up the interior of my expensive car is normal behavior."

"If you say so, bro." He grins and whatever dark cloud was hanging over his head appears to have lifted.

I move onto Pelham Road just as an alert pings on my phone. My cell is connected to the system in the car, so the automated text message pops up on the screen, and I curse as I read it.

Caleb sits up straighter in his chair. "Who the fuck is trying to access your office?"

"I have a pretty good idea. Log into the security system, and call up the camera outside my office." I'm strict about locking my office when I leave the room. There may be rare occasions where it's unlocked for a couple minutes at a time, but I'm careful not to leave my space unattended. All sensitive and highly classified files are stored in the side room off my office, and the room can only be accessed by fingerprint scanner.

Caleb pulls out his cell and taps away on it, hissing under his breath a few seconds later.

"Is it my temp PA?" I ask.

"It's her. What is the cunt up to?"

"I'm going to find out. I know she was thoroughly vetted before we hired her, but something doesn't add up."

I call HR and request a copy of her file to be emailed to me. I'll talk to Ben at the house and ask for the security file. There's a specialist division within Caltimore Holdings who conducts full background checks on employees for the five families upon request. No one is hired into the Accardi Company without a background check, so it's possible Lavinia is trying to access my office for legitimate reasons. But my gut is telling me she's up to something. I want someone to take another look at her file. If she's working for McDermott or the rat, someone's head will roll for this.

We head onto US-1 N, and the traffic eases considerably, and from there, it doesn't take too long to reach the Mazzone estate where Mom and Leo live in their own lavish mansion on the vast grounds of the property.

"Don't tell Mom what I told you," Caleb says as we grab the gifts for our stepdad from the trunk of my car. "She'll only worry."

I grab the bouquet of flowers from the back seat. "Dude, she'll always worry about us. It comes with the territory."

"Well, I don't want to add more worry onto the pile. She has her hands full with Rosa and Leif, her job, and her charity work." Mom went back to NYU as a mature student and completed her medical studies. Now, she is assigned to the official *mafioso* medical team. The team of surgeons, doctors, and nurses are employed by the five families to handle our medical needs.

Sierra Mazzone set up a foundation to help victims of human trafficking a couple of years ago in partnership with Moonlight, an organization founded by Keanu Kennedy's wife Selena. All the woman who volunteer at the foundation are *mafioso* wives, and they give their time for free so all the money raised through the various fundraising efforts goes directly to the people who need it. Mom works there two mornings a week while our younger half-siblings are at school.

"I won't say anything if you don't want me to." I lock my car as the front door opens and our sister and brother charge out of the house, making a beeline for us.

Caleb sets the gift bag on the ground to scoop our nine-year-old sister into his arms. "How's my little *principessa?*" he asks, nuzzling his nose into Rosa's hair as she wraps her arms and legs around him.

"Hey, Joshie." Leif winds his bony arms around my waist. "Wanna play PlayStation? I got the new Spider-Man game for my birthday."

"You betcha, little dude. I just need to talk to Uncle Ben first."

The kids run off to the playroom while we make our way toward the kitchen. Delicious aromas waft in the air as we walk through the house. "Fuck, I've missed Mom's cooking." Caleb runs a hand across his toned stomach. "I literally have wet dreams about her apple cake."

"You and me both, buddy," Leo says, chuckling as he steps out of his study on our right.

"Hey, old man." Caleb pulls him into a brief embrace. "I think I see more gray," he teases, squinting at Leo's hair. It's still dark, like our siblings, with only a few gray strands.

"Less of the old man, punk." Leo grabs Caleb into a head-lock. "Haven't you heard fifty is the new forty?"

"I thought I heard voices." Mom walks toward us with a wide smile, wiping her hands on the front of her apron.

"Hey, Mom." I lean in as she clasps my face in her hands, kissing both cheeks, before yanking me into her arms.

"I've missed you both." She envelops me in her warmth and the comforting smell of Chanel No. 5.

I hand her the flowers when we break apart. "From both of us."

Tears well in her eyes. "You're such good sons. Always so thoughtful." She hugs me again.

"Thanks, Caleb." She pulls him into a hug after releasing me.

"Something smells delicious," Caleb says, readily sinking into Mom's embrace.

"Happy birthday, Leo," I say, clapping him on the back. I don't give him our gift, already knowing Mom will want everyone to give him their gifts together after we've eaten.

"It's good to see you, kid. I hear shit's really hitting the fan on the streets."

"Yeah, it's not good, and we can't catch a break."

"Maybe the five of us should talk in the morning before you head back to the city."

"It can't hurt to discuss it."

Leo and Alesso are part of the Mazzone *famiglia*—as

underboss and *consigliere*—and not involved with the street trade. As "outsiders" they might have some suggestions we haven't considered. "I need to talk to Ben now about something that's cropped up. What time will he be here?" Dinner isn't until six, and we're early. I was figuring I could talk to Ben in the meantime about the Lavinia problem.

"I'm here," Ben opens the door from the inside of Leo's study, holding a tumbler of scotch in his hand.

"Can we talk?"

"Of course."

"You need me?" Leo asks.

"Nah. This won't take long."

The others wander toward the kitchen while Ben and I go into the study and close the door. I quickly fill him in, and he places a call to his team immediately, requesting another look at Lavinia as well as a copy of the report on file. In less than ten minutes, my cell pings with the document. "Thanks for this."

"Let me know if we missed something. I'll fire whoever fucked up."

"I could be wrong. She might just be a harmless flirt."

He perches on the edge of the desk. "Trusting your instincts will rarely steer you wrong. If you have a sixth sense about her, I'm betting you're right."

Chapter Twelve
Joshua

I play Spider-Man on PlayStation with Leif before I help Rosa make the finishing touches to her hand-drawn card for her beloved papa. The rest of the family arrives at six: Alesso, Serena, and their four kids come, and Sierra shows up with Rowan and his girlfriend and his two younger siblings. I'm not surprised to see that Frankie, Rico, and their family scored an invite too. Gia would ordinarily be here with her family, and I'm betting she'd love to be around the table with us. I'm kind of wishing she was here too, which I'm not in the mood to examine.

It's a boisterous affair with so many people around the table. There are a lot of young kids and plenty of laughter. Mom has excelled, and we help her to carry a mountain of different dishes to the table. It's all traditional Italian fare with most being Leo's favorites. There's apple cake for Caleb and cannoli for me for dessert because Mom never forgets. We're no longer the three-year-olds she inherited when she married our dad, but she still indulges us.

There has never been a time when I haven't felt her love. It always shines bright, and she means the world to me. She may not have had a happy marriage to our father, but Caleb and I lucked out when she became our mom. All we know of Juliet—our bio mom—is gleaned from photos and stories the others have told us. Caleb and I don't remember her because we were too young when she died. On occasion, it makes me sad, but it never lingers. I have never felt like I've missed out because Nat is my mom, and she's incredible.

After we finish eating, our stepdad opens his gifts while the adults drink champagne and toast the birthday boy. We all sing happy birthday to him as he blows out the candles on his cake aided by Leif and Rosa. It's these moments that mean the most to me.

Coming home always helps to ground me, and I didn't realize how much I needed it today. Caleb needed it too.

We grab Rowan, Romeo, Antonio, Cosimo, and Marco and make them help us with the cleanup so Mom can chat with her friends. The older men retreat to the study for bourbon and cigars. The younger kids are all in the playroom, getting up to mischief, no doubt. Elisa found her way into the kitchen too. That's no surprise. She always gravitates toward Caleb. I watch them chatting as they rinse and stack plates in the dishwasher, noting how good they look together. I'm drying the good silverware and putting it back in the wooden box Mom keeps it in as I survey my twin and the younger woman.

Elisa laughs at something Caleb says, tossing long strands of thick, dark, glossy hair over her shoulder. She shares the same reddish tint as her mom, and they have matching hazel eyes too. Elisa has really blossomed during her time at NYU, and she's a striking woman. But I've never been able to see her as more than a friend or a quasi-sister. Caleb says it's the same for him, but seeing them together today makes me wonder if it's the truth. There is an ease, a familiarity, between them that is wholly natural.

Caleb relaxes around her, and he genuinely worships the ground she walks on. He won't ever hear anyone saying anything bad about her. And God fucking help any guy she decides to date as my twin will put him through his paces to determine if he's worthy of his little Lili.

"They look good together, don't they?" Frankie says, sneaking up on me while I've been lost in thought.

"I'm not touching that," I say, drying the last fork and slipping it in the box. I push down the locks and pop the box into the sideboard where Mom stores it.

Frankie pins me with a soft smile. "You're a good man, Joshua. A good son. No wonder Nat is always singing your praises. Caleb too."

I shrug because I don't see it as a big deal. I might be a CEO of a multibillion-dollar empire and a skilled made man, but back home, I'm just a son who would do anything for his mother. "Today's about Leo, and Mom has already cooked up a storm. She deserves to put her feet up."

Frankie loops her arm through mine. "Walk with me?"

I stifle a groan. "I know what you want, and I can't tell you anything about Gia's assignment. I'm sorry, but it's confidential, and the less you know, the better."

Her face drops and I feel like a piece of shit. I'm sure she's really worried about her daughter, but I can't ignore protocol.

"I hate this," she says in a low voice. "I wish she had picked any profession but this one."

"If it's any consolation, Gia is capable and resourceful, and I have every faith in her. We all do, or we wouldn't have hired her to the team. Also, I'm personally overseeing her assignment and ensuring she's got every protection available."

She clutches my arm tight. "Don't let anything happen to

her. Please, Joshua. She's my only daughter, and I would die if anything happened to her."

"I'll keep her safe," I say, hoping I haven't just lied.

We're all nursing hangovers the following morning when we meet to discuss the situation on the streets. The adults stayed up late, drinking far too much, and I indulged more than I usually do. It was a good night and great to catch up with everyone. Unfortunately, Leo and Alesso don't have any suggestions we haven't already tried, but they make me promise to call them if there is anything they can personally do to help.

We hang around for another couple of hours to take our siblings out on their bikes, and we spend a half hour with Leo at the shooting range Ben had built on the grounds. Then we have lunch with Mom before making our way back to New York. Mom also asked me to keep Gia safe, and I promised her I would.

The weight of that promise is bearing down on me as I drive us back to the city.

"We're heading to Bar Havana for drinks at nine. Are you joining us?" Caleb asks when we're in the elevator on the way up to our penthouses.

"I'll come for a while, but I'm meeting Elizabeth later."

"You should cancel and come with us to Club H after the bar."

"No thanks. That's your scene, not mine." I have nothing against sex clubs per se, and Club H is the most prestigious of Ben's clubs, but I prefer to do my screwing in private.

"Don't bail," my twin says when we exit the lift. "You need to let loose, and Marino said he'd stop by. We should both be there to buy him a drink."

God knows our underboss has earned it. Benedito manages things for us at the ground level, and he is the person the *soldati* and *capos* report to. We have a recurring weekly meeting with him and Luca—our cousin and *consigliere*—where he updates us on things we need to know, but unless there's an emergency, we don't hear from him much. He runs a tight ship, and he's experienced, having worked with Luca in the same capacity when he was acting Don Accardi in our stead. He provides stability for the men and ensures everything runs smoothly at the grass roots.

"I'll be there. Perhaps you should ask him if there is more you can do at the grassroots level. If you want to dirty your hands, that'd be a good place to start."

Caleb shrugs. "Maybe."

"The more I think about it, the more I like the idea," I tell Caleb later that night when we're en route to Bar Havana. "It would be good for the men to get to know us better. The newer *soldati* already know you from initiate training, so it makes sense you're the one to do this. We know there's a mole or moles in the city. It could be within any *famiglia*, but the odds are it's within the Accardi or Maltese ranks. Maybe if you're more hands-on, you might glean intel we need."

"I've been thinking about it too, and I like the idea."

"Good." I pop the cap on a bottle of water while Caleb drinks a beer. "Set it up with Marino tonight, and I'll call a senior management meeting on Monday and reassign some of your work at the office."

"I'll send an email tomorrow with a summary of key items." I can already see some of the strain easing from my brother's

---

face. "I really hope the rat isn't one of us. That will seriously piss me off."

"We have to prepare for anything, and speaking of, Ben sent me an updated report on Lavinia just before we left. I haven't had time to read it fully, but the gist of it is her back history is fake."

"You didn't think to lead with that?"

"I was getting to it. Do you think we've been lax in not getting to know our men better? In letting Marino handle most of it?"

"I don't see how it's any different than how the other dons run their businesses. Cristian isn't hands-on either. None of us can be and avoid public detection to the extent it's required."

"I'm beginning to think that's a mistake. Maybe we're being too trustworthy." I finish my water, tempted to reach for a beer, but I want to keep my wits about me tonight while Gia is on her date. I've had confirmation she's at a Michelin-star restaurant with that Irish prick. I'll have a couple drinks at the bar, but no more, in case there's an issue and I'm needed.

"Luca trusts Marino. He wouldn't have suggested we retain him as our underboss if he had any concerns." Caleb drains his beer and grabs another.

"I know, and I'm not suggesting he's untrustworthy. He was great during the transition, patient with us as we learned the ropes, and he never criticized us for being young. He's solid, and he's got our backs."

"He respects us, and we respect him."

"Agreed. My point was more of a general one. This shit on the streets has shaken me up. We're not as in touch as we'd like to think we are."

"It's all the more reason for me to take a step back from the legit business and reconnect with our *soldati*." He flashes me a grin as our driver pulls the car alongside the curb outside the bar. "At least we have something to celebrate tonight."

We get out and head inside, making a beeline for our usual table at the back, which is always reserved for us.

The gang is all here, and I'm glad to see Cristian and Zumo have left their girls at home tonight. Vittus orders a round of drinks while I fall into conversation with Giulio. He's Luca's son, therefore, our cousin, but we only got to know him later in life. He's a few years older than us and a successful Wall Street trader. He gets pulled into *mafioso* business from time to time, but mostly he's on the fringes and not an active made man.

My phone pings with regular updates as the *soldato* shadowing Gia sends me texts and pictures. I grind my teeth to the molars as I stare at the most recent photo he sent. Gia and Liam have left the restaurant, and they're heading for a bar on foot. The jerk has his arm around her shoulders, tucking her in close to his side as they walk. She's laughing as she looks up at him. Her eyes look bright and there's color in her cheeks. He's gazing at her like he wants to devour her whole, and I'm growling under my breath before I've even realized I'm doing it.

"What gives, man?" Vittus asks, pouring another measure of bourbon into my glass.

"Nothing." I repocket my cell and attempt to shake my shoulders loose.

Caleb chuckles, smirking at me from his seat beside Cristian. "Told you that one was trouble."

Zumo sits up straighter, his face perking up. "Is there a girl?"

My nose scrunches in irritation. "Don't act stupid. Of course, there isn't." They all know my history with Bettina and why I've vowed never to be in a relationship again.

"He's lying," Giulio says, waggling his brows. "He's getting pics of some redhead on his phone," he adds, totally throwing me to the wolves.

Cristian eyeballs me over his scotch, scooting closer to my left side. "Something you want to share, buddy?" he asks in a low tone.

I look around, ensuring no one is paying us too much attention before I press my mouth to his ear. "Gia is on a date with that douche. I asked for updates."

"Did you now?" Cristian grins.

"It's not like that."

"It's totally like that," Caleb says, eavesdropping.

I flip him the bird. "It is *not* like that," I whisper-hiss, keeping my voice low on purpose. The other guys are discussing football and no longer interested, but I need to be careful what I say when I'm in a public place. "I promised Mom and Frankie I'd keep her safe. This is me trying to keep that promise."

"Liar." Caleb flicks hair out of his eyes. "You arranged it before they asked that of you."

I run my finger underneath the collar of my black shirt. "I didn't need it verbalized to know they'd want me to do this. Back the fuck off."

My phone pings again, and I'm almost afraid to look.

"I'm only messing with you," Caleb says, sensing my irritation. "We know you don't date."

I swipe my finger to access the message, almost vomiting when I open the picture. My fingers clutch my phone in a death grip, and my nostrils flare as I glare at the image of Gia pressed up against the wall outside a bar. Liam is devouring her mouth like an animal while his hand travels up her thigh. Her skirt has been pushed up higher, and she's showcasing a lot of skin. What the hell is she playing at? She's supposed to be acting coy, not letting him paw at her in public like a horny teenager who cannot control his hormones.

I'm beyond enraged.

Why? I have no fucking clue, and that only makes me angrier.

"I know that face." My twin pushes the bottle of Old Rip Van Winkle across the table to me. "Drink up, brother. You look like you need it."

Grabbing the bottle, I pour a generous measure in my glass and knock it back in one go. It does nothing to quell the inferno swirling inside me.

"You sure you haven't got a thing for her?" Cristian asks. His brow is puckered as he examines my face. "She sure seems to have you tied into knots."

"I don't have a thing for her," I snap, refilling my glass. "I just don't like seeing good women getting treated like trash by trash."

That's all it is.

Right?

Chapter Thirteen
Gia

Vigorously scrubbing my skin in the shower does nothing to alleviate the itch clinging to every inch of my flesh. Memories of Liam's disgusting hands all over my body sends shivers crashing over me, and I'm chilled to the bone despite the hot water raining down on me.

I am only a couple weeks into dating him, and it's already painful. But I know the worst is yet to come, and I need to find better coping mechanisms. I'm able to deal with his touch in the moment because I zone out, forcing my body to cooperate while my mind goes someplace else. It's the aftermath of our dates I have the problem with. Then I can't stop my brain from replaying everything. Knots twist my insides as I turn off the shower and get out. I wrap a fluffy white towel around my body as I remove the shower cap from my hair and toss it on the vanity.

Swiping at the condensation on the mirror, I stare at my reflection. I'm still not used to my new hair. It suits me, and I'm glad I had to change my appearance. It helps to separate "'real me" from "work me." Now, if I can just learn how to leave "work me" at the door when I come home each day, I'll be happy.

I drag a comb quickly through my hair before padding out of the bathroom into my bedroom.

"Oh my fucking god!" I screech, slapping a hand over my chest as my heart pounds painfully against my rib cage and blood thrums in my ears. "You almost gave me a heart attack! What the fuck are you doing here?" I glare at the tall, broad frame of the brooding man sitting bolt upright on the side of my bed. "And how the hell did you get in?"

"I have a key," Joshua says, running his eyes over me from head to toe.

"You can't be here! What if Liam has someone watching my place?"

"He doesn't. I canvassed the area thoroughly." Joshua stands. "And I came in through the rear entrance to the building and used the staff elevator."

"You can't just creep up on me like this! What if I'd been naked?" I wave my hands around before remembering I'm *in a towel*. I check it's secure and grip the top of it before leveling daggers at him.

"I'm your boss. I can do what the fuck I like. And you're not, so there's no need to throw a hissy fit."

"Get out!" I point toward the door.

He steps toward me. I grip my towel harder, gulping as he puts himself all up in my personal space. Fuck, why does he have to look so good and smell so good? The blue of his open-necked shirt matches the blue in his eyes as he stares at me with cold indifference. There is scant distance between us, and I'm acutely aware of every hard, toned inch of his tempting body. But a muscle ticks in his jaw, and heat rolls off him in waves, giving the game away. He's not as indifferent as he seems. He's *angry*. I'd bet money on it.

His fingers wrap around my chin as he tilts my head back. "No." His expression dares me to challenge him, but I'm not a woman who ever backs down, and I know how to pick my battles.

I shrug. "Suit yourself." Removing his hand from my chin, I take a couple steps back and smirk as I unknot the towel and expose myself to his greedy gaze. I keep my eyes trained on his face as I slowly dry my body, watching him watch me as I swirl the towel around my breasts, lifting the heavy weight to catch the moisture underneath. My nipples stand at attention under his heady look, and lust swirls in my belly as I drag the towel lower, patting my bare pussy dry.

Turning around, I run the towel against my ass before lifting one leg onto the bed and slowly drying it from foot to thigh. Then I repeat the motion with my other leg, smirking as I feel his eyes all over me. Planting both feet on the carpeted floor, I turn around to face him again, slowly running my hands all over my naked body.

"Stop that," he clips out, adjusting the front of his pants where a noticeable bulge is straining against the zipper.

"I like to be thorough," I say, deliberately lifting my boobs in each hand, inspecting the underswells with my fingers. "To ensure I got every drop of moisture."

His Adam's apple jumps in his throat, and I'm enjoying this.

"Put some clothes on."

His eyes devour me as I walk toward him, stopping with only an inch between our bodies. His nostrils flare as his gaze lingers on my tits. I'm betting it wouldn't take much to escalate things, but that's not what this is about.

I slide my hands across his firm chest. "It's after midnight. Why on earth would I get dressed?" I can't fight my smirk any longer.

He curses under his breath before stalking off and snatching my green silk robe from the back of my door. "Put that on."

"No." I plant my hands on my hips, thrust my chest out, and smile, loving throwing his word back at him.

"Don't push me, Gia, or you'll be sorry." He grinds his teeth, and his jaw clenches tight.

"Why, Joshua?" I reclaim the distance between us, putting my hands back on his chest. "What will you do to me?" I bat my eyelashes and pin him with my best sultry expression. "Will you throw me on the bed and fuck me until I'm screaming your name?" My hands roam higher, heading toward his shoulders. "Or will you spread my legs and bury your face in my pussy?" I push my boobs into his chest. "Push my tits together and fuck them?"

His pupils are practically black with lust, and the bulge tenting his pants is rock hard where it presses against my stomach. "Oh, you'd like that."

His eyes zero in on my mouth, and my tongue darts out, wetting my lips. I stop breathing for a few seconds as electricity simmers in the air. My chest heaves when he clasps the back of my head, pulling our faces super close. I gulp, resting my hands on his shoulders as my gaze bounces from his piercing eyes to his gorgeous full lips. Indecision resides in the minuscule gap between our mouths, and the moment is super charged.

My breath hitches, butterflies swoop into my chest, and blood rushes to my head. I'm confused over my reaction to him. To *us*. Part of me desperately wants him to kiss me, and I don't understand why, but the stubborn part of me won't concede easily.

The stubborn part wins out, and I break myself free of whatever spell he has me under. Lowering my hands from his shoulders, I push my tits together and rub my taut nipples with my thumbs. His body visibly trembles with the effort involved in keeping his hands at his sides, and I know I have him where I want him.

Stepping aside, I free my breasts and snag the robe. I pull it on, tightening the belt around my waist as I fix him with one of his signature ice looks. "Hell will freeze over before I ever let you anywhere near me. But thanks for letting me practice seduction techniques on you. Now I know that'll work on Liam, I'll be sure to reenact it."

His hands clench into balls at his side. "Watch it. You're on very thin ice, Gia. One word from me, and you're off the mission and out of the program."

"Try it, asshole." I narrow my eyes. "I dare you." I prod my finger in his chest. "I told you to get out. It was your choice to stay like some creepy perv." It's on the tip of my tongue to say he's no better than Liam, but I don't want to push him too far and I have lied enough.

The truth is my body is humming at the thought of Joshua's hands all over me, and there is nothing creepy or pervy about it. I'm not remotely pleased about this development. I don't want to be attracted to him. I never asked for this stupid chemistry that has sprung to life between us. I'd rather we go back to him ignoring me and me barely noticing he exists.

We stare at one another, neither of us backing down. Tension bleeds into the air as seconds pass. Joshua breaks first and smug satisfaction swells my chest. He moves to one side, combing a hand through his thick blond locks and messing up his careful styling. He's rattled, and it's good to know this freaky chemistry isn't one-sided. "I shouldn't have come here."

"Why did you?" I rotate my shoulders from side to side before sliding my feet into my slippers.

He sighs, dragging his hand through his hair again. He mutters something under his breath. "Let's talk in the living room," he says, like he owns the place. Okay, maybe he does. I never asked. He strides from the bedroom, and I take my sweet ass time following.

Dropping onto the couch beside him, I purposely let my robe part, showcasing my smooth thighs.

"I'm not the one you're being paid to seduce," he snaps, grabbing both parts of my robe and folding it over me. "Quit this shit."

My lips twitch. "I thought your job was to help me?" I purr, pressing my body up against his. My heart is thumping wildly behind my chest cavity as heat travels south, pooling in my core. Just brushing against him has me overheating. Imagine what touching him would do? "What if I need to practice more seduction techniques?"

"You don't need any practice," he growls, scooting sideways on the couch to get away from me. He thrusts his cell into my face. "Looks like you've already hooked your prey."

I stare at the pic on the screen as bile swims up my throat. Liam is ravishing me on the street outside the bar, in full view of passersby and the men Joshua has trailing us. I should feel proud, but I don't. That itch is back, creeping over my flesh, and I have a sudden desire to take another shower.

I hand the cell back to him. "You look angry. Why is that when I'm doing what's been asked of me?"

"Have you forgotten your research? He doesn't like easy women. You letting him paw at you on a busy street doesn't exactly scream sophistication, now does it?"

I bark out a dry laugh. "Jealous much, Joshua?"

His cold veneer shrouds his face, and his voice is lethally controlled when he says, "I don't want to see you crash and burn, Gia. If you fail, it reflects badly on me too. You can't afford to fuck this up."

Now he's seriously pissing me off. "You told me I needed to

progress things, to move it along faster. How the hell did you think I'd achieve that?"

"Not like this!" His fingers dig into the armrest of the couch.

"Then tell me what I'm supposed to do, Joshua? Either you want me to continue acting demure and let this play out over months or I do more of what I did tonight so I earn his trust faster. Which is it because your mood swings are giving me a serious case of mental whiplash!"

"I don't want you to compromise yourself," he says in a composed voice as his fingers ease their death grip on the couch.

"Then you shouldn't have assigned me to this job." I stand and walk to the island unit, grabbing the half-drunk bottle of red wine and a wineglass. I don't grab a second glass or intend to offer him any because I want him to leave.

Flopping down on the seat beside him, I pour a healthy measure of luscious red wine into my glass and then knock back a long mouthful. The instant I set the glass down on the coffee table, Joshua snatches it and greedily drinks from it.

My mouth hangs open. That is not a Joshua thing to do.

"What?" he asks after swallowing most of *my* wine. "You clearly weren't going to offer me any, and you're not the only one who needs it."

I rub at my aching temples. "Why are you here, Joshua?" I ask again. The stress of this evening is catching up to me, and I want to drink my body weight in wine and then crash.

His gaze falls over every feature on my face as he stares directly at me. "I wish I knew," he whispers.

"Did something happen tonight?" I ask, thoroughly confused.

His eyes bore into mine, and a frisson of electricity crackles in the small space between us. "I didn't like seeing you with him. I didn't like him touching you."

I open my mouth to speak, and he shakes his head. "Don't ask me to explain it because I can't." He grabs the wineglass and drains the rest of the wine. "Make of that what you want."

"Joshua, I—"

"Don't," he says, and my hand pauses in midair. "I shouldn't have come here." He stands, grabbing his jacket off the arm of the chair.

"Wait." I don't know what the hell is happening between us, but I want to put things back on a professional setting. He is my boss, after all, and my main point of contact. Tonight has been weird, and I don't want things to remain weird between us. "I want to show you what I've been working on." Walking over to the island unit, I hop up on a stool and open my laptop. I pull up the research report I was working on earlier today before I left for my date. "I was going to send this to you in the morning, but you might as well look at it now."

He leans one hand on the counter as he peers over my shoulder, staring at the screen. "What am I looking at?"

"I've spent the past two weeks examining surveillance cameras on Staten Island and along the route back to the city. I've hacked into street cams and private systems trying to piece together footage from the night of the robbery, and it doesn't make any sense."

"Elaborate," he clips out, and I'm tempted to flip him the bird.

"There is no trace of anyone getting onto the cruise liner or off it. I see you and Fiero and the men that were working that night but no one else, and nothing appears amiss."

"The surveillance systems were tampered with, and Mazzone's tech team has already investigated and reported on this."

"Why do you think I wanted to take another look?" That and I'm bored hanging around this apartment during the day. I wanted to make myself useful. "There is something very off about this whole scenario that goes beyond us having a rat working with the enemy." I angle my head to look back at him, spotting the confusion etched on his face. "You're not getting my point."

"Then make it more clearly." His warm breath fans over my face, and it's challenging to remain focused.

"I get they tampered with the systems around the port because whoever they have on the inside fixed it so they could get in and out undetected, but what I don't understand is why there is no trace of anything or anyone leaving the island or along the route back to the city. How the fuck do you transport a significant amount of drugs without leaving a visible trail?"

"They could have transported by air or sea. It's the conclusion we reached."

I shake my head. "I've checked radar reports, the ferry records, air and shipping logs from the night in question, and followed a camera trail along the island with a clear view of the ocean and the skies, and there is nothing, Joshua. There is no ship on the water or no chopper in the sky. I didn't detect any suspicious persons or activity on the ferry, and I've checked all sailings for a twenty-four-hour period before and after the robbery. I went through the footage very carefully, and it gives us nothing. It's like they disappeared into thin air."

"That's not possible." He pushes off the counter and straightens up as he scrubs his hands down his face.

"We're missing something, and I have a feeling it's the key to everything."

Chapter Fourteen
Joshua

"Gia has raised valid points," Massimo says at the next commission meeting, a few days after my ill-advised visit to her apartment.

"Valid points my team should have raised," Ben adds, frowning. "I'll have a conversation with Phillip." Phillip has been Ben's go-to IT guy for *mafioso* business for years, and he oversees the high-level specialist team at Caltimore Holdings. This team conducts top-secret research and information-gathering reports on behalf of all five families, when the need arises.

"Whoever is behind this is clearly way ahead of us," Fiero says. Worry lines pucker his brow as he sighs.

"It's hugely concerning we can't find any trace." Cristian props his elbows on the table. "How are we so in the dark with all the resources at our disposal?"

"That's the million-dollar question." I remove a piece of lint off the sleeve of my navy jacket.

"I say we grab McDermott and pull him in for questioning." Caleb drums his fingers on the table. "We don't need proof to know he's involved. Let's torture the prick and get some answers."

"We need to give Gia more time," Massimo says. "I am gravely concerned but not enough to burn bridges with our only ally. We can't go after McDermott without compromising O'Hara and forcing his hand. Remember there are plenty loyal to his brother and plenty who would rather see Liam running the show. Let's not play into their hands."

"We can't do fucking nothing!" Caleb snaps. "It's been almost a month, and we are no wiser than we were the night our shipment was hijacked. We're losing ground on the street, and foreign supply is flooding the market. We are losing control. We need less talk and more action."

It's a little worrying when my twin is the voice of reason around the table. "I agree with Caleb in relation to the street trade," I say. "We need to drive the foreign supply out. I propose we send teams of *soldati* out onto the streets to take out the guys selling that shit. Make an example with a few dealers, which will send a clear message to the others. We follow that up with threats. They buy from us and only us or they're next."

"This is why I wanted to distance us from things at street level. This is a waste of our resources and a distraction." Ben pours water into his glass as he speaks. "Maybe we need to discuss ending the street business permanently this time. Return to bringing product from Colombia solely for our private use, to supply our clubs and enterprises. Let the Irish handle the street business if they want it. They can clean up this mess."

"Seems only fair when they started it," Cristian concurs.

"Allegedly. We still have no proof," Fiero says. "And I don't agree with Don Mazzone. The street trade is very lucrative."

"It's less to do with money and more to do with control. Letting foreigners onto the streets sets a bad precedent,"

Massimo says. "It's why The Commission gave my wife control of all this when she first approached us years ago. If we let them have free rein, what's to stop them coming after our other businesses? Or partnering with our enemies when they get greedy and decide they want it all?"

"It's too risky." I wet my lips. "What if it's the Bratva? What if they're behind this?" I ask, eyeballing the five men around the table. "Things have been acrimonious with them in the recent past, and we drove them out. What if they've regrouped and this is revenge?"

"We can't rule anyone out, but our intel says they are preoccupied with things in Russia and across Europe. It seems unlikely," Mazzone says.

"But not impossible." Massimo leans forward, eyeballing each of us in turn. "I propose we implement Joshua's suggestion to try to regain control of the streets. Caleb, can you handle that?"

My twin nods. He's getting more hands-on, like we discussed, and this will suit him.

"Joshua, you stick with Gia. See what can be done to move that forward."

"She's cooking dinner for him at his place on Saturday. It's the first time he's invited her to his home. Hopefully, she might find something useful." I work hard to keep a neutral expression on my face and not show my distaste.

"Good, let us know immediately if she finds any intel."

"I think the rest of us should pay the other dons a visit," Fiero suggests. "Let's call it a pre-Thanksgiving catch-up. We'll split the key states between us. Spend a day or two on the ground, talk to the *soldati* and the *capos*, see if there is any gossip at ground level that might be helpful."

"You think the betrayal extends beyond the five families?" Cristian asks.

"Like I said, we can't rule anything out. We may be enjoying unprecedented peace within all Italian American *famiglie,* but that doesn't mean everyone is content. Power corrupts, and dons have been known to change their allegiances." Massimo sits up straighter in his chair.

"Maybe we should accelerate the plans for adding more members to the board," I say. "There is strength in numbers, and it would foster good will."

The plan is to move from a six-person board to a ten-person representation. Four seats will be opened up to member dons outside of New York for the first time ever. We have discussed using a voting system, to try to keep it fair and unbiased, but the truth is we need to retain the right of veto because there are several dons we would not welcome onto the board, for various reasons, and we need to preserve the integrity of The Commission.

"We could end up voting a traitor onto the board," Ben says. "I'd prefer we find the rat first."

Fiero stretches his arms up over his head before lowering them back to his sides. "What if we used these impending visits to discuss our ideas for The Commission with the other dons? We don't have to commit to anything, but it would give them a heads-up, they'll feel included, and we'll have an idea of which dons might apply."

We all nod our agreement.

"Okay, that's decided," Massimo says. "Let's wrap things up. We'll meet again after Thanksgiving unless there's a need to meet beforehand."

"I don't like it," Caleb says thirty minutes later as we eat lunch with Cristian at one of our favorite restaurants in Manhattan. "I think the board is too complacent."

"You mean Maltese, Mazzone, and Greco." Cristian smothers his burger in ketchup before popping the bun back on.

"This entire situation reeks, and their lack of action could cost all of us." Caleb bites a chunk of his burger.

"I don't disagree, but I understand Massimo's cautionary response. If we go after the Irish without O'Hara's approval, we risk making an enemy of them, and it seems like we've got enough of those right now." I cut my grilled chicken into even pieces before popping one in my mouth.

"Sometimes I wish it was the old days. When made men took action instead of fucking discussing every angle like damn politicians." Caleb swigs from his beer. "The others have lost their appetite for violence. They're too old and too set in their ways. They're glorified businessmen, and that's where their true interests lie."

"We're all businessmen these days because it's the only way to survive. The RICO laws are no joke, and our contacts in authority can't save us if there is evidence that can't be disputed." I pause eating to level my brother with a warning look. "That's why we can't run around the streets killing people." I glance around and lower my voice. "Do what you must to send out a message, but you have to be discreet, Caleb. Stay under the radar."

"I'm not an idiot. I just think Don Greco is making a mistake. You can send a clear message without conceding anything we've built or compromising our ally."

"I agree. We seem to be ten paces behind, and I sense big trouble brewing." Cristian dabs at the corner of his mouth with a napkin.

"You may get your war after all, brother," I deadpan before popping another piece of chicken in my mouth.

We chat casually over the rest of lunch, and I've just paid the bill when I get a call from the guy shadowing Gia today. "Boss, we have a problem."

I'm immediately on guard. "What's wrong?"

"She's at the Chelsea food market, and I've just spotted her talking with Elisa Salerno."

I close my eyes for a brief second. What the fuck is Gia playing at? She knows it's risky meeting anyone she knows in public. "Does Liam have anyone on her?"

"No, boss. She wasn't followed."

I find it strange Liam wouldn't vet his potential girlfriend. Perhaps he's satisfied with his background check and Gia is doing enough to convince him she's trustworthy. Still, she can't afford to take risks. "Okay, keep eyes on them. We'll be there shortly." I already know my brother will want to come with.

"What's up?" Caleb asks, throwing an extra fifty down on the table for the waitress.

"Gia is with Elisa," I explain as we exit the restaurant.

His face turns thunderous as he curses under his breath. "I'm coming with you."

"I figured."

"Good luck handling those two," Cristian quips, saluting us before he walks off toward his office building.

Chapter Fifteen
Joshua

We meet our guy outside the front of the market, and he gives us directions to locate the girls. "Alesso will freak if he finds out Elisa did this," Caleb says as we stride through the main concourse heading toward the wine bar.

"We're under no obligation to tell him. She's not a kid anymore."

"I won't be telling Salerno shit. He still hates my guts," Caleb says, winking as we pass a group of women gawking at us with their mouths hanging open. We're recognizable in the city. A consequence of having our faces plastered on billboards for years. Caleb is as notorious for his partying and his womanizing, but I like to think I've avoided being tarnished with that particular brush. "Ladies." Caleb grins and salutes them, and they legit swoon.

I barely resist an eyeroll. "He doesn't hate your guts. He doesn't want you around Anais. They are two totally different things."

"She's in Vegas. Has been for years, yet he still hasn't thawed."

I level him with a look as we move aside to let a woman with a stroller through. "Don't insult my intelligence, brother. I know you still fuck her when she's in the city."

"I can't help it. I'll never want to not drive a stake through that fucker's heart."

"I hate him as much as you do, but I still wish you'd cut all ties with her. She's poison, Caleb, and I don't trust her not to try and stick her claws in you permanently."

He barks out a laugh as we approach the entrance to the wine bar. "I know how to handle Mrs. DiPietro. No claws are being stuck anywhere in this body by any bitch. Trust me on that."

"So poetic," I tease as we push open the door and enter the rustic bar. Several eyeballs swing our way as we stand just inside the door, scanning the crowded room for Gia and Elisa. We stand out in our designer suits, and our tall, broad frames and similar looks always draw attention.

"There. In the back." Caleb jerks his head toward the far corner where the girls are tucked into a circular booth.

A waitress moves toward us, holding two menus and sporting wide doe eyes. "We're not staying," I tell her, barely making eye contact as we walk across the space. I'm checking the room, looking for signs of anyone who doesn't fit in but it's mostly women in here, chatting over wine and sharing plates. The few men in attendance don't warrant a second glance. I breathe a little easier knowing that but not much.

Gia's head lifts when we're a few feet away, and her lips pull into a grimace. Elisa has her back to us, so I don't notice she's crying until we stop at the table.

"Lili." Panic underscores Caleb's tone. "What's wrong?"

He slides into the booth beside her while I sit on the other side beside our troublesome informant.

"For fuck's sake," Gia hisses. "That asshole didn't have to call you." She spits fire from her eyes, and it makes her look even more beautiful. She's only wearing jeans and an off-the-shoulder sweater with minimal make up, but she's the sexiest woman in the room by a mile. Gia doesn't even have to try. It just comes natural to her.

"That *asshole* is an experienced made man who deserves your respect." I keep my voice low. "He's ensuring your safety and under strict instructions to call me if you pull any bullshit." I clear my throat and pin her with a dark look. "Hence why I'm here."

"This doesn't involve you, and I took precautions." She flings her hair over her shoulders, and a blast of perfume tickles my nostrils. "I'm not being followed, and I requested this table so I have a full view of everyone coming in and out of the place." She pulls her bag onto her lap. "I wore a wig leaving my building, and I'll put it back on returning."

"I can't believe you'd risk your best friend like this," I say, looking across the table where Caleb and Elisa appear to be exchanging heated words. Her eyes are red-rimmed, and her face is all blotchy. "It's too dangerous, and she's not equipped to fend off any attack. This was reckless and selfish."

"Fuck you, Joshua. She needed me, and I won't let her down. I would never risk my friend. Why the fuck do you think I met her in such a public place? In Manhattan? Liam is in Boston today, and he hasn't got anyone tailing me, so chill the fuck out. You're overreacting."

"I'm your boss," I remind her, trying not to focus on where our thighs meet under the table. "And I'm not overreacting. Grab your things. We're leaving."

"Like fuck we are."

"Gigi, it's okay." Elisa slides her hand across the table. "I shouldn't have called you."

I shoot daggers into the side of Gia's face.

"Fuck off, Joshua." Gia stabs her finger into my upper arm. "She called me on my personal cell not the burner." Gia eyeballs Caleb, her gaze lowering momentarily to his arm circled around Elisa's shoulders. "You need to take him out and get him laid because I'm liable to stab him if he keeps busting my balls when it's completely unnecessary."

Caleb arches a brow, but he's too concerned with Elisa to give me shit. I didn't tell him I blew Elizabeth off Saturday night. I had zero interest in fucking her after I left Gia's apartment. The only redhead on my mind all night was the spitfire currently sitting beside me.

"This is my fault," Elisa says, fixing pleading eyes on me. "I promise I won't call her again if you let this pass."

"Don't make promises like that!" Gia links her fingers in Elisa's. "I want you to call me." The women share a loaded look and Caleb is as tense as a brick. He's always been overprotective of his Lili.

"I don't want you to get in trouble."

"She won't," Caleb butts in, squeezing Elisa's upper arm. "You can't meet up, but it's safe to call her if you need to."

I count to ten in my head. It's either that or shoot him. "Take Elisa to her apartment."

"Call me later," Gia says as Elisa retracts her hand. "We're not done discussing this."

"Thank you," she whispers. Tears well in her eyes. "I love you."

"Love you too, Lise." Gia elbows me as Caleb helps Elisa out of the booth. I stand and let her pass. The girls hug and Gia whispers something to her friend as Caleb watches with concern written all over his face.

"Let's go, Lili," he says, a few beats later, taking her hand and pulling her away from Gia. Caleb wraps his arm around her. "I've got her."

"Guard her with your life, and message me when she's home safely."

They walk off as I throw a few bills down on the table. "Grab your things. We're leaving."

"You're such an asshole." Anger paints her beautiful face as she grabs her purse and her coat and a couple of shopping bags. "And I'm not telling you why she was crying, so don't waste your breath asking."

"Wasn't planning to," I truthfully admit. "Elisa Salerno is not my concern."

"You really are a cold prick. Do you care about anyone but yourself?"

My sharp gaze pins her in place. "You already know the answer."

She nibbles on the corner of her mouth but doesn't reply.

I take the bags while she puts her coat on, shaking my head when she tries to take them back. "Let's go." I gesture for her to go ahead of me, and I follow, ignoring the heated looks sent my way as we pass a few tables of giggling women.

I stop her outside the door, checking left and right to see which way Caleb went with Elisa, and then I steer Gia in the opposite direction. We head down to the lower level where the food market is. "Don't manhandle me." She shoves my hand away as we walk past the butcher shop. "It's bad enough I've got to walk beside you and endure your little groupies," she adds as a gaggle of college-age girls scream at me, trying to catch my attention.

"Jealous much, Gia." I smother a grin.

"Don't start with me." She grips the strap of her purse more tightly. "Oh, I want to pop in here to buy sauce for Saturday's dinner." She races into the hot sauce store like she's got a rocket up her butt.

I trail her inside the store, wondering at the viability of such an offering. But it must work because the place is crawling with people, and the till is ringing with purchase after purchase. I watch her inspect every bottle like it's life or death. "Buy the hottest. With any luck, he'll drop dead, and problem solved."

"You can't die from too much chili," she says, handing two bottles to the man behind the counter. "You'd have to ingest it in massive doses, but it can make you sick."

"Good, sprinkle his portion liberally." I swipe my card before Gia has even removed her wallet from her purse.

"That's not a bad idea. Maybe if he's sick, he'll let me stay over to nurse him, and I can snoop while I'm there."

"Second thoughts," I say, swiping the bag and gripping her elbow. "Go easy on the prick. We might need to interrogate him." I open the door for her, and we step outside.

A laugh bursts from her lips, lighting up her entire face, and it's like being sucker punched in the nuts. "You're too fucking easy to wind up."

"And you're beautiful," I blurt, like a teenager with zero game.

Her eyes widen as she stares up at me, and our surroundings fade into the background. My eyes drop to her plump lips, and I'm contemplating planting one on her when reality returns with a cruel slap to the face.

"Josh. Is that you?" an unfortunately familiar woman asks from behind me.

My heart slams against my chest as ice drips through my veins. Gia glances over my shoulder, her mouth forming an O shape. She doesn't fight me when I wrap my arm around her and turn us to face the woman who single-handedly decimated my heart.

I fight to maintain a disinterested look when my eyes instantly roam her rounded stomach. Bettina's smile is brittle as she glances between me and Gia. Her hands gravitate to her bump, and I don't see any rings on her fingers.

Of course not.

While this could be any man's baby, I know exactly who got her pregnant. I have known she's been with him all this time, so it doesn't take much to connect the dots.

Rage surges forward from where it's buried in a lockbox marked with my ex's name. "Wow. You let him knock you up? Is there no end to your foolishness, you stupid bitch?"

"Joshua!" Gia attempts to pull me back when I put my face all up in Bettina's, but I'm an immovable force.

I shuck her off and glare at my ex. I've waited years to say this to her face. "Was the thought of being my wife so abhorrent you'd throw it all away to be his whore?"

"Josh, it was never like that." Tears stream down her face. "I didn't set out to betray you. I couldn't help falling in love with him."

She couldn't help it? Rage pummels my insides, and my hands twitch at my sides with longing to strangle the bitch who deceived me and left me broken. But death would be too kind to her. Let her live and face what's surely coming. "I suppose you just tripped and landed on his dick?" I snarl.

"We didn't plan this. It—"

"Shut. Your. Lying. Face."

"I'm sorry, Josh. I'm so sorry. I didn't think you'd still be mad. I was just so happy to see you, and I thought—"

"You thought what, slut?" I glare at her, and she steps back, clasping a hand over her mouth. "That I'd forgive you for cheating on me, for months, behind my back, with that conniving prick just because it's been nine years since your betrayal?"

"Don't do this." Gia wraps her arms around me tight. "You're better than this."

I ignore her words but hold her hands tight around my waist, needing to distract myself so I don't strangle a pregnant woman in broad daylight. "Get one thing straight, whore. I will never forgive you, and I will never forget."

Although our birthday is in December, I've always felt I'm more Scorpio than Sagittarius. Like most Scorpios, I hold on to resentment with the tenacity of a nun protecting her virtue and I never forget betrayal. If you cross me, I'll cut you dead, remember it forever, and always hate you.

Sobs escape her mouth, and snot dribbles from her nose.

"I might have ended up with your whining, sniveling ass if you hadn't shown your true colors, so I guess I can thank you for saving me that torment. As for the rest, you're already dead to me, bitch. As dead as you'll actually be in a few months when that baby arrives."

"Joshua! Stop this. Oh my God." Gia's shocked tone doesn't deter me, and I'm not taking back anything I've said.

The bitch's tears stop, and her face turns pale.

A bitter laugh rips from my lips. "You didn't seriously think he'd let you keep it or even let you live? You know he doesn't love you, right? Please tell me you're not *that* stupid. He didn't marry you. You've been his piece on the side for years. You and countless others, so don't think you're special. And don't think he'll protect you when the time comes because he won't. He'll rip that baby from your arms and take it home to his wife to raise as their own."

"He wouldn't do that. She doesn't want babies."

Gia comes around to my side, peering up at me with horrified eyes. I'm not sure if she's worked it out or if it's more of a generalized state of horror.

"So fucking stupid." I snap my fingers in her face. "Wake

up and smell the coffee, Bettina. She can't conceive." I don't know that to be fact. I'm just guessing this is the reason why they've never had kids and why he's now resorted to using his whore as a last measure. "He used you to give him an heir, and you just spread your legs and let him. You deserve to die for being such a pathetic bitch." I grab Gia's hand. "If you're lucky he'll make it quick, but if his wife gets her hands on you, all bets are off."

She visibly shakes, and if I had any heart left, I might take pity on her. But I don't, and she doesn't deserve it. "Rot in hell, Ina. You deserve it."

Chapter Sixteen
Gia

I'm in the back of a taxi, en route to Liam's place, and I should be focused on our dinner date, but instead, I'm worrying about Elisa and still mulling over everything that went down between Joshua and his ex a few days ago. I have borne the brunt of Joshua's cold front before, but I have never seen him act so callously. He pulled no punches with Bettina, and he was brutally cruel. After she ran off, I tried getting him to talk to me, but he clammed up like an oyster, and I haven't seen or heard from him since.

He's clearly harboring a lot of resentment and hasn't fully moved on. It's been a long time, and my heart hurts for him carrying all that pain and hatred around for years. It doesn't mean I excuse or condone his treatment of his ex because I don't. Bettina did him dirty, but attacking her so viciously while she's heavily pregnant was out of line. He should have remained dignified and just walked away.

It was naïve of her to approach him in the first place. Why on earth would she ever think he'd want to talk to her? Especially when she's pregnant with the other man's baby? I never knew the specifics of what went down only that she had been cheating on Joshua with another made man for months before he found out.

The car pulls up in front of a fancy apartment building in historic DUMBO, right beside the trendy waterfront, and I crane my neck to see the top of the steel-and-glass façade of the high-rise. Figures Liam would live someplace like this. The man is all about appearances and he loves the sound of his own voice. Conversations we've had where he was bragging about his new apartment make sense now.

I pay the driver and leave with my purse and my grocery bag, entering the plush building a minute later. The concierge adds my name to a guest book and escorts me to the elevator that takes me to the penthouse apartment Liam is currently renting. I press on both earrings to activate the recording device just before the elevator doors part on the top level.

My fake new boyfriend is waiting to greet me, leaning in to kiss me before the elevator doors have even closed behind me. I go through the motions while I run through the menu I'm creating in my head until it's over.

"I'm glad you're here," he says, looping his arm through mine as his gaze devours me from head to toe.

"I'm happy to be here," I lie, smiling at him. "I love cooking, and I can't wait to cook for you."

He steers me across the lobby, ogling me like I'm the meal, and into his penthouse. Unlike Joshua's place, this is flamboyant and garish with a bright red leather couch and a cowhide fur I really hope is fake on the floor. There are no homey touches, but Liam hasn't been living here long, and it's only a rental.

"Wow, the view is stunning," I say, gravitating toward the tall floor-to-ceiling windows offering expansive views of the harbor, the Manhattan skyline, and the Brooklyn Bridge in the near distance.

"It is, and this place is quite historic. The Battle of Brooklyn took place on these streets in 1776. It was the biggest battle of the revolutionary war. Washington crossed from here by way of the ferry landing because the bridge wasn't around then. It was built in 1883, and it was the largest suspension bridge at that time."

"I didn't know that," I truthfully admit.

"I researched the area after I decided to base myself in Brooklyn, and I rented this place mostly because of the balcony and those views," he says, jerking his head to the side where a large balcony juts out from the building overlooking the water and the bridge. "Pity it's too cold for outdoor eating." His arm winds around my shoulders while mine aches a little from holding the bag laden with ingredients. "We'll eat outside in the summer. I'm hoping you'll be living here by then."

My brow arch is natural, and he chuckles. "In case it's not obvious, I'm serious about you, Emma. Very serious." His fingers sweep over my cheeks. "I put in an offer to buy this place today. Made it so the owner won't refuse."

"Wow. You don't waste time."

"Life is for living." He swats my ass and waggles his brows.

I work hard not to slap him. "I need to get started, or we'll be eating dinner at midnight."

"Knock yourself out, sexy." He points toward the kitchen. "I have some work to finish so I'll leave you to it."

He walks off, disappearing into a hallway, as I head to the kitchen tucked at the rear of the main living space. He didn't even offer to give me a grand tour. His manners suck, and I don't think much of how his mother raised him. My mom would berate my brothers if they ever treated their girls like this.

Shucking out of my coat, I place it and my purse on the back of a high stool and set about unpacking my supplies on the large island unit. I switch the oven on before walking off in search of the bathroom, purely so I can locate where Liam is and get my bearings. I leave my shoes in the kitchen and pad in my bare feet down the hallway that leads to the rest of the apartment.

Quietly, I open each door, finding a couple of guest bedrooms, a small home gym, and a family bathroom. I take pictures of everything with my camera pen. Muffled voices can be heard coming from the door of the last room on the right. That must be his office. I inch the door open on the left, poking my head inside what is obviously his master suite. I'm tempted to snoop now, but it's too risky when he's in the room across the hallway even if he appears to be occupied on a call.

I press my ear to the office door, but I can't hear anything. I make a mental note to ask Joshua if we have any kind of tech device that can penetrate walls.

There was lengthy debate over whether I should bug Liam's place, but it was deemed way too dangerous. Most made men regularly check for surveillance equipment, and we can't risk Liam discovering one. His list of suspects would be short, and I'd most likely come out on top. So, for now, we're not planting any bugs.

I tiptoe back to the kitchen and get started on our meal, compiling the apple tart first and getting it in the oven. Then I work on the carrot and coriander soup and the shepherd's pie. I decided to cook him an Irish meal in the hopes it will impress him and garner more trust. His comment about me moving in took me by surprise, but I'm not unhappy. This is working out perfectly. Now, if I can just get the intel I need so I can cut him out of my life sooner than later that would be the cherry on top of the cake.

When the apple tart is cooling, the soup is simmering, and the pie is in the oven, I make him an Irish coffee using a bottle of JD I find in his liquor cupboard, and I head toward his office. I knock on his door and wait for him to call me inside. "I thought you might like a drink." I smile as I walk toward him. Papers are strewn across the desk, and I'm itching to go through them, but I keep my eyes fixed on him as I walk around the desk and set the tall glass mug down in front of him. He flicks a button on his keypad, and the screen saver appears on the large desktop Mac. "Dinner will be ready in thirty minutes." I lean in to kiss his cheek.

I yelp when he pulls me down on his lap, narrowly avoiding elbowing the drink and spilling it. "I really like having you here," he says before slamming his mouth down on mine. He grabs my ass, holding me in place, and I feel his disgusting erection growing underneath me. I kiss him passionately as I slip my pen from the pocket of my dress and discreetly take pics of his desk. "Damn," he says, breaking our lip-lock and nuzzling my neck. "You make me so horny." He thrusts his hips up. "I need to fuck you, baby."

"Patience." I press my lips to his to distract him while I slip the pen back into my pocket. "I told you I'm not that kind of girl. I don't hop into bed with just anyone."

"I like that about you." He runs his hand up my back and fists it around my hair, tugging my head back a little. "I like you're not a slut, but I have needs, baby, and if you won't service them, I'll find someone who will."

"Go fuck yourself, Liam." I struggle against him, trying to get free, but he tightens his hold on my hair. "Let me go." I let my anger flow freely because Emma wouldn't tolerate such blatant manipulation and disrespect. "If I'm only a fuck toy to you, we might as well end this right now. I'm going home."

"Don't be so sensitive." He squeezes my ass with his free hand. "You should be proud I'm so hot for you."

"I don't know what kind of women you're used to, Liam, but I won't be spoken to like this by anyone. Now get your fucking hands off me. You've ruined the mood, and the last thing I feel like doing now is eating dinner with you." I shoot daggers at him, gripping his arms tight when he doesn't budge.

"Don't go." He softens his tone. "I didn't mean to piss you off. I just want you. Is that so bad?"

"You can't rush me, Liam, and threatening to fuck someone else because I won't put out is hurtful and disrespectful." I have zero doubt he's fucking other women behind my back and he'll continue to do so for the entire time we're dating. It's second nature to arrogant dickheads like him. "We've only been dating a month. I really like you, Liam. This feels serious between us already, but I won't let any man push me before I'm ready. I thought you understood that?"

A heavy sigh escapes his lips, but he finally frees my hair and loosens his tight grip on my ass. "I do, and I'm trying to be patient, but it's hard."

"Try harder." I lock eyes with him in a brief stare-off.

"Okay, but I won't wait forever, Emma."

God, he's insufferable. "I won't make you," I lie. I slide off his lap. "I'm going to set the table and you should drink your Irish coffee before it goes cold."

I subtly scan his office as I make my exit, blowing him a kiss before I close the door. I wait a couple minutes until I hear him on another call, and then I take a calculated risk and slip inside his master suite.

I snap pictures of his king bed dressed in black silk sheets and the two samurai swords crossed and mounted to the wall over the bed. Slowly, I open the drawers of each bedside table, quickly inspecting the contents, but it's nothing of importance.

Then I check out his en suite bathroom and his closet, looking for any boxes that might be hidden underneath or over the wardrobes, but I find nothing. The only discovery is a safe with a lock hidden behind a framed picture on a side wall in his bedroom.

Ducking out of his room, I close his door super slowly, adrenaline coursing through my veins as I tiptoe down the hallway and back to the kitchen. My breathing levels out after a few minutes, and I breathe a sigh of relief I got away with it.

Liam appears in the living area just as I'm ladling soup into bowls. I warmed up the brown bread I made at home this morning, and it's residing in a bread basket on the table. "Something smells delicious, and I'm not talking about the food." He snakes his arms around my waist from behind and nuzzles my neck.

He's so freaking cliché, and it's a miracle I don't gag. "Go sit and I'll serve you."

"Oh, I love the sound of that."

Of course, you do, you arrogant, misogynistic prick. It feels good to curse him out in my head, but I'd much prefer if I could say it to his face. I hope, at some point, I get to tell him my true feelings. I'd love to wipe that smug grin off his face.

His hand trails up under my dress, and I swat it away, barely resisting the temptation to stab him with a fork.

"Behave," I warn with narrowed eyes. "I've gone to lots of trouble to cook you a traditional Irish dinner, and it's not going to waste." I gave each course a unique flare of my own, like adding a couple spoons of hot sauce to the shepherd's pie to give it a little kick, but it's still a traditional menu.

"You did that for me?"

I nod. "Of course. Why do you sound so surprised? You told me you're proud of your Irish heritage and my great-great grandmother was from Ireland," I lie. "It was fun researching recipes, and it helped me to feel connected with my roots."

"I'm going to take you to Ireland someday. You'd love it there."

I serve the soup, and we sit down to eat. Butter melts on the chunky homemade bread, and it's to die for. After, we eat the shepherd's pie, and I dish up the apple tart with cream for dessert, but I can't manage more than a few mouthfuls I'm so full. Liam has seconds, so I consider it a win.

"That was fucking incredible." He reels me into him as I begin clearing the table. "You're perfect, Emma. So fucking perfect."

"I'm glad you enjoyed it. I did too."

His hand slides under my dress and creeps up the back of my thigh. Everything I've said tonight seems to have gone in one ear and out the other. How does any woman put up with this slimeball? "Go sit, and I'll fix you a drink before I clean up. You worked hard today, and you deserve to chill out." I already know he won't offer to help with the cleanup because he has the manners of a pig.

"Like I said, perfect." He waggles his brows, and I peck his lips before clearing the table. I stack the dishes on the counter and fix his whiskey, handing it to him before I return to the kitchen. I take my time rinsing and stacking dishes and covering the leftover food. He calls for me several times, and I know I can't delay this any longer.

The instant I sit beside him on the couch, he jumps on me, groping and kissing me as he pushes me flat on my back. "Liam." I move my head to the side and shove at his shoulders. "You promised you'd be patient."

"You've got to give me something, Emma." His hand glides up the inside of my thigh, and his fingers brush against my lace panties.

Panic flares as I grip his wrist, stopping him before he goes any farther. Dark eyes drill into mine, and I know I can't stall him any longer. "Let me do something for you." He's selfish at his core, so this should work. I can't bear the thought of touching him intimately, but it's preferable to him touching me.

His eyes flash with lust as he lifts himself off me. "I like the way your mind works," he says, sitting back and spreading his legs as he pops the button on his jeans.

I discreetly press my earrings to turn off the audio before lowering to my knees on the floor. I can't do this if I think Joshua might be listening.

Blanking my mind, I rest my hands on his thighs and lean in as I take one for the team.

Chapter Seventeen
Joshua

Three things are responsible for my perpetual shitty mood this past week—the run-in with my ex, Lavinia pulling the wool over my eyes for the past couple months, and Gia's dinner date with that Irish prick on Saturday. Blood boils in my veins every time I think about the way he treated her. I was listening in live, and I almost puked when she turned off the audio for obvious reasons. Thinking about her blowing that asshole makes me want to riddle the fuckface with bullets. For the first time, I'm regretting suggesting this assignment for her. It feels wrong to force her to do these things. Even if the photographic intel from his desk has proven useful. Gia wasn't able to properly capture each document, but we have enough to piece together the evidence.

Liam had detailed blueprints of the plant in Cali on his desk. This means the mole could be on the Colombian side, rather than in the city. Or the mole is within our ranks, he got his hands on classified intel, and they are planning a hit on our plant to disrupt our production and completely fuck up the supply chain. Either way, it's not good, but at least we are one step ahead this time.

Massimo and Fiero were in Florida when the intel was confirmed, and they quickly hopped on a plane to Colombia where they met with their plant manager, Juan Pablo. He has denied any involvement, and Don Maltese and Don Greco believe him. Not sure the rest of us do. Anyway, they installed surveillance equipment without his knowledge, and we've sent a team of fifty trustworthy men to guard the plant and report to us. We also have drones in the area, and if anything goes down, we're confident we'll capture it.

"You seem preoccupied." Ben materializes beside me at the window of his home office, staring out at the vast secluded Greenwich estate.

Sierra and Ben are hosting Thanksgiving this year, and the whole crew is here. Including Gia and her family. I've been hiding from her, but I know my reprieve is only short-lived.

"What's troubling you?" my uncle asks.

I shrug, not sure I want to discuss it with him. But if I was going to confide in anyone, it would probably be Ben.

I've always looked up to him.

Always gone to him for advice.

I'm close to Ben in a way I'm not with Leo.

Don't get me wrong, I love Leo. He's good to my mom. He is a good stepdad to Caleb and me and a great father to Leif and Rosa. I'm just not as close to him as Caleb is.

I can't say why Caleb confides in Leo and I confide in Ben. Or why neither of us go to Luca more. He's our *consigliere*. It's his role to advise us, and he ran the business and sat on The Commission for years after Dad was gunned down while we were too young to take on the responsibility. We do consult him on all relevant matters, but more often than not, we rely on Ben or Leo. Having them support and mentor us has been a godsend these past two years since Caleb and I took our rightful seats at The Commission.

"Would this have anything to do with Gia?" he asks, moving to his liquor cabinet.

"Why would you ask that?" I turn around and watch him fixing drinks.

"Call it a hunch." He adds ice cubes to his bourbon and my scotch.

"She's part of the issue." I have never lied to Ben, and I'm not starting now.

He hands me my drink, and we walk toward the leather couch in front of the blazing fire. "Is Bettina the other?" I stare at him, and he answers my unspoken question. "Made men talk, Joshua. They're worse gossips than women sometimes. She was seen running out of Chelsea market in tears. It didn't take much to connect the dots."

"I don't regret the things I said to her, but it was reckless to place Gia in danger like that. I drew attention to us in public. Anyone could have seen and reported it to Liam." It's part of the reason I've been in a foul mood. I should have walked away from my ex and protected Gia. Instead, I let emotions overrule me, and I made a bad judgment call.

"True, but Gia seems competent, and there's nothing you can do to change it now." He swirls the amber-colored liquid in his glass. "Is the baby Cruz's?"

I nod.

"Fuck." Ben claws a hand through his hair. He will be fifty next year, but he doesn't look it. He has a few lines on his face, but he's in great shape, and there is no hint of gray in his dark hair. "Alesso will be furious."

"I don't know why he cares when Anais barely gives him the time of day."

"She's his last link to the father he never knew, and she's family."

"If she was my family, I'd have cut her loose a long time ago."

"I'm with you, but Alesso is not us. He cares about his cousin even if it's not reciprocated."

I knock back my drink. "Cruz is a loose cannon. Are we sure he's not involved in this? I wouldn't put it past him to try to usurp us. He knows we'll never let him join the board, and as long as Cristian holds a seat, he'll never be the New York don."

"Cristian visited him this week. He didn't spot anything out of the ordinary."

"Cruz is a prick, but he's smart. He's not going to risk his brother seeing anything, and they hate one another. It's not like he'd ever confide in him."

"Agreed." We turn around as Caleb saunters into the room. "I know how we can get the intel we need," he adds, confirming he was eavesdropping.

"No." I shake my head, already knowing where this is going.

"She's already messaged me wanting to meet up. Anais is the perfect person to spy on Cruz. She hates him, and she'll want to bury him when she finds out he knocked Bettina up."

"Alesso will string you up by your balls, Caleb." Ben stands and moves in front of the roaring fire.

"He can try. This is bigger than all of us."

"You have no proof Cruz is involved," he adds. "You two have had a hard-on for him since everything went down. Don't let bias cloud your judgment."

"I don't need proof." Caleb claims the seat Ben just vacated. "He's a power-hungry motherfucker who hates us all for various reasons. We know we have a mole on the inside. We know it has to be someone senior. Cruz has links between

Vegas and New York, and he bought an airline last year. Red fucking flag if you ask me."

Ben scrubs a hand across his chin. "It's suspicious for sure, but going after another don could cause a full-blown war, and we can't afford that right now."

"Which is why my plan makes sense," Caleb crosses an ankle over his knee.

Ben slowly nods. "I hate to agree, but it's the easiest way of keeping tabs on him."

"Provided she says nothing to him. She's not exactly reliable."

"You leave Anais up to me. I know how to handle her."

***

We conduct a quick conference call with Don Greco, and he approves Caleb to approach Anais to spy on her husband. I really hope it doesn't blow up in all our faces. Then Sierra calls us in for dinner. I take a seat at the farthest end of the table from Gia, sitting beside Sierra and Serena's mother Georgia and her husband David and across from Rowan and Raven. With twenty-five around the table, it's easy to avoid looking at her.

But my reprieve ends twenty minutes after dinner when Gia charges over to me with a determined look on her face. Caleb chuckles as we finish stacking the dishwasher. "She's going to roast you over the coals, brother." He slaps me on the back. "You should just fuck her and get it over with."

I glare at his retreating back as Gia stomps up to me. "I'm done with this avoidance bullshit." She tugs on my arm. "We're going for a walk."

"I have nothing to say to you," I calmly reply, removing her hand from my arm.

"Well, I have plenty to say to you."

"Don't care." I cross my arms over my chest.

She waves her finger in my face as her nostrils flare. "I didn't take you for a coward, but you are one."

"I'm not a coward. I just don't want to talk to you."

"Liar, and you don't get to say that." She cocks her head and smiles sweetly. "You're my handler on this assignment. You need to make yourself available to me."

"You want to talk about work stuff, fine? But everything else is off-limits."

She glances over my shoulder and smirks. "We're having this conversation whether you like it or not. It's your choice if you want to do it with an audience."

I briefly close my eyes before turning around. Mom, Sierra, Serena, and Frankie are stopped in the doorway watching our interaction go down.

"Want some popcorn?" Caleb asks them with a wicked glint in his eye.

"That's not a bad idea." Sierra grins.

"Fine," I grit out, glaring at Gia. "I'll walk with you."

"I'm not mad if that's what you're thinking," I say as we're walking through the woods at the rear of the estate. It's dark out now, but there are spotlights bordering the path, guiding our way, and tall lamps are sprinkled along the walking trail every now and then.

Her brow puckers as she rubs her hands through her gloves. "Why would you be mad?"

I pull my collar up and tighten the scarf around my neck. "I know you had to do it. He backed you into a corner."

"You think this is about Liam?"

"Isn't it?" I arch a brow as we walk close together.

"That's not what I wanted to talk about, but if you need to get something off your chest, go for it."

I don't hesitate to accept the offer, which is not usual for me, but I've been feeling out of sorts for weeks, and I'm sick of it. I'm going to put it all out there, and she can do with it what she likes. "I hate you have to spend time with him. I hate you have to kiss him. I hate your mouth was anywhere near his vile dick."

"How do you know it's vile?"

"Are you saying it's not?"

"I'm just wondering when you got up close and personal with McDermott's cock."

"Gia. Stop." I rub at my temples. "You're giving me a headache."

A pregnant pause ensues for a few beats. "Why do you hate him so much?" she asks in a softer tone.

"Because he gets to do the things I've been fantasizing about doing," I blurt without a second thought.

She stops, yanking on my arm. "You've fantasized about me blowing you?"

"Multiple times." I peer directly into her blue peepers. "Especially since I saw you naked. You're exquisite, and I can't get you out of my mind."

She stretches up and brushes her lips against mine. It's only fleeting, but it heats all the frozen parts inside me. "If it helps, I've been daydreaming about you too."

"Is it as annoying for you as it is for me?" I ask as we resume walking.

Laughter bubbles up her throat. "Extremely. I don't understand this"—she moves her hand between us—"like at all."

"Makes two of us." I shove my hands in the pocket of my coat before I'm tempted to grab her and kiss her.

"What do we do?"

I shrug. "Fuck if I know."

We're both quiet as we walk. "I hate him. I scrub myself raw in the shower after every time I'm with him. He literally makes my skin crawl. I have to purposely tune out to kiss him and work extremely hard not to flinch or shy away when he touches me, which is far too often for my liking."

I'm glad we only have audio. If I had a visual of every time he grabbed her, I'd have stormed his place and put him six feet underground by now. "It was wrong to ask you to do this."

"No." She pulls me over to a bench, and we sit pressed against one another through layers of warm clothes. "You were right to assign this to me. At least we've gotten some intel now, and I know I can get more."

I turn to face her, loving how cute she looks tucked up in a woolly hat with flushed cheeks and a red-tipped nose. "I don't want anything to happen to you."

"I'm being careful."

"Neither of us are being careful." I drill her with a knowing look. Searching his bedroom when he was in the room directly across from her was reckless as fuck. "I shouldn't have argued with my ex in public while you were there. I risked exposing you. I'm really sorry, Gia. I should have showed more restraint and put your safety above my need for revenge."

She blinks several times, and I quirk a brow in silent question. "You're being nice to me. I can't decide if I like it or not."

A genuine smile ghosts over my mouth. "If this is the benchmark for niceness, you haven't set it very high."

"Well, I have been hanging out with that sexist pig. Most any man would measure higher against that misogynist prick."

"True, but I meant it. I am sorry for putting you in danger."

She places her hand on my arm and smiles. "Don't beat yourself up. Nothing has surfaced online, and Liam has been normal with me, so he's not aware of our ruse. We got away with it."

"Let's agree not to put you in a similar position again, and that goes for you putting yourself in danger. Don't take unnecessary risks, Gia. You're not dying on my watch." Even the thought of it sends shards of pain hurtling through my chest.

"I'm going nowhere, Joshua, and I'm going to find more intel. I know we need more to go after Liam, and I'm determined to get it."

Chapter Eighteen
Gia

"I want to talk about Bettina." I eyeball him so he knows he's not getting out of this conversation.

"She is the last thing I want to talk about." He blows on his hands and averts his gaze.

"Which is exactly why you should." I touch his arm again. I seem to be unable to help myself. I have this irritating urge to be near him all the time. It's only getting worse, and it pisses me off as much as it excites me. A shrink would have a field day in my head at the moment. "You need to unburden yourself, Joshua. I didn't realize how much you're still hurting over her until last week. You're carrying so much anger and pain."

"So?" He shrugs, stabbing me with a harsh look.

"Don't." I cup his face in my gloved hands. "Don't put your shield back up. Talk to me."

"Why?" His hand lands on my hip over my coat. "Why do you even care?"

I swallow a bout of nerves. If I'm asking him to be vulnerable in front of me it's only fair I return the favor. "Because I care about you. And I hate to see you suffering. I want to help. I know it might not seem like it, but I'm a good listener, and I promise I won't judge."

He stares at me for an indeterminate amount of time, and I wish I knew what was going through his head. His eyes lower to my mouth, and my heart kicks off, going crazy behind my chest cavity. Warmth heats me from the inside as he clasps the back of my neck in one large firm hand and draws me toward him. Our eyes connect, and we hover on the precipice of something monumental as we hold still with our mouths a hairbreadth from one another.

He's so beautiful. Can you say that about a man? All I know is it's true. Joshua is shielding nothing from me now, and staring into his gorgeous deep-blue eyes is like staring into his soul. Joshua is good. It's innate, but he's buried it so far inside it rarely surfaces. He's been showing me glimpses, and I'm reminded of the boy he used to be—sweet, kind, considerate, and he always had a smile for everyone. He smoothed Caleb's rough edges and jumped in as peacemaker so many times.

"This isn't a smart idea," he says, his warm breath fanning over my face.

"I know," I whisper.

"But I need to taste you, Gia. I need it more than I need air to breathe." He bridges that final gap and presses his hot mouth to my lips.

I expect him to devour me. To brutalize my mouth with punishing kisses and pent-up need, but he gives me the opposite. His lips are tender, worshipping, respectful as he moves them against mine, and I'm floating on air, melting against him, sucked into his warmth and his strength and his virality. Enveloped in the confidence that comes from slow, sensual kisses when it would be far easier to give in to our baser desires.

It's everything.

I never want him to stop kissing me, and it scares me.

Eventually, we pull apart before we both develop lockjaw. Warmth blankets me from head to toe despite the chilly night. My lips are swollen, and my heart is careening around my chest.

"You terrify me, Gia," he says, tucking a few stray strands of hair back into my hat. His eyes are shining with emotion as he peers into my face. "The things I feel for you terrify me."

"I share that sentiment," I truthfully admit, dragging my fingers slowly through his silky, blond hair. I've been dying to do that for weeks. "This has hit me out of nowhere. I have never felt this way about any guy before."

"I had feelings like this before, and I got burned."

I sweep my thumb across his cheek. "I'm not her."

"I never thought she'd betray me. She was so sweet, and she seemed happy. She *was* happy. We were happy." His eyes glaze over as he remembers the past.

I release his face and take his hands in mine, urging him to continue with my eyes.

"We were together four years when she started sleeping with Cruz DiPietro behind my back. She was eighteen, and he was thirty-three and married."

"I suspected it might be Cruz that day at the market." I rub his bare hands with my gloved ones. "Is that why Caleb fucks Anais?"

He nods. "He targeted her deliberately in retaliation."

I have all kinds of feelings on that, but my focus is Joshua.

"My brother always has my back. He's one of the few I know I can count on."

Despite their vastly different personalities, there is no denying how close the twins are. They have a tight bond, and they are always there for one another. To come at one is to come at both, and woe betide anyone going up against the

Accardi twins. Few live to tell the tale. I've seen it countless times over the years.

"You won't want to hear this, but Bettina could be a victim," I say. "Cruz may have targeted her on purpose. Groomed her to be his whore. How long was he married to Anais before this happened?"

"About four years, I think. I might have believed that theory back then but not now. She's a grown woman. She could walk away anytime, and she doesn't."

"She could be trapped. We don't know what he's holding over her or what kind of shit he's telling her to keep her by his side."

"Or she's just stupid enough to believe a married man's lies."

"That could be true, but what if it's not?"

"I don't care! I don't give a fuck about them!" he snaps, yanking his hands back.

"But you do," I quietly reply. "It hurts you she's still with him when the truth is if she hadn't cheated you two may have broken up anyway."

"I can't say what would or wouldn't have happened. I loved her. I wanted to marry her. And she chose him."

"So, you cut yourself off from feeling anything, and you keep women at arm's length now. You're letting her restrict your choices, and you don't even know why she did it. You don't know if it was a choice or if she was forced into this."

"You heard her the other day! She said she couldn't help falling for him."

"That doesn't mean she wasn't manipulated." I stand and face him, knowing it's risky to push him like this, but he's not facing up to it, and it will continuously hold him back in life until he does. "Are you hurting because she left you for him or because you think you failed to protect her from him?"

"I hate her for discarding everything we shared like it meant nothing. I hate her for throwing my love back in my face like it didn't matter. I hate her for all the lies and the deceit, for how foolish she made me look. But most of all, I hate her for changing me. There isn't a single part of me that feels even a tiny shred of guilt. She made her bed; now she can rot in it."

"That's not what I meant. I—"

"Drop it. I'm done talking about that cunt." His Adam's apple bobs in his throat, and he grabs fistfuls of his hair. "I can't do this. I can't do this with you. Tonight was a mistake. Forget it happened." Before I can reply, he's walked off, looking like he's carrying the weight of the world on his shoulders.

Chapter Nineteen
Joshua

"I'm coming with you," I tell my brother three nights later when I can't stand the voices in my head any longer.

"Okay." Caleb scans my black top, cargo pants, boots, and the Smith & Wesson strapped to my hip.

"She was my assistant. I fucked up letting her into the company. She's my problem to fix." Ben's specialist tech team found evidence Lavinia's file was a complete fake. Whoever put her up to this is good. They left no clues. The intel online matched perfectly, and her fake IDs were flawless. The team had to dig deep to find the truth. She's the sister of a two-bit gangster from New Jersey. We have no clue how to connect her to everything else, but it can't be a coincidence.

The Commission discussed how to handle it, and we chose to let her stay, under constant surveillance, in the hope she might lead us to vital intel. The hunch paid off, and something is going down tonight in Atlantic City. The irony isn't lost on us. A.C. was the birthplace of organized crime and the Italian American *mafioso* back in the day. Now, it's known for its casinos and the legendary boardwalk.

"I said okay. You don't have to convince me." Caleb thrusts a bulletproof vest at me. "You want any other weapons?"

I shake my head. "I'm good."

"Let's hit the road then."

We park several blocks from the construction site where the meeting is going down at midnight and make the rest of the way on foot. The development is at the northernmost point, a couple miles past the boardwalk, facing the water. This is an industrial part of town, and there are little signs of life. A perfect location if you're up to no good.

Caleb and I lead our group of ten *soldati* toward the meeting point, sticking to the shadows along other buildings as we quietly advance forward. A bunch of dusty cars and mud-splattered trucks are parked out front. Scaffolding scales the front elevation of the high-rise building. Raised voices greet our ears, and we split into two groups after we enter the building at the lower level. One group goes up the stairs while Caleb and I take four men and move toward the sound of voices.

Heavy-duty plastic sheets sway softly in the light ocean breeze where they cover what will be windows. Caleb gestures with his hand, and the *soldati* crouch down under the window with their backs to the wall. My twin deposits the duffel bag with the rifles and extra ammunition on the ground beside a large pillar. We take up position on either side, and it offers us a good vantage point.

A small gap in the sheet allows us to see outside. Three portable lights shine brightly on a group of armed men as they form a circle around a short stocky man with long hair tied back in a ponytail and my assistant. All the men are wearing custom suits and expensive watches, and some have chest straps with rifles on their back. Others have guns holstered to their hips. Lavinia is dressed in yoga pants, sneakers, and a hoodie underneath a denim jacket, and she's shifting from foot to foot as she wraps her arms around herself in a protective gesture.

Caleb and I exchange glances. These men are no two-bit gangsters.

What the fuck is going on?

"Should we call for backup?" I mouth to my twin.

"No time," he mouths back.

"It's not good enough, Liv," the dude with the tail says.

"His office is like Fort Knox," she says in a shrill voice. "And even when I got inside, everything is locked up. I'm guessing anything of importance is in the side room, and it's got a retinal scanner on the door. I don't know how you expect me to penetrate that."

"I'll give you something that can penetrate," some douche says, cupping his cock through his pants, and a burst of laughter rings out.

"Enough," the guy in charge snaps. "This is not a laughing matter." He eyeballs every man surrounding him with a deathly look. "Do I need to remind you of what's at stake? We've only come this far thanks to our allies. If we fail to deliver the intel, they become our enemies, and I'm sure I don't need to tell you what a shit show that'd be."

The air sobers, and there's no more joking. The dick with the long hair returns his attention to Lavinia. She's visibly trembling now.

"It's not her fault," a man on her left says. "I shouldn't have involved her."

I'm guessing he's the brother though they look nothing alike.

"She's involved now, and that means she's accountable." The man pulls a gun on her. "You have had ample time to do this, and you're a shit informant."

"I've given you information," she shrieks. Panic is splayed across her face. "I gave you the cruise liner schedules, client listings, and contracts, and I shared his calendar with you."

That little bitch. Thank fuck I only log legit work meetings on my business calendar. I hate that these assholes have a list of our client dealings, but I don't think it's any threat unless they plan to set up a competitor shipping or clothing business. They could pass it to our competitors, and it would hurt, but I don't think that's what they're after. This feels more personal, but I don't know why. Call it a sixth sense.

I agree with the guy's assessment if that's all the intel she supplied. The calendar would have given them jack shit except for my location at any given time. Those schedules are public knowledge too. Something we've always joked about because we've blatantly brought narcotics in right under the nose of the authority. But none of us are laughing now. We've already stopped using the cruise liners for the Cali runs, and an order was placed for another cargo ship recently.

"Bitch, that information was worth a whole ton of nothing." He prods his gun under her chin, and she's shaking all over.

I look at Caleb, wondering if we should step in now and stop this. If we rescue her, I'm pretty sure she'll tell us everything she knows. Except I doubt she knows much. We need the guy in charge or one of his men. Then maybe we'll get the intel we need. Excitement races through my veins at the prospect of a fight. I've been on edge for weeks, especially in the last few days, and beating the shit out of a few motherfuckers is just what the doctor ordered.

Caleb nods, reading my expression clearly. Or maybe it's just we know one another inside and out. Either way, we're on the same page, and I know he's dying to get his hands bloody. The street stuff he handled recently didn't even whet his appetite.

"You couldn't even seduce him," the long-haired dick says. "You're a pathetic excuse of a woman."

"No woman could seduce that cold prick!" she shouts. "He's gay or bi or something, but he's definitely not into women."

The man backhands her with the gun. "He fucks women. You just didn't do it for him." He drags his eyes up and down her body in a derogatory fashion. "Can't say I fucking blame him." He presses the gun to her brow. "We don't tolerate weak links. Weakness almost ruined us last time but not under my watch."

"Dude, your sister just pissed herself!" some guy shouts, and every set of eyes lowers to the pool of urine spreading across the asphalt.

"Get ready," Caleb mouths to our men as he slowly unzips the duffel and distributes rifles. I step back and press on my earpiece, whispering instructions to our second group.

"Please," Lavinia pleads over a sob. "Please don't kill me. I'll try harder. I'll get him to trust me. I'll get you what you need." Her voice elevates a few octaves with each sentence.

"Too late, bitch. You had your chance, and you blew it." He pulls the trigger, and the light dies instantly in her eyes.

"You bastard!" the brother yells, raising his gun. "You said she wouldn't be hurt! Fuck you!" He points his weapon in the man's face, but he's not watching his back, so he doesn't see his buddy creep up behind him and put a bullet through the back of his skull. He falls forward on top of his sister.

"Anyone else have something to say?" the man asks, kicking Lavinia's lifeless body as he steps over the dead siblings.

Caleb looks at me and smirks. I return his grin as we get into position behind the sheets.

"I do," Caleb shouts as we push the sheets aside and jump out onto the debris-strewn ground. "Which one of you mother-fuckers wants to die first?" We step out into their line of sight just as gunfire rains down on them from the level above.

Chapter Twenty

Joshua

Our crew takes out four of their men before they've even realized they're under siege. The others dive for cover behind dumpsters full of building materials, large equipment, and a corrugated steel hut, which I'm guessing is the foreman's office.

We trade gunfire, Caleb and I sticking close together as we take aim and shoot. Their guys are dropping like flies because they are outmatched and outmaneuvered. "Fancy going old school?" Caleb asks when there are only three guys left standing.

"Thought you'd never ask." I grin at my twin.

We shoot the firearms from the enemies' hands, leaving them unarmed and surrounded. Tucking my gun back into my holster, I glance at my brother as we walk calmly toward the men. Our guys hold back, weapons trained on the three goons as Caleb and I charge at them with our fists raised.

They enter into the spirit of things, and we throw punches and duck and dive like we're in a ring. Caleb spars like a warrior, thanks to his time in Nepal, and though I'm not on his level, I'm not too shabby either. What I lack in skill, I make up for in enthusiasm and adrenaline as I pummel my fists into a dark-haired dude's face and kick him in the gut, winding him. I sweep his legs out from under him as Caleb attacks the man in charge. The other guy is out cold on the floor.

Pouring every ounce of futility, frustration, and pent-up anger into my thrusts, I pound the guy's face and head until his skull caves and the light goes out in his eyes. Blood coats my hands and splatters my face, and sweat sticks the clothes to my back. Adrenaline courses through my veins, and I wish there were ten more motherfuckers for me to beat. This has barely quenched my bloodlust.

"Enough, brother. He's dead." Caleb pulls me off him as I continue to lash out at his corpse.

"Accardi scum," the long-haired dude says from his position on his knees. Several guns are trained on him, but our soldiers are under orders not to kill these survivors. We want them alive to interrogate them.

"Who are you?" I swipe blood from my face with my sleeve.

"Fuck. You. Pretty Boy."

Caleb grabs him by the hair and yanks his head back hard. He hates that moniker. The New York media have called us The Pretty Boys of New York for years. Other, braver journalists have referred to us as The Poster Boys for the Mafia in New York. Those articles never last long on the web, and those journalists never live to write another accusation. "You're in no position to throw shade, shit for brains." Caleb taps his gun against the man's face. "In case you hadn't noticed, your friends are dead, and you're next."

"Tell us what we want to know, and we'll make it quick." I sidestep the blood pooling underneath the dead man's skull. "Deny us the truth, and we'll torture you to the brink of death and bring you back, over and over, until you tell us what we want to know."

"You can try it, Pretty Boy, but I won't break. I'm not telling you shit."

Caleb punches him in the solar plexus, and he falls forward on his palms, wheezing and heaving.

"We need to leave," I say, checking the sky for drones. This place is a virtual ghost town but we've just littered the air with gunfire, and someone might have heard. "Grab the two live ones and take them to the bunker." We have a hidden bunker, buried deep underground, on Staten Island where we bring men for interrogation.

"No one is snitching on my watch," the long-haired guy says, snatching a fallen gun from under a hunk of rock and peppering his colleague with bullets.

"No!" I shout as one of our men shoots him in the chest. "For fuck's sake," I snap when the long-haired asshole falls on his side and blood bubbles in his mouth and flows from the wound on his chest. "What part of 'don't shoot to kill' didn't you understand?" I level a lethal look at the *soldato* in question, wondering who he is and if that was an innocent mistake caused by an eager trigger finger or a deliberate action to ensure we get no intel. Or maybe he was genuinely trying to protect Caleb and me. The jury is out. Did he pull that trigger on purpose? Is he working with the mole? Or a loyal made man? We need to find out. I eyeball our *capo*, and he instantly swings into action, disarming and restraining the man. Guess we'll be interrogating someone after all.

"You're all dead," the fallen man says in fits and spurts as blood drips down his chin. His eyes are manic as his gaze locks on mine. "You have no idea who's coming for you. He's going to kill everyone." His head lolls to the ground as all the life leaves his body.

"This is really starting to stink bad," Caleb says three hours later when we're finally back home. We separated to shower and clean off the blood and grime before reconvening in my penthouse. I refuse to step foot in Caleb's messy den of iniquity.

"This has stunk from the start. What do you think he meant?" I ask, pouring us both a scotch. I pad across my living room in my bare feet and cotton pajama pants, handing him his drink.

"Who the fuck knows? He made it sound like whoever is behind this is not anyone we're expecting."

"Does he mean other Italian Americans?"

Caleb shrugs. "It's a minefield, and my brain is too tired to decipher it at four thirty a.m."

"I'm not sure I can sleep," I admit, sinking onto the couch. "I'm still wired."

"You get it all out of your system?" Caleb side-eyes me.

"Not even close."

"What's going on?" He dangles one sweatpants-covered leg over the side of the recliner chair as he sips his whisky and stares at me.

"I kissed Gia."

He swirls the liquid in his glass. "You like her."

"More than I should."

"Why shouldn't you like her?"

"Because I can't. I swore I was never letting any woman in again, and I meant it."

"You were made to be in a committed relationship, J. How long are you going to continue denying yourself?"

"I'm not denying myself."

"Sure, you are, big brother."

I groan. He only ever rolls out the *big brother* sentiment when he's trying to prove a point or get his way about something. Most other times, he'll argue it doesn't matter that I was born first, eleven minutes before he made his grand entrance.

"You don't believe in love either," I remind him with a knowing look.

"We're not talking about me, and are you saying you're in love with Gia?"

"No. Fuck no." I almost spit my scotch all over my polished floors.

"I think you protest too much." He flashes me a mischievous grin. "It's okay to admit it."

"Like you'll admit you have feelings for Elisa?"

"Of course, I have feelings for her. She's my friend. I love her like a friend. That's all."

"Are you trying to convince me or you?" I ask, and he flips me the bird. I burst out laughing. "We're both such delusional pricks."

"The difference is you have a shot with Gia, and you should take it, brother. You've been miserable since things ended with Bettina, and your little list of fuck buddies doesn't satisfy more than an itch."

"I don't even know why we're talking about this. We have more pressing problems than women."

"Don't deflect. If you really like Gia, you owe it to yourself to give it a shot. Not every woman is a backstabbing ho like your ex."

"Gia thinks Cruz might have groomed Ina. She thinks my anger comes from my failure to protect her."

"I definitely think some of your anger comes from your inability to keep her away from that asshole, but a lot of it rightly comes from betrayal." Caleb finishes his drink and stands. "And if the grooming theory was correct, why the fuck is she still with him? I don't buy he's had a hold on her all this time without someone intervening. She's got a big family. Lots of brothers. If they thought Cruz was forcing her to be with him, I'm sure they'd have found a way to extract her, don or not."

"I agree." I swallow the last mouthful and climb to my feet, stifling a yawn. "She knew what she was doing."

"This is gonna sound hypocritical, but you need to let go of the hurt and the anger. You won't move forward until you do. But fuck showing that bitch any sympathy. She doesn't deserve it." He clamps a hand on my shoulder. "It's time to let it go, broski. Put her behind you, and open yourself up to Gia. I have a feeling you won't regret it."

Chapter Twenty-One
Gia

Joshua will probably bust a nut when I show up at The Arena, the VIP club where the twins are hosting their twenty-seventh birthday party tonight, but I didn't want to miss it. Hence why I ditched my bodyguard, again, and I'm currently in the back of a taxi enroute to the venue. I'm wearing my wig, and I traded my green contacts for brown ones. My thigh-high, body-hugging, glittery gold and silver dress and knee-high silver boots are a far cry from the tamer, sophisticated wardrobe I'm sporting as Emma Brown.

Tonight, I'm neither Emma nor Gia, and I don't think it's too risky to show up for a brief interval. I won't stay long. I'll have a quick drink, give them their gifts, and hopefully Joshua will let me apologize and give him a birthday kiss. I haven't seen him since our hot make out session at Thanksgiving, and I'm suffering withdrawal symptoms.

Of course, I had to go and blow it by mentioning his ex. I shouldn't have pushed so hard. I guess I'm just trying to find an explanation for it because it doesn't make sense to me. Cruz DiPietro is a creep, and he's old. Joshua was an amazing boyfriend. I was there. I saw it firsthand. He loved Bettina good, so why would any eighteen-year-old girl ditch her childhood sweetheart for a married man? It doesn't add up, and for Joshua's sake, I want there to be another reason.

But maybe there isn't one.

And I probably need to let it drop.

The taxi pulls up to the curb. I pay the driver and climb out a tad awkwardly in my tight dress while carrying my two gifts.

I push my way through the crowd, heading toward the VIP section where the party is taking place.

"Name," the guy at the door says, looking bored as he scans a list on his clipboard.

Shit. I hadn't thought of this. I'm debating who to call when Cristian opens the door behind the bouncer. "Oh good, Cristian, vouch for me, yeah?"

His eyes widen as he steps in closer, inspecting my face. His lips twitch. "You're playing with fire, G. This is reckless with a capital R."

"I just wanted to stop by and say hi. I'll be in and out before anyone sees me. Besides, it's an opportunity to see my bestie. I miss her."

"She isn't here," he says, grabbing the clipboard off the older man with the bushy 'stache and scribbling a name before adding a tick beside it.

"She must be." I know she was upset, but it's hardly the first time. There's no way Elisa would miss Caleb's birthday. She's been on a countdown to tonight for weeks, and she finished his birthday painting months ago. It's a tradition at this stage. Something that began when she was young and she started drawing and painting pictures for Caleb on his birthday. She does the same for her stepdad too. Alesso's home office walls are decorated with every one of her pictures, and if it wasn't obvious how proud he is of his daughter, that would seal the deal.

"Maybe she's running late." He shrugs before thrusting the clipboard at the man. "You can let her in."

"As you wish, Don DiPietro."

"You look hot," he whispers in my ear. "I can't decide if that will save your ass when our boy sees you or make it worse."

"I'll take my chances." I kiss his cheek before slipping around him and climbing the stairs to the upper VIP level.

Reaching the top, I set Caleb's gift down on the long table pushed against the wall just off the stairs. There is barely space to leave my gold-wrapped parcel because the table is swamped with a multitude of gifts.

Laughter and lively conversation compete with rhythmic beats as the DJ plays tunes for the large crowd jumping around the dance floor. The room is packed, and I spot several familiar faces. Thankfully, no one notices it's me though I am garnering plenty of admiring glances. I edge my way around people as I scan the space for Joshua. All the blood drains from my face when I locate him at the end of the bar with Sorella fucking Caprese of all people.

She has him pushed up against the wall, and her body is flush against his. He's holding a glass in one hand and his other hangs loose at his side as she roams his torso with her greedy talons. His lips lift in amusement at something she says, and I gulp over the lump in my throat. Pain stabs me in the chest when she leans in and kisses him.

And he lets her.

I contemplate stomping up to him and throwing my gift in his face, but I've got more class than to make a scene. Besides, it's not like I have any claim on him. We made out and confessed to feelings. It's not like we're in a relationship or have made any commitment to one another. Clearly not if he's still screwing his fuck buddies.

No, I'm not going to embarrass myself.

Fuck him.

That's the last time I let him touch me.

I'm not going to become a sidepiece.

Tears prick my eyes as I spin around on my heel, bumping into people in my haste to get the fuck out of here. I debate taking the gift home and donating it to charity, but I had the onyx chessboard custom-made for him by a renowned company in Florence. I even had it engraved for the prick. I plonk the gift-wrapped box on the table and leave. Let him find it there and know I showed up. Let him realize I saw him with his date.

Pain rattles across my chest as I make my way outside the club. I hurry toward a taxi at the curb, currently depositing a couple on the sidewalk. Climbing into the back, I give my address and try to paper over the cracks in my heart.

Joshua doesn't date. Everyone knows it. He never brings a date to his birthday parties, and though some of his supposed fuck buddies often attend, he never engages in PDAs with them. So why now? And why her? Does he know she took my brother's virginity or that she blatantly flirts with all my boyfriends purely because Tommy Fusco dumped her to date me three years ago? Did Joshua pick her as his date on purpose as some form of payback for the things I said about his ex?

I stare sullenly out the window as we whizz by streets crowded with people enjoying their Saturday night. Removing my cell from my purse—to call Elisa—I remember I only brought my burner phone with me tonight in case Liam called. An incoming call lights up the screen as if my thought just summoned him.

Fuck my life. I'm in no mood to deal with that Irish prick.

Slamming my head back into the headrest, I wonder what

I've done to deserve this shitty night. Working hard to compose myself, I pull my "Emma'" persona on and answer his call. "Hey, babe."

"My sweet, sexy Emma. Where are you?"

I'm tempted to lie and say I'm at home, but if he's shown up at my place, I'll be caught out in the lie. Better to stick to as much of the truth as I can. "I'm in a taxi on my way home."

"Home from where?" Suspicion threads through his tone.

My heart thumps faster. "I stopped by a family party, but it was lame, so I left quickly."

"I'm at the bar. Join me." He hangs up before I've had time to say anything.

I curse him under my breath before relaying the change in destination to the driver.

I've been at the Irish bar twice in the past ten days. It's owned by a friend of Liam's who is clearly either Irish mafia or a trustworthy supporter. Liam has set up his interim base there, and it's where they appear to conduct their business. The Commission was pleased I've been invited into the inner sanctum even if Liam hasn't told me outright he's part of a criminal enterprise. All he said was the men at the bar were business acquaintances and I was to keep my mouth shut about anything I saw or heard while there.

Not that I heard much. I was recording the entire time, but the men he hung around with were careful with their words. I managed to capture several of them on film, and we're compiling an extensive dossier on the men who seem loyal to him. O'Hara is helping with identification.

"Pull over," I say around the corner from the bar. "I'll get out here." I pay him in cash so there's no trace and get out. I wait until he's driven off before I ditch the wig and the brown contacts in the nearest trash can. I won't risk carrying anything on me that might give the game away.

Ducking into an all-night diner to use the bathroom, I put in my green contacts, freshen my makeup, and spritz some perfume before pressing my earrings on. I'm supposed to message Joshua, but he can fuck right off. He's probably too busy sucking face with that Caprese bitch to notice anyway. There is always someone listening, so if anything happens, they'll report to him like the good little lapdogs they are.

When I walk toward the bar, an older guy with a bad combover and a pervy smile is waiting to take me inside to Liam. Wolf whistles and catcalls ring out as I walk through the crowded bar. Three older women sitting on stools at the bar send daggers in my direction. They seem to be the only other females here tonight.

Nerves fire at me as the perv opens a door to the basement and gestures for me to walk down the stairs. I feel his heated gaze on my ass as I descend the steps, willing the anxious feeling in my chest to die down.

All eyes swing my way when I reach the bottom. Smoke clouds cling to the low ceiling in the dimly lit space. My heels click off the concrete floor as I plaster a smile on my face and advance toward Liam. He's seated around a large circular table playing cards, drinking, and smoking. Apart from a few crates stacked against one wall, the table and chairs are the only other items in the vast basement. Briefly, I wonder if this is where they torture their enemies.

It's not a good thought to have when I'm surrounded by evil men.

Six assholes sit around the table with Liam, all of them fixing me with hungry eyes as I approach. I wonder if any of them are the men Diarmuid has watching over me or if any of the men upstairs are. These perverted pricks creep me the fuck out, and I'm struggling to maintain composure. Panic lays siege to my insides, and I can scarcely hear over the thrumming in my ears.

"What the fuck are you wearing?" Liam snaps, looking anything but pleased.

I'm tempted to sass him, but I'm not completely reckless. This is where I must play the docile submissive girlfriend. "I came straight from the party because I thought that's what you wanted."

His chair slams to the ground as he stands abruptly, gripping my chin painfully. "You're my woman, and no woman of mine dresses for other men." His eyes narrow over my shoulder. "Lower your eyes unless you want to fucking lose them," he barks.

"Sorry, boss. We meant no disrespect."

Liam's gaze returns to mine. His fingers loosen their grip on my chin before he smashes his disgusting mouth upon mine. "I'll let you make it up to me," he says, instantly raising my heckles. "Get on your knees."

Just when I think this night couldn't get any worse, it does.

"What?" The tremble in my voice is not fabricated. Surely, he doesn't mean what I think he means?

"You hard of hearing now, Em?" He shoves me roughly to my knees, and I bite the inside of my cheek to stifle a cry as pain shoots through me. "Suck my dick."

I gulp as I look over my shoulder.

"Eyes on me," he roars, grabbing the back of my head and squeezing.

"Liam, please," I whisper. "Don't make me do this in front of those men. Ask them to leave, and I'll do it."

I can't swallow my cry this time as he backhands me without warning. Stinging pain skates across my cheek, and I'm torn between abject terror and furious rage. I consider biting his dick, but I think that'd earn me a bullet in the skull.

"I won't ask you again." He unzips his pants. "Prove you deserve a place at my side, Emma. Show these men who you belong to, and we'll forget this little act of rebellion."

It was only a fucking minidress, for fuck's sake, I want to yell. But I value breathing.

"Come up here," he says, smirking at his men. "Make sure you get a front-row seat."

Chapter Twenty-Two
Gia

"Good girl." Liam pats me on the head like I'm a dog when it's over. Pain obliterates me on the inside as I hold on to a chair and climb awkwardly to my feet. I have never been more humiliated or objectified in my life.

I vow here and now that I'm going to kill him.

No one else is doing it. It's going to be me. Every single humiliation I've endured will become his to bear. I will make this fucker pay.

I purposely don't look at the men standing behind Liam. If I see lust in their eyes or their hands sliding underneath their pants, I'm liable to say fuck the mission and kill as many of them as I can before I'm put down.

"Ready the vehicles," Liam instructs. "And leave us."

I glare at him when the men are out of sight. "Fuck you. We're done."

He grips my wrist, twisting it at an angle that hurts. "We're done when I say we're done, and we're only getting started, sexy."

"You're hurting me." I drill him with a contemptuous look.

"I'll hurt you worse if you ever disrespect me again."

I want to scream and pummel my fists in his face, but I force myself to remain calm. "I'll bury you if you disrespect me ever again."

A chuckle bounces off the walls. "If you were anyone else, Emma, I'd kill you for that threat. But I know it's empty." In a flash, he has me pinned to the wall by my throat. "I've played things your way, and I'm all out of patience." His fingers tighten around my neck, and I'm trying not to panic. "Now we're doing things my way." He loosens his grip, and I suck greedy lungsful of air in through my mouth. "It's quite simple, really. You do what I tell you, without argument, and I will treat you like a queen."

I bite the inside of my cheek hard to resist the urge to flinch when he sweeps his fingers across my face before moving them lower. "You're mine, Emma. My perfect little doll." His hand slides under the top of my dress and beneath my bra, and it's a miracle I don't puke. He fondles my bare breast without permission, and I want to gut the motherfucker until he stops breathing. "I want to fuck these so bad, but it'll have to wait." I breathe a sigh of relief when he removes his hands completely from my body. "Go home. I've got business to attend to. Be at my place tomorrow at eight. You will cook for me, and we'll have a nice night. Put all this behind us."

I suck in a gasp when he presses a gun to my head. "Don't even think about crossing me, babe. I love you, but I won't hesitate to riddle you with bullets if you disobey me or try to run." He pushes the muzzle in tighter. "Swear you'll be a good girl and behave."

I nod, unwilling to push anything with this psycho because he's legit crazy.

"Say the words," he grits out over a snarl.

"I will be a good girl and behave."

He arches a brow. "And?"

"I'll be at your place at eight tomorrow, and I'll cook you dinner."

Without warning, he slams his lips down on mine, forcing his revolting tongue into my mouth.

"I love tasting myself on you." He grabs my ass, hauling me up against him. "Bring a bag with you. You're sleeping in my bed tomorrow night."

With those parting words, he stalks off, stomping noisily up the stairs. When the door slams upstairs, I clutch the wall and bend over as a sob rips through the eerie air, traveling directly from the depths of my soul. My breathing gushes out in exaggerated spurts, and nausea swims up my throat. I'm hyperventilating and barely holding it together when I remember my earrings.

Horror washes over me along with a fresh wave of humiliation at the realization some of our men heard what just went down. Joshua couldn't have been listening as he's at his party, but I've no doubt they back up the audio, and the thought he might hear that sends me spiraling.

Until I remember I'm still in the devil's lair and I need to get the fuck out of Dodge. I pull myself together and quickly inspect the crates. They only contain bottles of beer and whiskey, which is disappointing but not unsurprising. Finding a side door at this level, I flee through it, avoiding the walk of shame upstairs.

I emerge in a back alley and turn right, immediately jerking back when I spot the cavalcade of blacked-out SUVs. I hide behind an alcove as car doors open and shut. Risking a peek to the left, I spot the open trunk and make a split-second decision, crawling into the space and pulling a coarse blanket over the length of me. My heart slams against my rib cage as I lie still, breathing quietly through my nose and praying this wasn't a mistake.

About a minute later, footsteps approach, and I hold my breath, hoping I don't pee my pants. When the trunk slams shut a few seconds later, I offer a prayer of thanks and settle down for the journey.

It seems like we're on the road for ages. Whoever the driver is, he needs to go back to driving school. I'm betting I'll have bruises all over my back from being thrown about as he speeds over bumps and potholes and swings dangerously around corners.

Eventually we slow down, and I prick my ears, listening to the myriad of doors opening and closing. Footsteps crunch over gravel, and I wait until there are no sounds, until it's completely quiet, before I make a move. I press down on the lever on the back of the trunk and push with my shoulder until the seat moves forward.

Adrenaline courses through my veins as I climb into the back seat, keeping down low. I drop to the floor and take a minute to compose myself, remembering others are listening and they know where I am thanks to the tracker in my arm. Breathing deeply, I shove the seat back into place and briefly lift my head.

We're at a construction site with row upon row of scaffolding on the front of the high-rise. I count nine cars in total. Five appear to belong to Liam and his crew, meaning they are meeting others here.

Very carefully, I open the back door and crawl out of the car, shutting it quietly behind me. Crouching down, I move between the cars, keeping low in case any men are watching the parking lot. Rounding the front of a Lincoln town car, I dart into the open doorway of the building undetected.

Muffled voices filter into the room through large thick

sheets of plastic covering the window spaces on the other side. I can't risk being heard, so I sit on the dusty floor and remove my boots. The salty air and icy breeze confirm we're close to the ocean. Wishing I had taken my warm coat tonight instead of my flimsy jacket, I wrap my arms around myself to ward off the chill as I tiptoe carefully across the space, sidestepping bits of rubble and trash littered on the floor.

When I reach the far wall, I kneel behind one of the window coverings and extract my cell, setting it to record because I don't know if the audio will pick up everything.

"It's not our fault Rizzo took one for the team," Liam says in that haughty voice I've come to know and loathe.

"He was our don," a man with a slight southern twang says.

Liam snorts. "Don't play dumb. Rizzo was a don in name only. You ran the show. Like me, everyone knows you're the true leader. They did you a favor. I wouldn't be grumbling if I were in your shoes."

"We lost other good men that night, and we lost men to the water the night of the hijacking." He pronounces water like wooder, and I immediately recognize the Jersey accent.

Excitement trickles through my veins at the prospect of gleaning some decent intel.

"You knew what you were signing up to, Calabro. Casualties are normal during war."

"The Barone knows that better than anyone! We have painstakingly rebuilt our *famiglia* after we were all but wiped out. The boss promised retribution, but there won't be anyone to avenge our name if we all die before D-day!" Anger underscores his tone as I'm wracking my brain trying to remember where I've heard the name Barone before.

"Calm the fuck down," Liam snaps. The clicking of multiple weapons ensues, and I hold my breath to see how this plays out. "Acting like a hysterical schoolgirl who just got her period is not helping your cause."

"Those backstabbing *bastardi* must pay."

"And they will. You just need to wait a little longer."

"We've waited years," he hisses before adding, "Lower your weapons. The Irish aren't our enemy."

"Stand down," Liam tells his men. "You can wait another few months. You need to learn patience."

I clamp a hand over my mouth to smother a snort. That asshole could benefit from listening to his own advice.

"Don't pull that shit again," Liam warns. "I'm showing you a courtesy by giving you a free pass. If the boss knew you went after the boy alone, you'd already be swimming with the sharks."

What boy? I ponder.

"I'm grateful for your mercy, McDermott."

"You're all out of free passes. Remember that."

"Remember who brought you in on this."

"Remember who we both report to," Liam retorts. A few tense beats ring out before he adds, "Get the fuck out of here. We'll be in touch when we get instructions from the boss."

Gravel is noisy underfoot as the men separate and leave. I hold myself still, afraid to even breathe. I don't budge for ages after I hear the last car pull away. When I'm certain the coast is clear, I walk across the space and put my boots back on.

Walking out through the open doorway, I inspect my surroundings, looking for any sign of a bus or taxi stop, but there's none. Industrial buildings and warehouses surround me. On my left, in the distance, I spot the boardwalk, confirming I'm in Atlantic City. It's going to cost me a small fortune to Uber it home from here, but I've got no choice. I'm not calling Joshua to come get me.

I'm opening the app on my cell when a black Land Rover

swings around the corner and pulls into the lot in front of me. Headlights pin me in place as I flick the button on my cell to withdraw the small dagger embedded inside. I'm preparing to fight when the driver's door swings open and a familiar face comes into view.

A look of thunder is etched upon Joshua's face as he stalks toward me. If glowering was a weapon, I'd be dead ten times over by now.

"What the actual fuck do you think you're doing?"

Chapter Twenty-Three
Joshua

"My job, Joshua," she snarls, curling her lips in disgust as she rakes her gaze over me. "Not all of us have time to party." She touches her earrings to turn off the audio, clearly not wanting anyone to listen to me rip her a new one.

I stalk toward her, working hard to leash my anger. Though she's responsible for some of my foul mood, Gia isn't the only reason I'm pissed off tonight. "Your job is to call me before you make any move!"

She jabs her finger in my chest. "An opportunity presented itself, and I went for it. I couldn't call you."

"I'm talking about you going to meet Liam without reporting it."

She snorts out a bitter laugh. "You were too busy shoving your tongue down Sorella's throat to notice even if I had!"

My eyes pop wide. "That's why you didn't stay?" I've been fuming all night since Cristian told me she showed up. I was angry at first. That she'd risk her cover to attend and for Cristian's comments of how hot she looked. Then I was hurt that she couldn't even say hi or wish me a happy birthday. "I don't know what you saw, but—"

"Don't try to deny it. I saw you kissing her."

"She. Kissed. Me."

"You fucking kissed her back!" She shoves at my chest.

My lips kick up at the corners as realization dawns. "You're jealous."

"What? Don't be ridiculous. You can fuck around with whomever you like just like I can."

She plants her hands on her hips, and it's hard not to notice how fucking sexy she is in that showstopping dress and matching boots. Images of her boot-covered legs wrapped around my head surge unhelpfully in my brain. Sporting a boner now is not a good idea. Which reminds me. We need to get out of here. I don't know if they installed any cameras after the shootout went down. I don't want to hang around and find out.

Grabbing Gia, I toss her over my shoulder and stride toward my car.

"Let me down, asshole." She wriggles and writhes while pounding her fists into my back. "I'm sick of sexist pricks manhandling me tonight."

I'm guessing that remark refers to Liam. I haven't received any intel on what went down in the bar. The call was to notify me she was in an unidentified vehicle on a route out of the city. It was enough to concern me that I had the guys send me the coordinates so I could follow her. When I realized where she was, I almost wrapped my car around a tree. I was terrified she'd be discovered before I could get to her.

I slap her butt hard, chastising her for the blatant disregard for her own safety. Expletives spew from her mouth, and a smile touches my lips. No other woman sends my emotions seesawing from one extreme to the other like Gia does. I purposely ignore her while I open the passenger door and carefully set her inside.

She's still cussing me out when I climb behind the wheel and start the car up.

I wait until we're out on the road, away from the construction site, and sure we're not being followed before I speak. Gia has her arms folded and she's pouting as she glares out the window. "What happened with Sorella was entirely one-sided. If you'd stayed you would've seen me pushing her away. She wasn't invited. None of the women I used to fuck were invited because I didn't want any of them there."

Gia turns her head to face me. "*Used* to fuck?"

"I haven't fucked anyone in weeks."

"Why?"

"Why do you think?"

"I wouldn't have fucking asked if I knew!" She flaps her hands around, and I have to bite my tongue to trap my laughter.

"You're adorable when you're lying to yourself." She flips me the bird, and this time, I can't stop my laughter. She glowers at me, and my dick really loves it, jerking a few times behind my pants. "I haven't fucked anyone because of *you*, Gia. Don't pretend like you don't know."

"I thought I knew." Her shoulders slump, and the look of anger on her face transforms to hurt. "But then I saw you smiling and laughing with her, and I don't care what you say; you didn't push her away immediately when she kissed you. I would have seen if you did."

"I was trying to spare her feelings. I didn't want to embarrass her in front of everyone."

"What about my feelings?"

"I didn't know you were there at the time."

"And if you did?" Her expression challenges me.

"Then I would have immediately pushed her away because sparing your feelings is more important than sparing hers."

She nibbles on her lip as a full-body shudder works its way through her. "Good answer," she whispers. "I should probably feel bad for Sorella because she has more claim over you than me, but I can't find it in myself to feel anything but contempt for that woman."

I pull off the road onto the shoulder and kill the engine. I cup Gia's face. "She has no claim on me. None of those women do. It was only ever sex."

"Okay." Her big eyes latch on to mine, and she looks so vulnerable.

I don't fully understand why. Or why I feel the insurmountable urge to reach over and hug her, but I do. Her arms cling to my neck, and I feel her entire body shaking against me. I ease back a little, concern creasing my brow. "You're shaking."

"It's the adrenaline. It's been a pretty crazy night."

My eyes skate over her body. "Are you hurt? Did—"

"I'm fine."

It's a clear lie because she's still trembling against me as she rests her head on my shoulder. I hold her for a few minutes before slipping out of our embrace. "Stay there," I say, hopping out of the car and moving to the trunk. I pop it and grab the supplies I need before climbing back behind the wheel. I hand her the blanket and a bottle of Gatorade. "Put that on and drink that. It'll help with the shock."

"Thank you." Tears well in her eyes, and my concern is growing.

"I'm sorry for shouting," I truthfully admit when we're back on the road. "I just panicked when I realized where you were. You can't wander off without telling me, Gia. It's too dangerous."

"I would've used the alert button on my watch if I thought I was compromised."

"That's not good enough. The deal is you notify me when Liam has summoned you. You don't take off by yourself without informing me."

"I was mad at you," she softly admits, huddled under the blanket, sipping the sugary drink.

"And that is why us starting something is not a good idea. You can't endanger yourself or your safety because you're jealous of another woman."

"I know it wasn't professional, but I can't switch my feelings off where you're concerned."

"Is this because it was Sorella?"

She shrugs, looking contemplative. "Seeing you kiss any girl would make me mad but especially her. We don't like one another."

"Why?" I slow down as I approach the last junction before the highway.

"She took my brother's virginity and taunted me about it. When she mocked his performance in front of others, I swung at her. Knocked her unconscious, and she got a concussion from hitting her head on the ground." A mischievous grin spreads over her lips. "My parents went ballistic, and I was grounded forever, but it was worth it. No one talks shit about my brother and gets away with it."

I think I fall in love with her right in this moment.

"Then a few years ago, a guy she was dating dumped her to date me," she continues, turning sideways on the seat under the blanket and staring at me. "I didn't know he'd been seeing her, but of course, she blamed me. Said I did it deliberately. Since then, she flirts like crazy with my boyfriends or any guy who shows the slightest interest in me. It's kinda pathetic."

"I had no idea she was like that. I was already planning on

formally ending my arrangement with her, but I'm not wasting time now. I'm going to do it tomorrow."

Gia's eyes blink rapidly.

"What?" I ask, moving onto the highway.

"You'd do that for me?"

"I won't be a pawn she uses against you, and I told you she means nothing to me."

"Ouch."

"I'm ending it with the others too."

Her eyes drill into the side of my head, and I'm sensing she wants to ask more, but it's late, and I refuse to have a serious conversation in the car. I don't really know where my head is at. Just that I have no desire to sleep with anyone else, and I missed Gia tonight. I wanted her at my party. By my side. Helping me to celebrate my birthday. My brother's words have been playing on a loop in my mind, and I think I want to try things with Gia. It's a big step and not one we can take yet. She needs to finish her assignment, and then we can discuss what happens next.

"Did you hear anything important tonight?"

She nods, sitting up a little straighter. "Does the name Barone mean anything to you? I've been wracking my brain trying to remember where I know it from."

My brows knit together in concentration. "I've heard that name too, but I can't recall the context." I glance at the clock on the dash. "If it wasn't after two, I'd call Ben or Leo, but it'll have to wait until morning. What else happened?"

She fills me in on the conversation and I listen intently.

"I'm guessing ordinarily that'd be enough to confirm Liam is knee-deep in this," she says when she's finished explaining. "But now we know Italian Americans are involved, and there's some mysterious big boss calling the shots, I'm guessing it'll be better if we halt making a move on McDermott and I keep close to him."

"That seems like the smartest play, but it'll be up to the board. I'll call Massimo in the morning and ask him to set up a meeting."

"Have we found evidence of the rat yet?"

I shake my head and sigh as I switch to cruise control and coast along the quiet I-287. "Caleb and I met with our under-boss, Marino, earlier today. He's gone through our list of men, crosschecking their trackers and locations to see if there are any anomalies. He also double-checked to see if anyone was close to the vicinity of Staten Island the night of the hijacking, or close to any of the delivery vans that were attacked, and there is no evidence of any corruption within our *famiglia*."

"That's a good thing, so why do you look so glum?"

"The other dons have gone through their lists too, and they can't find anything either. Either the rat isn't in New York or it's someone super fucking smart who's covering their tracks. If it's the latter, how the hell will we ever smoke them out?"

"Maybe we need to set a trap," she muses, tapping her finger on her lip. "Maybe we should create some fake intel. Something our enemy would find useful. Create different intel for each *famiglia* and spread it out. Then if it's acted on, we'll know which *famiglia*, if any, is sheltering a traitor."

"That's not a bad idea. I'll raise it at the board."

"What else?" Her eyes pierce mine. "I know something else is bothering you."

"We were finally able to identify the remaining men who died on the ship." While our *capos* were able to identify most of the men, some of the bodies were so mutilated their tracking chips were gone and we had to pull dental records and organize autopsies to confirm who we lost. "Three of them were Accardi *soldati*. Caleb and I visited their families today to tell them.

189

One of the men was a father to four-year-old triplets. His wife was inconsolable."

She reaches out and touches my arm. "I can guess why that'd be especially harrowing."

I smother a yawn, conceding what I'd chosen not to confront earlier today. "It's always awful having to relay such horrible news, but it affected me more than usual. On the drive back, I kept thinking that must've been how my dad reacted when he was told about Juliet." My eyes flick to hers. "My bio mom," I add, in case she isn't aware that was her name.

She nods, and her eyes shine with understanding.

"It was a sobering moment for both of us." Caleb rarely lets anything in when it comes to our bio parents. Especially our father. But I could tell it impacted him too.

"You must miss them."

"I miss my dad, sometimes, even though he was a pretty shitty dad. Especially at the end. It's different with Juliet. I don't remember her, and Nat is the only mom we've ever known. She was our only present parent growing up, and we owe her everything."

"I love Nat. I know she's my godmother, but she's more like my second mom."

"Man, how did this conversation get so heavy?"

"I don't know." She yawns, finishing the Gatorade and placing the empty bottle into her purse.

"You should sleep. We still have at least an hour to go."

Chapter Twenty-Four
Gia

J oshua dropped me off a block from the apartment. It was on the tip of my tongue to ask him to come home with me because I don't want to be alone with my thoughts. But I held back. He's right. We need to keep things strictly professional between us until I'm finished with my assignment.

I take a shower and try to think of anything but what happened in the basement earlier tonight. But my mind refuses to let me forget it. The first tear falls as I'm leaning my head back, rinsing suds from my hair. They continue falling as I get out, run a towel over my body, and blow-dry my hair. I brush my teeth four times and use half a bottle of mouthwash rinsing my mouth, but I can still taste his disgusting cum tainting my insides. By the time I'm dressed in my comfy long-sleeved pajamas and I have crawled under the covers, I'm completely under siege. Wracking sobs rip from my chest as I curl into a ball on my bed and totally lose it.

I clutch a pillow to my body as I expunge pain, grief, humiliation, and fear.

I don't even feel the bed dipping behind me at first or have time to panic that someone got in my apartment without me noticing. "It's me, Gia. I've got you," Joshua says, carefully turning me on my side to face him.

I'm in too much pain to shelter my emotions from him. I don't care how weak I must look. I can't do anything but give in to the deep-seated pain battering me from all sides. Tears pour from my eyes like a waterfall, and I can barely see him through my blurry vision.

"You should have told me. I'm so sorry you had to endure that tonight."

I almost choke over the sobs as anguish tears me apart on the inside. "Hold me," I rasp in between sobs, needing someone to make it better.

His arms wrap around me without hesitation, and I sob into his chest. He's still wearing his dress shirt and pants, and I drench the crisp white cotton with an avalanche of tears. The entire time, he holds me secure in his strong embrace, dotting kisses into my hair and encouraging me to let it all out.

Eventually, I run out of tears. I close my eyes and press my face to his shirt, inhaling his comforting scent and sinking into the protection of his arms. "Don't leave me," I whisper. "Please stay."

With the tenderest touch, he tips my chin up so our eyes meet. "I'm going nowhere, and you don't have to beg. Not where I'm concerned." He dusts his lips lightly across my brow, my cheeks, and the tip of my nose before softly kissing me. When his eyes lift to meet mine again, I see nothing but concern and compassion. "Did he hurt you physically, Gia? Did more happen than we heard on the tape?"

I shake my head. "All my pain is inside." I cringe at how hoarse my voice sounds. "Actually, that's not quite true," I add, feeling a throbbing ache in my hips and along my back. Alarm blazes in his eyes. "Not because of Liam. From the car ride to Jersey. The driver had the skills of a sixteen-year-old who just got his learner's permit. I got thrown around a bit." I didn't feel it before because my internal pain overrode everything else.

"I'm going to take care of you." He kisses me again, and it's a feather-soft touch of his lips against mine. "I'll be back," he adds, rolling off the bed.

After he exits the bedroom, I sit up against the headrest, ignoring the spasm of pain the motion produces. I scrub at my stinging eyes and shove messy strands of reddish-brown hair behind my ears. I'm exhausted from my crying stint but I feel lighter too. I needed to vent that.

Joshua returns with a mug and a tube of arnica cream. Sitting on the side of the bed, he hands the drink to me. "It's honey and lemon. It'll help. Mom used to always give it to us when we had a cold or a sore throat."

Fresh tears prick my eyes for a different reason. "Thank you." I take a sip, and the liquid is like a balm flowing down my throat.

"I'm going to kill him." He says it real matter-of-fact as if we're casually discussing the weather.

"If anyone is killing that prick it's me."

"We'll do it together," he says. "I'll help, and you can deliver the kill shot."

"Deal." A small grin slips over my mouth in between sips of the sweet citrusy concoction.

"You're not going to his place tonight. It's far too dangerous now."

As much as the thought of it disgusts, enrages, and terrifies me, I'm not bowing out. I can't fail, and I can't fall apart at the first true hurdle. I shake my head. "I have an assignment to complete, and we're finally getting somewhere. I can't back out now."

"Please, Gia." He sweeps his fingers across my cheek, leaving a trail of fire in his wake. "I don't want anything to happen to you."

"I'll use the sleeping aid. I'll put it in his food or his drink. I can make it look natural, so he won't suspect anything."

"I don't want you going near him again."

"It's my job, Joshua," I softly say, finishing my drink and setting it down on the bedside table. "If I was a man, would you ask me to step away?"

A muscle strains in his jaw. "This isn't because you're a woman. It's because you're you." He gently clasps my face in his hands. "It's because I care. I won't see you hurt on my watch, and it's too dangerous now. He thinks he owns you. He's liable to do anything."

"It won't come to that."

"It did tonight."

"Because I was caught off guard, and I acted recklessly."

"That's my fault." He averts his eyes, clenching and unclenching his jaw.

"It's not. I was the one having a hard time separating personal from professional. If I'd been thinking straight, I would have gone home to get changed before going to the bar. Then none of it would have happened."

A harsh laugh escapes his lips as he turns to look at me again. "Honey, it really wasn't anything to do with what you were wearing. He wanted to exert his control over you with an audience. If it wasn't the dress, he'd have found another excuse. Don't think he didn't plan it, because he did."

I reach for him, needing his solace again. Joshua leans back against the headrest, mirroring my position, and hauls me against him. "I ruined your shirt."

"I don't care. I have forty-nine more like it in my closet."

"That's a very exact number." I peek up at him.

"I keep an inventory of my wardrobe." His sheepish expression tells me he knows how that sounds.

"There is nothing wrong with being coordinated and well prepared. You could probably teach me a thing or two." I crack a grin.

"I don't know how you can joke after everything you've endured tonight."

I trace circles on his hard chest through his damp shirt. "Crying helped. Having you here helps too. And if I don't laugh, I'm liable to fall apart, and I refuse to let that bastard turn me into something I'm not. He thinks he's broken me, but he hasn't." My eyes bore into his. "It's why I need to finish this. I'm not bailing on this assignment."

"So brave." He kisses my brow as I yawn. "Let me freshen up in the bathroom, and then I'll put some cream on your back, and you can sleep."

"Sounds like a plan."

When he returns a few minutes later, I have removed my pajama top and I'm lying on my stomach with my back exposed. "How bad does it look?" I ask, glancing over my shoulder. I gulp as I trek my gaze over his semi-naked form. Joshua sets his neatly folded pants and shirt down on the chair before sauntering toward me in only his boxers.

He says something, but I don't hear it. I'm too busy ogling the smooth expanse of skin stretched tight across defined muscles. He's got abs to die for, those V indents at his hips, and his arms are shredded, way more so than they look in his clothes.

He chuckles, and the most disarming smile spreads across his face.

"You're beautiful," I blurt. "So fucking beautiful."

His smile expands as he climbs onto the bed. "I don't think I've ever been called that before."

"Well, that's a travesty because it's true."

"You're great for my ego, Gia." He flashes me a smug grin as he uncaps the tube of arnica cream.

I roll my eyes before putting my head back down on the pillow. "Your ego does just fine without my compliments."

"I think you're confusing me with my twin."

I snort out a laugh. "I'm not, but I get the point, and I completely agree."

"I'm going to put this on now, okay?"

I glance back at him. "Yes." His tender concern is doing funny things to my insides. I flinch when his cool fingers land on my back.

"Relax. Take deep breaths." His large palms glide carefully over my back as he applies the anti-bruising cream.

"Is this our thing now?" I say in a sleepy voice.

"I sincerely hope not." He massages the cream in with confident strokes. "I don't like seeing you hurt."

"They're only bruises." I'm hurting way more inside, but I don't share that sentiment. He doesn't need me to anyway.

"Turn over."

I lift my head and look back at him.

"I'm not trying anything, Gia. That is the last thing you need tonight, and I will never take advantage of you."

I mock pout because I wouldn't say no to some sexy time, but he's right. It's been a testing day, and it's not the best time to make those kinds of potentially life-changing decisions. I already know sex with Joshua is going to be transcendental, and I'd rather wait until I'm not emotionally wrought and in pain. "I know you wouldn't. You're a good man, Joshua Accardi," I say as I turn over, exposing my tits and my stomach.

"I'm *not* a good man, but I can be good for you." His eyes drill into mine, and he purposely avoids looking at my chest, gently rolling the waistband of my pajamas down until my hips are exposed. He's diligent in applying the cream and avoiding looking at my intimate parts. It only makes my heart beat harder for him. His touch warms my skin, sending delicious tremors skating across my flesh as he works the ointment in. I can't stifle my whimper in time. I'm a strange combo of sleepy and aroused, and my core is pulsing with the need to feel his fingers in me and on me.

"There. All done." His voice is gruff, his pupils are dilated, and he doesn't hide when he adjusts his erection behind his boxers.

Tension crackles in the air as we stare at one another. Leaning down over me, he presses a passionate kiss to my lips. Our chests brush in the process, and my body is totally down for this. But he pulls back, grabbing my top and helping me back into it. "Not tonight, honey." He lies down, guiding me to his chest. "I don't want our first time to be tarnished with the things that happened tonight. And you need rest." He kisses the top of my head. "Sleep, darling. I've got you."

I nestle into his side and fall asleep way too fast for my liking. I would have preferred to savor the joyful memory of being held and adored by him as we slept side by side for the first time.

When I wake, Joshua is already gone. His side of the bed is still warm, so he hasn't been gone too long. There's a note beside my bed explaining he had to attend an emergency meeting of The Commission and confirming he left breakfast for me in the kitchen.

The fact I'm smiling as I crawl out of bed is all thanks to Joshua. He transformed one of the worst days of my life into one of the best. I know I'm falling for him, and as I survey the decadent breakfast awaiting me in the kitchen, I can't find a single reason why I shouldn't.

Chapter Twenty-Five
Joshua

"We asked Leo to attend today as he has vital intel that could shed light on the situation," Ben says after we are all seated around the table at Commission Central.

"What exactly did Gia overhear?" Leo asks, and I repeat it for the room.

"Shit. That is not good." Leo shakes his head, looking deep in thought.

"Tell us what you know," Massimo says.

"The Barone were a group of made men from Jersey. They were a bit of a laughingstock in our circles. Disorganized and a chaotic mess. They lost control of their business, and they started taking on jobs to pay the bills. They became known as the hit men of the *mafioso*." He levels a look at Caleb, Fiero, and Massimo. "Though none of them could hold a torch to you three." All three men trained in Nepal, and Massimo was a contract killer for years, in secret, before he gave it up to take control of his *famiglia* and marry Donna Conti.

"Why don't we know anything about them?" Caleb asks.

"Because we took them out," Leo calmly explains. "Carlo Greco was the original Greco heir, and your mom was contracted to marry him. He was a monster."

"The worst kind," Massimo agrees. He has never defended his now-deceased older brother.

Leo grips the arms of his chair. "Carlo hired the Barone to kidnap your mother a few months before their wedding." Anger flares in his eyes. "They would have succeeded if I wasn't there to stop them." He rubs at his shoulder. "I took a bullet to ensure they didn't get their hands on her."

"Why would he do that?" Caleb looks confused. "It doesn't make sense."

"Nothing ever did when it came to my brother."

"It doesn't matter now," our stepdad says. "What matters is we wiped them from existence. Or so we thought." He sighs, scrubbing a hand across his chin.

"Who was involved, and how did it go down?" Fiero inquires, fidgeting with the collar of his shirt.

"This was almost thirty years ago, and my memory's a little rusty. I was only a *soldato* back then, and though Angelo often took Mateo and me into his confidence, we weren't privy to all the facts." Mateo was Don Angelo Mazzone's eldest son. He was gunned down on the streets, in his prime, and that's when Angelo yanked Bennett Carver from his normal life into this one. Ben had no clue he was Angelo's bastard son or that his father was the most powerful *mafioso* in the entire US.

"From what I remember," Leo continues, "it was Gino Accardi, Maximo Greco, and Angelo Mazzone who were mostly involved though all five families were there the day we annihilated the Barone in Jersey. A few might have escaped the bloodbath, but we thought we covered everything. Rizzo was only a kid then. Maybe ten?" He shrugs. "Anyway, we sent him, along with his sisters and his mother, to Italy, telling them not to come back."

"I should have been informed," Ben says, placing his palms flat on the table. "I could have kept tabs on them."

"They fell through the cracks. Mateo died less than a year later, and we were all preoccupied."

"We have to assume Rizzo came back from Italy and began rebuilding the Barone in secret," Caleb says.

"How the fuck did we not get wind of it?" I ask, propping my elbows on the table. "Surely someone would have heard something."

"It doesn't make sense," Cristian agrees.

"It does if the people who got wind of it decided to ally with the Barone and their partners." Ben looks suitably worried.

"We have more than one rat." Fiero verbalizes all our suspicion, articulating our worst fears.

"It's safe to assume we have rats and informants in all of our families," Massimo says.

A heavy silence descends over the room.

"They have been plotting this for years." Ben raps his fingers on the table. "We're not just talking about some drug war. We're talking about the ultimate war."

"They intend to take New York from us," I surmise.

"Let them fucking try." Caleb cracks his knuckles and grins. "They want a war. Let's give them one."

Everyone looks at his smiling face like he's grown ten heads.

"What?" He throws his hands in the air. "Don't pretend like you won't relish gutting those motherfuckers."

"Do I need to remind you we're still completely in the dark?" Massimo says.

"Not completely," I say. "Thanks to Gia, we now know

about the Barone. We know Liam and his crew are allies and that there's a big boss ruling everything."

Massimo's features soften. "I heard what happened last night. Is Gia okay?"

"What happened last night?" Cristian leans forward, eyeballing me with concern.

"Liam staked his claim very publicly in front of his men. He's taken his gloves off, and he's done playing nice."

"Shit. How is she holding up?"

"She's hanging in there. He commanded her to be at his place tonight to cook him dinner and stay the night. I think it's time we pulled her out." Gia will bust my balls if she finds out I went against her wishes, but I'll take her vitriol over her being dead any day. "It's too dangerous, and I'm not sure how much more useful Liam could be now we know he's not the one in charge."

"Liam could know a lot more," Fiero says. "My money says he does."

"So, let's tell O'Hara we have the proof and haul the prick to the bunker. We'll torture the intel out of him." Caleb's grin is now firmly planted on his face.

"We'll show our hand," Ben says.

"Our best option now is to pretend like we know nothing," Massimo agrees. "Gia needs to stay on the assignment."

"We're risking her life," I snap, digging my fingernails into my thigh. "I know she's skilled and resourceful, but the stakes are too high now."

"You need to separate your personal feelings for her," Ben says not unkindly.

"If this has become a conflict, I can reassign Gia a new handler," Massimo says.

"I'll do it." Cristian seems very keen to push me aside.

"That won't be necessary." I glare at my oldest friend. "I'm perfectly capable of doing my job and protecting Gia."

Massimo stabs me with a look. "This is bigger than all of us, Joshua. We're already at a disadvantage, and we can't afford to fall further behind. If this is a problem, you need to tell us now. No one will fault you if you need to step aside. I know I'd feel compromised if it was the woman I love."

My natural instinct is to deny I'm in love with her, but who the fuck am I kidding? I'm already halfway there, at least. So, I say nothing. I didn't think it was possible, but Caleb's grin is even wider. If he keeps this up, it'll split his face in two. I level him with a cool look. "Shut up."

"I didn't say a word," he teases, waggling his brows.

I return my focus to Massimo. "I'm a professional, and I'm fully invested in keeping Gia safe and finding these pricks who think they can stroll in and steal our turf from under us. If anything changes, I give you my word I'll talk to you immediately."

Massimo stares at me for a few tense beats. "Okay."

"There's something else Gia heard that's concerning and requires discussion," Ben says.

"What *boy* they were talking about." Massimo rubs at a spot between his brows.

Tension bleeds into the air again. "Whoever it was, it seems like the attempt was foiled, and Liam warned him about taking matters into their own hands, so I don't think they'll try it again," I say.

"That isn't much consolation," Massimo says.

"We know this is about us, so I think it's safe to assume the 'boy' could be any number of our sons or close relatives." Ben's expression is grave, and he's no doubt thinking of Rowan and Rhys.

"It could mean the twins or me," Cristian says. "We're still regarded as 'boys' by many of the older generation."

"Let those motherfuckers try to take any of us out and see what happens," Caleb snarls.

"We need to assign extra protection to our families," I suggest. "At least until we know more."

"Agreed," Fiero says. "You should assign some to yourselves too."

"No thanks," Caleb says. "I can protect myself."

"We'll be more vigilant, and we won't take unnecessary risks." I drill my brother with a look he ignores.

"Don't compromise your safety foolishly," Ben says. "For now, I agree you take precautions until we have more intel. If it becomes clear you're targets, then you *will* be accepting a security detail."

Caleb grumbles under his breath but doesn't fight it. We know what Uncle Ben means. He'll rope Mom in. She'll freak and want us surrounded by tons of bodyguards, and we'll concede because neither of us can ever deny her anything.

"We can't stretch our men too thin. We've already sent a team to Cali, and we might need every man available in the coming weeks if this turns into war." Massimo combs a hand through his hair.

"Use your security firm," Cristian says. "This is what those men are trained for. Hire them to protect our families."

"That's a great idea and the perfect solution," Massimo agrees, raising his eyes at Caleb. "Any objections?"

Caleb shakes his head. "My concerns were regarding official *mafioso* business. Protecting our families won't expose them to too much, and it's the logical decision."

Leo stands. "I'll get that set up right away. Unless you need me for anything else?" His gaze bounces between Ben and Massimo.

"You're excused, Leo. Thanks for your help," Massimo says.

"Let me know if I can do anything else." He nods at Ben, Caleb, and me before exiting the room.

"Gia suggested we try and trap the rats in a lie." I explain her plan.

"It's smart," Caleb says.

"It can't hurt to try. Let's do it," Massimo agrees. "I'll devise a different lie for each *famiglia* and pass it over to you by the end of the day. Feed it into your ranks, and let's see what comes of it."

"What about the plant in Colombia?" Cristian asks. "Do we have an update from our men on the ground?"

"The plant is clean. No rats or spies," Massimo says.

"I think they were planning or *are* planning to hit the plant," Fiero adds.

"We need to assign more men to protect it," I volunteer.

"We're already on it," Fiero confirms, slouching in his chair a little. "Juan Pablo is recruiting a hundred local men. Most are ex-military thanks to his contacts. If they go after it, we're confident we can hold our own."

"What about Vegas?" Ben asks.

"Anais hasn't offered up anything yet, but I'll be seeing her in two weeks at Christmas, and hopefully she'll have something for me then."

"Has she agreed to spy?" Cristian asks, looking a little wary.

Caleb bobs his head. "She was champing at the bit after I told her about that whore carrying her husband's baby."

"I'm not sure I trust Anais." Cristian reiterates a sentiment he's expressed many times over the years. "Be careful, Caleb. There has always been something a little off about her."

"I know how to handle her. Your warning is redundant."

"I didn't get a sense of anything being out of place in Vegas when I was there," Cristian adds, rubbing his hands down his

Siobhan Davis

face. "But my gut is telling me Cruz is all tangled up in this. I wouldn't rule out Anais being aware and having her own agenda. She might know what he's planning, and you're her backup plan. I'd smother my dick in latex if I was you."

"I've had the snip." Caleb puts it out there like it's no biggie.

"What? When?" This is news to me.

"A year ago."

"That's quite a drastic move for someone so young," Ben says.

"I don't want kids."

"What if your future wife does?"

"I don't want a wife either."

Fiero bursts out laughing. "You sure you're not my son?" he teases.

"Don't tell me you've had a vasectomy too?" Cristian asks looking genuinely shell-shocked. I'm guessing Caleb told no one.

"Nah, but it's not a bad idea."

"You're missing out," Ben says.

"It's always reversible if he ever changes his mind," I say over a shrug.

"Well, that was a fun way to end our meeting." Massimo grins, and at least it's helped to ease some of the tension. "Stick close and watch your backs. We'll meet biweekly from now on until we've got to the bottom of this and ended the threat. I'll have my assistant reach out to yours and add the dates to your calendars."

I groan at the reminder that Ben sent Sorella's younger sister to my office as my new temp PA until Ruthie returns from maternity leave. The decision has been made to recruit temporary staff for our businesses solely from our community going forward so no outsiders can get close to us. I'm grateful he

206

found someone for me fast, but couldn't it have been someone without the last name Caprese? I have a feeling Sorella is going to become a problem.

After the meeting breaks up, I ask to speak with Cristian alone.

"What's up?" he asks as we stand at the window in the conference room looking down on the city and the park below.

"That's what I'd like to know."

His brow creases. "I'm not following."

"I asked you this before, but you blew me off. I want the truth this time. What happened between you and Gia because I know something did."

He turns to face me. "I don't kiss and tell, man. You know that."

"She's important to me."

"We all see that, and I'm really happy for you, Joshua. She's perfect for you, and you don't need to worry about the past. It wasn't serious, but you should still ask her. It's her place to tell you, not mine."

Chapter Twenty-Six
Gia

"Leave them, and get over here," Liam demands as I move to take our plates away. He cleared his dinner while I just moved my chicken and pasta around the plate. Despite a stern inner talk, I'm on edge. I hate being here. I hate even looking at his gloating face. I hate playing the mute docile girlfriend. And I especially hate how he's been pawing at me all night.

I feel sick as I plaster a smile on my face and walk over to his side of the table.

"Show me your tits." He levels me with a challenging look as acid churns in my stomach.

Lifting shaking hands to the straps on my dress, I pray the diphenhydramine kicks in soon. I put 150 milligrams into his beer twenty minutes ago. It's double the recommended dose, but Liam is a big guy, and I figure he'd need more than the average person. I want to ensure the sleeping aid knocks him out long enough for me to search his place thoroughly and pretend like I was sleeping beside him all night.

I was sorely tempted to give him an overdose and rid the

world of him, but unfortunately, we need the creep. Joshua updated me on the meeting, confirming the board wants me to continue. I was mad when he told me he asked them to extract me, but it wasn't for long. At least he was honest about it, and I know his motives were purely coming from a protective place. Although I'm not happy he tried to undermine me, it shows he cares, and that means a lot.

My mouth is dry, and my palms are sweaty as I lower the straps of my dress and my bra, exposing my chest to his leering gaze.

"Fuck, these are incredible," Liam says, flicking his fingers at my nipples. He tweaks and rubs them until they stiffen, and I feel another part of me die inside. "Lean down. I want to suck on them," he says, ensuring my mortification is complete. I hate that Joshua is listening to this. He's having a hard time with me being here tonight, and I promised him I wouldn't shut off the audio no matter what.

I zone out as Liam sucks and bites my breasts, tugging painfully on my nipples.

He pulls his mouth back and peers intensely at me. "Hmm. I'm not sure you've learned your lesson yet." His conniving expression sends icicles crawling up my spine. "On your knees, whore."

I hold my head up as I lower to my knees and reach for his zipper, panicking that I didn't give him enough sleeping liquid. Shouldn't he be sleepy by now? I swallow back bile as I pull his limp dick from his pants. He's soft and floppy, like jelly in my hand. I stroke him a few times before he shoves my head down over him. I almost gag on his disgusting shaft, but I visualize all the ways I'm going to make him pay before I kill him, and it helps. Sucking his cock doesn't induce an erection either, and I'm guessing it's a side effect of the medicine.

"You're fucking defective," he snarls, slurring his words a

little as he slaps me away and tucks his flaccid cock back in his pants. "You can't even make me hard."

How the fuck am I the defective one?

He wraps his hands around my throat, but there is no strength to his touch, and I know he's got to be close. I need to get him to his room.

"Baby, come to bed. Let's get naked, and I'll get you really hard."

"You better." He releases my throat, grabbing my hand and yanking me toward his bedroom with a frown. He sways a little in the hallway. "What the fuck?" he says over a yawn.

"Which one is yours?" I ask, pretending like I don't know.

"Stop talking." He pulls me into his room. "Less talking, more fucking." He flops down on the bed on his back, beckoning me forward with his fingers. Another yawn escapes his mouth as his eyes struggle to remain open.

Thank fucking God.

I saunter toward him sexily, smiling as I shimmy my dress down my body, leaving me in only my lace panties. Crawling up the bed, I grin as his eyes open and close. I untie his shoes and remove his socks, hiding my grimace at the strong smell emanating from his feet. Ugh. His toes are hairy and oddly shaped, and his feet are all veiny, which I know is a sign of health, but his feet are seriously gross. Grabbing his pants, I unzip them and yank them down along with his boxers.

A snore rips from his lips, and when I look up, he's completely conked out. I slump on the bed beside him for a few minutes, staring up at the ceiling, thanking whoever invented that drug for its existence. Then I spring into action. Removing his shirt is a bit of an ordeal, but I finally manage to get it off him. I take pics of him naked before I shove him under the covers. You never know when it might come in handy.

Checking he's out for the count, I scan his apartment for

cameras with the device Joshua procured for me. None show up, which is a relief. Then, I begin a thorough inspection, starting with the kitchen and ending back in the bedroom. Using another gadget Joshua gave me, I crack the code to his safe and open it. But the contents are disappointing. There are a few bundles of cash, some watches, and the deeds to a house in Boston along with a couple of fake passports and driver's licenses. I take copies of everything and immediately send them to the cloud so the team has access to them.

I go through his closet, his drawers, and bedside tables again, growing frustrated I have found nothing of use. If he's storing everything at the bar, I can't see how I'll ever be left alone there to get my hands on it. I'm lost in thought as I rummage through the second bedside table, and I almost miss it.

My eyes flit back to the small silver cylindrical object, and my breath hitches as I stare at it. "No way," I whisper, staring at what appears to be one of our tracking chips. How did Liam get his hands on this, and why does he have it? My mind churns with ideas as I take pictures of it, making sure to zoom in on the numbers on the underside. Each number corresponds to an individual chip, so if this was an active one, we'll be able to identify where it came from.

Did he remove it from one of the *soldati* on the ship? The Commission assumed the dead men missing their chips lost them during their torture. But what if it was deliberate? What if they mutilated them beyond all recognition to hide the fact they wanted their chips? It would seem like the logical answer. I wish I could take it for Ben so it could be fully analyzed, but it's too risky to remove anything.

After a second search of his place, I'm satisfied I have found the only evidence here. I glance at my watch. Three a.m. is too early to leave. I can't risk Liam checking the cameras downstairs. He expects me to spend the night, so I shall. I plonk my butt on the couch and pull up a book on my phone to read. There is no way in hell I'm risking falling asleep. In case I doze off, I set my alarm for five thirty, but I don't need it. I'm still awake and itching to get out before he wakes up. I have no clue how long that stuff will keep him in the Land of Nod.

I tiptoe into his room and slowly climb into the bed beside him, watching him the entire time for any signs he might be waking. But he's completely comatose. He hasn't even budged position all night. I wriggle a little in the bed to mess up my side, only getting out when I've left enough body heat. I spritz a little bit of my perfume on the pillow, smirking when I deliberately smudge his brand-new white silk pillow with my mascara. Satisfied I've done enough to "prove" I spent the night, I go out to the kitchen and write him a note, confirming I have left to go to the gym before an early-morning meeting with a client.

I leave it beside him on the bed, staring at him as he snores like a freight train, debating whether to grab the pillow and smother him with it. I hightail it out of his place before I'm tempted to do it.

When I arrive home, I discover I have a guest. Joshua is pacing the floor in the living room like a madman, scrubbing his hands down his face and tugging on his hair. His head picks up when he hears my heels clicking across the floors. Bruising shadows paint the skin under his eyes, worry lines furrow his brow, and his usually pristine hair is sticking up every which way.

"Thank God." His giant strides eat up the gap between us in no time, and then he's reeling me into his arms. "I was so worried." He almost squeezes me to death he's hugging me so tight. "I couldn't sit still for a second all night. I was going out of my mind." He clasps my face in his large hands. "I shouldn't be here, Gia, but I couldn't not come. I wanted to be here when you returned to make sure you are okay with my own eyes. It was hell knowing you were over there, dealing with all that shit, and I couldn't do a damn thing to help you."

"I'm okay," I say, my voice muffled as he tucks my head into his neck and holds me tight.

"I barely stopped myself from going over there. I fucking hate that prick, and I want him dead," he growls. "I know we have a deal, but please let me cut his hands off, one finger at a time."

"Only if you let me slice his revolting dick from his body."

"I'm gutting his balls."

I giggle as I lift my head. "I want his ass. I have a few creative ideas for it."

"Fuck, you were made for me," he says before claiming my lips in a hard kiss. Joshua is normally so careful with me, but he's not holding back tonight, devouring my mouth with panicked intensity.

"Wait," I say, easing back a few minutes later. "I want to shower and get his stench off me."

"I'll make coffee, and I picked up some pastries from that bakery on the corner. The board has convened another emergency session to discuss the chip you found. They want you to attend."

"Thanks for coming in on such short notice, Gia," Massimo says as he sips from a paper cup of coffee.

"It's no problem. I haven't actually gone to sleep yet."

"You are doing a fantastic job under difficult circumstances," he adds. "We are grateful for your loyalty."

"Thank you, Don Greco."

"I called Philip the instant Joshua forwarded me the images you took of the chip," Ben says.

"I'm guessing it is from one of the dead men on the ship," I say.

"You would be correct," Ben confirms with a grim smile.

"How many more were missing?" Joshua asks, linking his fingers with mine under the table.

"Seven in total," Cristian confirms.

"That's why they completely disfigured those men," Caleb muses, leaning back in his seat as he draws the same conclusion as me. "It was to disguise the fact they took their chips."

"Are the chips still active?" I ask. "Are they using them to hide their spies within our ranks?"

Fiero shakes his head. "We thought that too, but none of those chips are active any longer."

"They were all deactivated the night their owners were killed," Ben confirms.

"So, what are they doing with them?" Joshua asks.

"We'd all love the answer to that question." Massimo's gaze dances around the table. "I have a feeling it's a vital piece of evidence."

Joshua squeezes my hand under the table.

"When are you seeing Liam again?" Fiero asks.

"Not for a while. He told me last night he's going to Ireland today with his family for Christmas. He won't be back until January third."

I felt like throwing a party when he told me. It required every ounce of acting talent to pretend to be sad. At least I'll have a reprieve from the stress of spending time with him, and I'll get to spend the holidays with my family and Joshua. I'm hoping the assignment might be ended before Liam returns and I've seen the last of him.

"That's unfortunate. Hanging around the bar might have proven beneficial. The holiday spirit can often lower guards and loosen tongues."

"Can't we ask O'Hara to send his men there to keep their ear to the ground?" Cristian suggests.

"We can, and we will," Joshua says. "I really don't see how there is much more Gia can do. She won't get an opportunity to search the bar even if invited back."

"I think we should stage a little breaking and entering," Ben says. "If Liam is keeping anything there, we'll find it. We'll hire outside the family. Make it look like a Christmas robbery so we're not showing our hand early."

"I think that would work," Massimo says. He turns to face me. "We'll extract you fully in January. You'll have to go into hiding until this blows over. Liam will not take kindly to you disappearing on him."

Thank fuck. I breathe a sigh of relief.

"You can stay at my house," Ben offers. "It's completely secure, and we have tons of room. The east wing is free right now. You can stay there, if you like." Ben has gone to great lengths to keep the location of his home a secret, and no one knows he lives in Greenwich or the coordinates of the estate. He has round-the-clock guards and top-notch security measures including a large basement-level panic room, equipped with full supplies.

"Or you can stay with Mom," Joshua says. "You know she'd love to have you too."

I smile at both men. "Sounds like a plan. Thank you."

Chapter Twenty-Seven
Joshua

"I 'm glad you're here," I whisper in Gia's ear as we sit side by side at the long, noisy table. Christmas is being hosted by Serena and Alesso this year, and everyone is here including Gia's family. The Salerno house is also on the grounds of Ben's vast estate, which is handy because it means everyone can stay over. Gia, Gia's parents, and her siblings are staying at Mom and Leo's house, so I'm hoping for a sleepover of our own.

Gia's assignment is all but over, and she'll be moving permanently into one of Mom's guest rooms in a few days. I'll feel more at ease when I know she's safely tucked away here. I'm going to help her pack up her stuff when we get back to the city in a few days.

Dinner is a lively affair, filled with tons of delicious food, expensive wines, and lots of laughter. But it's the girl sitting at my side that makes it the most special. I'm done denying my feelings for Gia and done denying myself what I want. The situation is still critical with the threat looming over us, but I'm refusing to think about *mafioso* bullshit today.

Today is about family and making new memories with the woman who has come to mean so much to me.

"Here, Mom. I forgot to give these to you earlier," I say, creeping up on her in the living room after the men and kids have finished with the cleanup. I hand her the box of chocolates I picked up at the White Plains Chocolaterie. They are her favorite.

"You are really spoiling me, Joshua. You and Caleb have already given us too much!" We gave them a cruise trip to Italy with a babysitting voucher so they can enjoy a romantic vacation together. Caleb and I will split the time in half and clear our schedules so we can be out here to take care of Leif and Rosa. It won't be a chore. I don't get to spend enough time with my little brother and sister, and I'm already looking forward to it.

"You're our mom, and we love you. Nothing will ever be too much."

Tears glisten in her eyes as she pulls me into her arms. "She is so good for you. She's bringing you back to life," Mom whispers in my ear.

I haven't said a peep to anyone about the status of my relationship with Gia, but I guess it's probably obvious by now. We were practically sitting on top of one another at dinner and grinning like lovesick loons.

"I'm thrilled for you." She grips my arms. "You deserve all the happiness in the world. Embrace it, my love." She kisses both my cheeks, smiling as she swipes at the tears in her eyes.

"Look what I found!" Raven shrieks, waving a sprig of mistletoe in the air. Her eyes scan the room, settling on Marco Bianchi with determination.

"Here comes trouble," Gia murmurs, grinning as she sidles up next to me.

My arm wraps around her waist of its own volition. Mom

practically floats off the ground. Across the room, I spot Frankie whispering to her husband and smiling as she looks in our direction.

"Does Ben know his little princess is crushing on Gia's brother?" I ask Mom, chuckling as I watch Raven dangle the mistletoe over Marco's head. At eleven, she is almost as tall as he is at thirteen.

"Oh, he's aware, and he's not happy." Mom smiles. "Raven will always be his little girl even when she's all grown up. She reminds me of Elisa at that age."

"I'd better warn my little brother," Gia teases, leaning into my side. "Though he'd be lucky to have Raven adore him the way Elisa adores Caleb."

"She's far too good for my brother." I'm only repeating what Caleb has said so many times, but Mom's not happy.

"Stop that." She playfully swats my chest. "Your brother is a catch. If he'd only allow himself to believe he's worthy of love and happiness, Elisa could be the best thing that's ever happened to him."

I'm tempted to ask if she knows he got the snip, but it's not my secret to share.

"Poor Marco." I'm chuckling as I watch him trying to avoid a mouth kiss, but Raven is a determined little thing and way more forthright than Elisa has ever been. She's going to be a complete stunner when she's grown up, and Marco most likely will not be ignoring her then. His cheeks stain red when Raven gets her way, planting a quick kiss on his lips. Thank fuck Ben isn't in the room. He's off somewhere with Alesso and Leo. Those three are thick as thieves. Have been for years.

"Marco is super shy," Gia admits. "But he's the best of us."

The mistletoe makes its way to Frankie and her husband Rico. He dips her down low, supporting her with one arm around her back, while holding the mistletoe over their heads.

It's quite an amorous display, and catcalls and wolf whistles ring out.

"Get a room," Cosimo shouts, and his parents break their passionate lip-lock with wide smiles on their faces.

Rowan and his girl have a turn next, and then I snatch the sprig and turn to Gia, hoping she is game to do this. I press my mouth to her ear. "Is this okay?"

Her big blue eyes widen as she stares at me. "You're sure you want to do this? There will be no coming back from it."

"I don't want an out." My expression turns solemn, and my heart is beating like crazy behind my chest as I ask my next question. "Do you?"

She rigorously shakes her head, sending waves of reddish-brown hair tumbling over her shoulders. She's decided to let the dye naturally fade, rather than getting the color stripped. "Nope. I'm all in, Joshua."

My shoulders relax. "I'm all in too."

She beams at me, and I grin back at her. This feels surreal. Like it's happening to someone else. If you'd told me last Christmas I'd fall in love with Gia Bianchi, I would have asked what you were smoking. I never could have predicted this.

"Kiss her already!" Rowan yells.

"Yeah, Joshie. Kiss her," Leif adds, and a chant of "kiss her" starts up around the room.

"Don't want to disappoint our audience," I say, reeling her into my arms as I elevate the plant over our heads.

"Definitely not," she agrees, winding her arms around my neck. "And we need to one-up my parents. Can't let the rents steal our thunder."

"Mission accepted," I say, leaning down to kiss her. Our mouths melt in a scorching-hot kiss as we cling to one another with burning intensity. I prod at the seam of her lips with my tongue, and her mouth parts, granting me entry. Our tongues glide sinfully against one another like we've been doing this our entire lives. We're so lost to the moment that our surroundings fade. Gia jumps up, wrapping her legs around my waist as I toss the mistletoe away and hold her upright.

"Ahem." A loud throat clearing finally pulls us apart as whistling and giggling bounces off the walls. I stare at Rico Bianchi's red face. His nostrils are flared, and his hands are clenched at his side. Oops. "There are kids in the room, and that's my only daughter."

"I'm aware." I bundle Gia in my arms as I spot Caleb and Elisa watching us from opposite sides of the room. Elisa has a smile on her face, but it's tinged in sadness, and Caleb looks miserable. I frown, wondering what is going on there. Elisa didn't sit beside Caleb at dinner, which basically never happens. I eyeball my twin, and his unhappiness is glaringly obvious.

"Relax, Dad." Gia punches him in the upper arm. "We got a little carried away, but there's no need to get your panties in a bunch. We've seen you and Mom do way worse."

"Take a chill pill, Rico." Frankie loops her arm through her husband's. "They're in love. Leave them be."

Mention of the L-word doesn't induce the panic-riddled fear it usually would, but I'm not wholly comfortable either.

"We're going for a walk," Gia announces, dragging me away. "Sorry about them," she whispers, "I know they're a lot."

"I like your parents. They're cool." I'm distracted watching my twin.

I peck her lips. "Wait by the side door. I just need to have a quick word with Caleb. I'll meet you there in five."

I spot Elisa making a beeline for Gia as I walk across the room to my twin. "What's going on?" I ask, lifting one shoulder and gesturing toward the corner of the room away from prying ears.

"It's nothing for you to worry about. Go be with your girl."

"Caleb." I pierce him with a knowing look.

Air whooshes out of his mouth, and we walk over to the corner. "It appears I've done something to upset Lili. She won't talk to me or tell me what it's about." He shrugs. "It's probably for the best. Things were becoming...complicated."

"We're definitely talking about this, but I've got to go. Gia is waiting. I can ask her if she knows anything?"

He shakes his head. "Don't get involved." He clamps his hand on my shoulder. "You two look good together. Don't fuck it up."

I grab him into a hug. "Love you, little brother."

"Fuck off. We were still born on the same day."

My grin is off the charts. "I still entered the world first."

He shoves his middle finger up at me, and I'm laughing as I walk off to meet my girl.

"Hey there, beautiful." I lean down and kiss her.

"Hey, that's my line!" she quips.

I nip her earlobe before she pulls a wooly hat down on her head. I cover up in a warm coat and scarf, and I remember gloves this time. We leave the house and set out on the walking trail, hand in hand. The air is brisk, lifting strands of Gia's hair, but it's not unpleasant. A warming heat filters through my veins that is all Gia's doing.

"Are you having a good day?" I ask, lifting our conjoined hands to my lips and kissing her knuckles through her gloves.

"This is the best Christmas I've enjoyed in a long time."

"Me too."

"Please tell me you're feeling this. That I'm not alone in it."

"I'm feeling it all over, honey. All over." I waggle my brows, and she giggles as she snuggles into my side. My arm encircles her shoulders, like it was made to fit there.

"I want to spend the night with you." She looks up at me with a look that is a mix of vulnerability and confidence.

"I would love that."

A gorgeous smile ghosts over her lips, and I can't help swooping in and claiming them.

"Oh, Joshua," she rasps when we finally break apart. Her hands land on my chest. "I could kiss you all day and all night and never grow tired of it."

"I plan to keep kissing you for a long time, Gia. You won't get a chance to grow tired of it."

Her eyes probe mine. "You mean that."

"I do. I told you I'm all in, and I'm serious."

"So, we're like..." She swallows audibly and worries her lower lip between her teeth.

"Boyfriend and girlfriend doesn't quite seem enough, but it'll do for now if that's what you want."

"It is," she rushes to reassure me.

Our lips meet again, like two magnets drawn together.

"We better stop," she says in a breathy voice. "Before I push you into the woods and have my wicked way with you."

"I'm not opposed to outdoor fucking, but I'd rather my dick didn't shrivel from frostbite."

She giggles, taking my hand and dragging me to the bench. "I need to talk to you about something."

"Cristian," I surmise, circling my arm around her and keeping her tucked in close.

She nods. "I would always have told you before we slept together, so don't think this is because Cristian said I needed to tell you. I would not have kept it from you."

"Yet you did when I asked before."

"You were an ass to me then, and you had no right to any part of my personal life. Things are different now."

"Did you fuck him?" I hold my breath, waiting for her answer.

Slowly, she nods, and I try to get a grip on my emotions.

"I thought he might have said something to you."

"Cristian is a gentleman. He never divulges details, and he hasn't said anything about you, not even when I asked him."

"Then I'm glad I did it with him."

I frown.

"I lost my virginity to Cristian when I was seventeen," she quietly admits.

Removing my arm from around her body, I rest my head in my hands. "He means something to you." A girl like Gia doesn't just give her virginity away flippantly.

"It's not what you're most likely thinking." She places a palm on my back. "It actually wasn't planned. I was a couple months away from graduating, and I didn't want to go to college a virgin. I had been planning to lose it with my boyfriend at the time, but we broke up. I was at a Maltese party, and Cristian was there. We got talking, and he'd just broken up with someone too. We flirted a bit, and then one thing led to another."

"Was that the only time?"

"Yes."

I'm battling with a whole slew of emotions. "He better have made it good for you."

"He took care of me. He made my first time memorable, and it was only special because it was my first time. I don't have feelings for him, and he doesn't have feelings for me. It was a onetime spur-of-the-moment thing."

"Okay." I lift my head.

"Are you mad?" She nibbles on her lower lip.

I shake my head. "I'd be a prick to be mad about something that happened years ago before I was on the scene." I expel heavily. "I'm jealous, Gia. He got to be your first."

She wets her lips a few times, opening and closing her mouth.

"Just say what's on your mind."

Fear flickers across her face briefly before her head lifts and her shoulders straighten. "You could be my last."

I hold her stunning face in my hands. "I could be." I move to stand, needing to make love to her now.

"Wait a sec. I have something else to tell you."

I groan. "Fuck. I'm not sure my heart can take this."

"I always want to be brutally honest with you, Joshua. Not just because of what you've been through in the past, but I believe all relationships need to contain complete honesty from the very start. I don't want you caught off guard by someone saying something to you. I want you to have the full facts."

"How are you only twenty-two? How are you so wise?"

"I've learned from the best. My parents have an amazing relationship built on open communication, trust, respect, and loyalty. I want that for me. For us."

"I've seen that with Nat and Leo too, and it's what I want. I need it after what Ina did to me. I don't trust easily, Gia, but you have effortlessly woven your way into my heart."

"Are you still afraid?"

"Yes, but the best things in life are scary."

She kisses my cheek. "I agree."

"I should probably tell you the names of the girls I've slept with as all are *mafioso*, and I don't want you caught off guard either."

"I don't need to know the names of everyone, Joshua, but if it makes you feel better, then absolutely tell me. I'll try not to be jealous."

I reel off the names, and she listens quietly. "I thought there would've been more," she says when I've finished.

"Gee, thanks."

She sits closer, and our thighs press together. "Your reputation makes it seem like it's more."

"I think people confuse me with Caleb a lot." I shrug. "What was it you wanted to tell me because I'm eager to move this to the bedroom." I purposely brush my lips against her earlobe as I lean in. "I have fantasized about making love to you for months, and I can't wait a minute longer to get my hands on you, so make it quick."

"God, Joshua. The things you do to me with just your words." A full-body shiver crawls over her, and I don't think it's anything to do with the cold.

"Stop deflecting."

"I'm nervous. I'm worried you might think differently of me after I tell you this."

"Impossible." I tweak her nose. "Now spill."

"I've had a foursome. Multiple foursomes."

"Okay, wasn't expecting that." I tuck a stray strand of hair back into her hat. "Three girls and a guy or..."

She smooths a hand over her head. "Me and three guys."

Chapter Twenty-Eight
Gia

S hock splays across his face, and I wish I didn't have to tell him, but made men are the worst gossips, and I'd hate for Joshua to hear this from anyone else. "It happened in Nepal. I was the only female there, spending months training with a ton of sexually frustrated made men. It was bound to happen."

A look of horror washes over his face, and I can guess where his mind has gone.

"I didn't sleep with all of them!" I rush to clarify in case he thinks I'm a total ho-bag. "I was having sex with the same three guys for a few months while there. Sometimes one on one. Sometimes it was a threesome or a foursome." I take his hands in mine again. "A few times a couple of the guys got it on." That was seriously so freaking hot. As long as I live, I'll never forget being nailed by Aldo while watching Marrone drive his dick into Cascio's ass alongside us.

"Jesus. I'm not sure I want details."

"I don't want to go there either. I wanted to make you aware in case anyone says anything."

"Who were they, and have you had sex with them since you returned to the US?"

I shake my head. "We drew a line under it when we left Nepal. It's been strictly professional since then." I give him Marrone's and Cascio's names. "The other guy was Aldo," I add in a softer voice. "How did he die?"

Joshua winces a little. "You really want to know?"

I nod. I already know it wouldn't have been pleasant.

"He was staked to the wall of the ship and barely recognizable. They had ripped him to shreds. He was one of the men who had his chip hacked out."

Pain sits on my chest. I didn't love him, but we had some good times together. He helped make Nepal more bearable, and he was one of the good guys. "He didn't deserve to die like that."

"He didn't. None of them did."

I lean into him, and his arms automatically go around me. "How many more will die gruesome deaths before this is over?"

"Too many." His voice is solemn and laden with the burden of responsibility I know he must feel.

I climb to my feet and offer him my hand. "Then we should live every moment to the fullest. For us and for those who are no longer here. They died so we could live to see another day. I don't want to spend any more time talking about death or the *mafioso* or our past lovers."

"Amen to that." He takes my hand and stands. "Thank you for telling me."

"Do you feel differently about me now?"

"I would never hold something you did before you met me against you. And it doesn't change how I feel about you. But there is one thing you need to know." He holds my face in his hands. "I won't share you. Not ever. You're mine and only mine."

"I feel the same way. I won't share you either, and I don't want any other man. I only want you."

"You're sure about this?" he asks, pulling me into his bedroom when we get back to his parents' house.

I dump my weekend bag on the ground and circle my arms around his neck. "Surer than I've been about anything in a long time."

"Thank fuck." His hands curve around my ass. "I think I'd die of blue balls if you changed your mind."

"Fuck me, Joshua. Make me yours."

He scoops me up in his arms, like I'm precious cargo, and walks over to the ginormous king bed, carefully setting me down on the mattress.

I watch with lust-fueled eyes as he slowly undresses, removing his cuff links and watch first and placing them down on the bedside table. Leaning down, he kisses me, and I hook my hand around his neck, driving my fingers into his soft hair, desperate to feel him moving inside me. I move to unbutton his shirt, but he pulls back, shaking his head. "Patience, honey. We only get this first once, and I want to savor every second."

God, this man. How he has gone from cold and closed off to *this* in the past few months is beyond me. It's like the cage is gone and he's finally setting himself free. Emotion crashes into me as I watch him remove his shirt, socks and shoes and pants until he's only in his boxers. The hard outline of his erection is clearly visible through the material, and I clench my thighs together and lick my lips as he crawls up the bed and over me. "Your turn." His husky voice is doing things to my body, and liquid lust floods my panties.

He kisses me softly as he undresses me, and we don't speak

as he slips my heels off and sets them neatly by the side of the bed. Next, he removes my pantyhose and my dress leaving me in my bra and underwear. Joshua dots kisses on my feet and brushes his sinful mouth along my legs until he reaches my thighs. I'm already a quivering mess, and he's barely touching me. When his lips brush against the crotch of my panties, I almost lift off the bed. His soft chuckle and adoring gaze hold me in place as he moves over me, leaning down to kiss me again while he deftly unclips my bra and discards it.

Joshua sits back on his heels, inspecting my almost bare body. We're both now in just our underwear, and I'm close to combusting.

"Please," I purr. "I need you."

"Where do you need me? Tell me what you want," he asks, sliding off the bed and opening the bedside drawer. Tossing some condoms on the bed, he smirks as he shoves his boxers down his legs and kicks them away. One hand wraps around his long, hard impressive length and I almost come on the spot.

"You in me right fucking now," I pant, moving my hands to my panties.

"Not a chance." He slaps my hands away to hook his thumbs in the lace and oh so slowly drag them down my legs. His heated gaze burns my skin every place it lands, and he takes his sweet-ass time devouring every inch of me. "Fuck, you're so beautiful," he says, parting my thighs and bending my knees, placing my feet flat on the bed. "So goddamn sexy," he adds, staring at my most intimate part with wide eyes like a kid in a candy store.

"Are you wet for me, honey?" he asks, gently swiping one finger along my slit.

"So fucking wet," I pant.

"Lift your arms and hold the top of the bed. Thrust your chest out," he says, climbing off the bed.

I do as he asks because it's fucking hot.

He stands at the end of the bed, with a hawkish gaze, raking his eyes over me from head to toe. It's the most delicious torture, and I'm so worked up. "Look at you. So gorgeous and all mine for the claiming."

He gets back on the bed, and adrenaline spikes in my veins. I'm excited but a little nervous too.

"Bring your knees in to your chest. I want to inspect my pussy and my ass."

With anyone else, I'd tell them to fuck off. Unwilling to expose myself so vulnerably. But I obey without question because I trust Joshua. I know he won't hurt me or humiliate me. He doesn't have it in him.

He lies on his stomach between my legs, staring. He parts my folds and swipes his tongue over my clit, and a loud moan slips from my lips. His tongue moves carefully over my slit, from top to bottom, and I close my eyes and relish the blissful feeling. A gasp escapes my mouth when he pushes two fingers into my pussy, pumping them in and out in a leisurely fashion while stoking my desire to the next level.

"You're so tight. So perfect. Feel how you're hugging my fingers."

A strangled sound rips from my chest when he curls those fingers, hitting the perfect spot inside me. "Oh god, Joshua. Please. I need your cock inside me."

"We're in no rush, and I plan to devour you all night." He removes his fingers, briefly tasting my juices on his skin before gliding them lower. I tense as one finger rims my asshole. "Has anyone been here?" he asks, softly teasing my forbidden hole.

"No," I admit over a gulp. "I'm not sure I'd like it."

"You'd love it with me," he says, pressing the tip of his pinkie inside.

My pussy and ass clench as a host of emotions washes over me.

He looks into my eyes. "We can work up to it if you decide you want to try. But I won't ever force you to do anything you don't want."

"I'll think about it," I say, both relieved and a little disappointed when he withdraws his finger from my ass.

He disappears into the bathroom for a minute before returning to settle between my legs. His erection is leaking precum, and I'm desperate to get my hands on him, but he tells me to hold position as he goes to town on my cunt with his fingers and his tongue.

I explode into tiny blissful particles a few minutes later as the most intense orgasm lays claim to my body. Then Joshua is rolling on a condom and lining up his shaft at my entrance.

Covering my body with his, he kisses me passionately until I melt into the bed. Slowly, he inches inside me, keeping his eyes locked on mine the entire time. "Fuck, you feel so good, honey."

My inner walls clench against him, and I whimper as he pushes inside me, inch by slow inch.

"Are you okay?" he asks when he's fully seated.

"I'm peachy." I drag my fingers through his hair, wondering if he can feel my heart beating superfast against his warm bare chest.

He holds himself still while he kisses me, and then his mouth lowers to my tits. Sucking one nipple into his mouth, he works it over while fondling my other breast. All while looking me in the eye. It's one of the hottest moments of my entire life. He gives the same treatment to my other breast while his cock jerks inside my clenching pussy. "These are fucking magnificent," he says, cupping both tits in his palms. "Every part of you is."

"Joshua, please." I'm not beyond begging at this point.

"What is it you want?"

"You to move, you sadistic fucker!" I playfully slap his hands. "This is the worst form of torture."

"Or the best foreplay," he teases, sucking on that sensitive spot under my ear. When he lifts back, the teasing expression is no longer evident on his face, replaced with a dark look of lethal intent that has me tingling all over. "I'm done torturing both of us. Hold on tight, honey. This won't be slow."

I grip the top of the headrest as Joshua makes good on his promise, slamming in and out of me like a wild beast. My body jostles on the bed, and every nerve ending is on fire as he throws my legs over his shoulders and pounds into me with virile strength. Sweat glistens on his broad, defined chest, and the muscles in his toned abs flex and roll with his skillful thrusts. I can only hold on for dear life as I enjoy the ride of a lifetime.

"Are you close?" he asks sometime later, and I nod as sensation builds and builds down below.

He forces my legs back as he leans down, slamming his cock in and out of me in brutal thrusts as expert fingers rub my swollen bundle of nerves. I scream, and he roars when we climax together a few minutes later.

After we've both come down from our high, we curl up on the bed, limbs entwined and hearts beating in sync, staring deep into one another's eyes as we silently contemplate how perfect this moment was and how perfect we are together.

Chapter Twenty-Nine
Gia

"I'm surprised you can walk at all," Elisa whispers as we stand outside while Joshua loads our bags in the trunk of his Maserati. I've just been filling her in on how fast things have developed with Joshua and our official relationship status. Joshua and I just enjoyed a delicious lunch prepared by Natalia, and now we're heading back to the city.

"Same, girl." We've had two incredible days here, mostly spent in bed, exploring one another's bodies and experimenting with different positions. "Not sure what it says about me, but I'm still craving him like I'll die if I can't feel him moving inside me."

Elisa cocks her head to one side, examining my face. "You love him, don't you?"

Slowly, I nod. "Yeah, I do. I'm not sure how it happened. It just snuck up on me."

"Sounds perfect, and he clearly feels the same. The way he looks at you. Gawd. It's beautiful, Gigi. He looks at you like you're the only woman who has ever existed. Like you're his entire world. He looks at you the way I wish Caleb would look at me, but it will never happen." She averts her eyes for a second, and when she looks at me again, I see the hurt hiding behind her eyes.

"Oh, Lise." I yank her into a hug. I hate seeing her hurt, but I'm glad what's happened seems to have brought her to her senses. "Your knight in shining armor is out there waiting for you. I bet it happens when you least expect it. Just how it's happened to me."

"I told Seb I'd go out on a date with him," she blurts as we separate. I watch Joshua hug his mother at the door.

My brows climb to my hairline. "When did that happen?"

Fire dances in her eyes. "I texted him Christmas night."

I'm betting it was after Caleb left to meet Anais.

"Good for you. He seems crazy about you, and I really hope it works out. You deserve to be happy."

She looks miserable as she forces a nod, and my heart hurts for my bestie. It feels wrong for me to be so ecstatically happy when she's dejected and heartsore.

Joshua glances over his shoulder, communicating with his eyes. I loop my arm through Elisa's and we walk to the entranceway of Nat and Leo's homey house. "Thanks for everything, Nat. It's been a wonderful Christmas."

Leo snorts out a laugh, and his wife shoots him the evil eye. He promptly shuts up, and I can't hide a grin. Gotta love seeing a dangerous made man humbled by his wife. Someday, I want that to be me. To be *us*. My eyes are drawn to Joshua like a string being pulled between us, and I can tell he's thinking similar thoughts. A rosy-red flush creeps up my cheeks, and I literally radiate happiness.

"We loved having you here." Natalia bundles me into a hug. "Thank you, Gia. Thank you for bringing my son back to us. I couldn't be happier you two are together. It's the best Christmas gift of all time."

"Enough conspiring." Joshua pulls me out of his mother's embrace to wrap me up in his. "And stop hogging my woman."

"I wouldn't dream of it." His mom beams and wipes a tear before she wraps Elisa into a warm hug. She whispers in her ear as Leo saunters over to us.

"You kiddos take care in the city. Watch your backs and don't take any risks. It's dangerous out there."

"I won't be there for long," I say. I'm mostly heading back to the city because my team is meeting up tomorrow night in honor of Aldo and Pisano, and I want to be there. "I'll just pack up my stuff, say goodbye to my folks, and then I'll be on my way back."

"We look forward to having you stay with us, and you're welcome for as long as you like."

I reach out and hug him. "Thanks, Leo. I appreciate it."

"You're family, Gia. You always have a place with us."

"Let's hit the road before traffic builds," Joshua says, nodding at his mom and stepdad as he walks Lise and me to his car. He helps Elisa into her seat as I climb into the passenger seat, and then he climbs behind the wheel.

We wave to his parents as we pull out, driving down the long entrance to the front gates.

Elisa falls asleep after ten minutes, and I lower the music so it doesn't wake her.

"Is she okay?" Joshua asks in a low voice.

"She will be."

"Do I need to kick my brother's ass?"

"Is that a rhetorical question?" I lift my eyes.

"Do you want me to talk to him?"

"And say what? You can't force someone to love."

Joshua glances briefly into the back seat through the mirror. "He loves her. The only women Caleb truly loves are Mom and Elisa. It's because he loves her that he stays away. He knows he's not good enough for her. That he can't give her the things she needs. He's trying to do right by her."

Yeah right. If he knew the things I knew, he wouldn't say that. But Elisa made it clear she doesn't want me or Joshua getting involved. And I think this was the breaking point. I think she's finally ready to move forward with her life, and I'm not doing anything that might cause her to regress. She needs to forget about Caleb Accardi. He's not the one for her.

"It's a moot point now anyway. She's over him." I almost blurt about her date, but that's not my business to share.

Joshua quirks a brow but doesn't question me, and I'm glad.

"I spoke with Ben this morning, and we've had a little breakthrough."

The leather squelches under my butt as I turn to face him. "What kind of breakthrough? Did my plan work?"

His face contorts into a grimace as he signals to move into the left lane. "Unfortunately not. None of the lies we spread were sent out into the community. Somehow, the rats knew it was a trap."

"Well, that sucks."

"It does, but we hired some guys outside the *famiglia* to break into the Irish bar, and they struck gold."

Excitement bubbles up my throat. "What did they find?"

"Paperwork with intelligence reports submitted to Liam from informants inside all our families. We have a list of names now. It's most likely not exhaustive, but it's a good starting point."

"What is The Commission going to do? Will they take them in and interrogate them?"

"I'm heading to a meeting at HQ to discuss it after I drop you and Elisa home, but my guess is we'll leave the guys in situ so we can watch them. We risk exposing ourselves if we round up these men for questioning. Pretending we aren't on to them is probably the smartest course. We'll watch what they are up to and see what extra intel we can glean. It will help to ferret out other spies and rats, and then we can plan an attack on several fronts to take our enemies down."

I stretch my leggings-clad legs out and cross my feet at the ankles. "Will Liam not suspect you know after the break-in?"

He shakes his head. "The guys got in and out without breaking anything or taking anything. They copied all the files, and Philip's team doctored the cameras in the bar, the alleyway, and streets outside, so if anyone looks, nothing will seem suspicious. Liam won't know we know until it's too late."

"What about O'Hara?"

"He's preparing to clean house. We added more names to the dossier we were compiling from your intel on Liam's crew. We have a substantial list now. Diarmuid is going to take them down and restore order within the Irish mafia. We have offered our support, and in return, he will help us defeat the Barone and whomever they're working for and with."

"There are a lot of angles at play and a lot of risk."

"There usually is," he says, taking the exit off the highway.

"Do we have enough manpower? We don't know how many we'll be up against."

"The decision was taken before Christmas to open applications for four new positions on the board. We're going to move fast and add new dons this month so we will have their backing when it's time to draw the enemy out."

"Sounds like you guys have thought of everything." It's reassuring to know they are finally getting ahead of this thing.

"We've had more emergency meetings these past couple of months than the entire two years Caleb and I have been on the board. It's been exhausting, but we work well as a team, and our skillsets complement one another."

"I hope that dynamic doesn't alter too much after the new dons join the board."

"You and me both," he says, heading for the city.

We drop Elisa at her apartment first. We hug, and she promises to let me know how her date with Seb goes. We stop by Joshua's penthouse next because he wants to get changed for his meeting.

I inspect the collection of books in his small living room library annex while he gets dressed. "Damn, you make a suit look good," I say when he emerges from his bedroom wearing a sharp black suit with a deep-blue shirt and a blue, black, and silver tie. "No wonder your brand is one of the most in demand." I slide my hands up his solid chest. "Having you and Caleb as the face of the brand was a stroke of genius. Every man wants to be you, and every woman wants to have you. It's a win-win."

"It doesn't hurt the bottom line, that's for sure."

I nuzzle my face in his neck, inhaling his gorgeous scent. "You smell divine too. Thank fuck you're only meeting men, or I might get jealous."

He tips my chin up with two fingers. "You don't need to be jealous. I'm yours. Only yours."

"I won't ever tire of hearing that."

"Good." He presses a hard kiss to my lips. "Because I'm going nowhere. I'm in this for the long haul, Gia." His eyes probe mine.

"I love you." It feels like the right moment to say it.

His Adam's apple jumps in his throat as shock splays across his face. He stares at me with unnamed emotion flooding his face.

"It's okay," I add, softly stroking his cheeks. "I don't need to hear it in return." I know that is a big step for him, given his past, and I'm fine to work up to it. "I see it in the way you look

240

at me and in the things you do for me. I don't need to hear those words yet."

"I don't think I'm worthy of you." Joshua reels me into his strong arms.

"You are more than worthy."

He releases me with a resigned sigh a minute later. "I wish we didn't have to go, but I'm under pressure."

"It's cool. I know we'll be forced to separate until this is all done. I'm prepared for it." I'll hate it because Joshua is like oxygen to me now, but he's going to be in the city working with The Commission to take our enemies down and reclaim order while I'll be hiding in Greenwich until Liam's no longer a threat.

"I'll fly back as often as I can to see you. Ben will be traveling back and forth, so I'll probably travel with him."

"I'd like that. Is it strange to say I'm already missing you?"

"Not at all. I feel the same." He brushes his lips against mine and takes my hand. "Let's go."

We are waiting for the elevator in the private lobby when the door to Caleb's penthouse opens and someone I loathe appears.

The door snicks shut behind her as she walks toward us. Anais's dark-blonde hair tumbles down her back as she sashays her hips and cocks her head to one side. She's a stunning woman, always dressed immaculately and expensively, but it's all fake. The resemblance to her half-sister is strong, but where Catarina Greco is a natural beauty, her younger sister is like the cheap knockoff version. She's caked in makeup with thick dark brows and bright red lips. Her lips and boobs are surgically enhanced, and her frozen forehead speaks to a Botox obsession.

Her eyes roam over Joshua and I, lingering on his arms around my waist as I lean back against him. Her lips kick up at the corners. "Slumming it again, Joshua?"

"Shut your hideous mouth, Anais, or I'll shut it for you." Joshua isn't holding back but he rarely does when it comes to Mrs. DiPietro. She is not well liked, and that's a universal truth.

"Trying something new?" she asks, fingering my red hair.

"Don't touch me." I snag her wrist and thrust her arm away. "And it's none of your business."

"Red is so tacky, and it really doesn't suit you," she adds as the elevator pings and the doors slide open.

Joshua opens his mouth to retaliate, and I shake my head. "I don't care what she thinks," I say, not lowering my voice, as we walk into the elevator. "Her opinions are as inconsequential as her existence." I turn to face her scowling features as the door shuts and we start moving. "In case that got lost in translation, it means you don't matter."

"How's your little virgin friend? Still pining after something that's mine?" Her haughty laugh grates on my ears, and I have to bite my tongue not to snap at her. There is no point entering into a war of words with her, and I won't lower myself or Elisa to respond to her ridiculous claims.

"Caleb will never be yours," Joshua says, holding me flush against his body as we ride the elevator with the bitch. "Tell yourself whatever delusional bullshit you like, but the cold, hard truth is you're a convenient hole to fuck. That's all."

The doors ping open, and she sidles up to us, pressing her hand on Joshua's chest. I shove her away, baring my teeth and snarling. "I don't think I'm the delusional one, Josh. You might want to look in the mirror." Tossing her hair over her shoulder, she saunters off looking like the cat that got the cream.

"I do not know how Caleb tolerates her. He might deserve a medal," I mumble as we exit the elevator and head toward Joshua's Land Rover.

"She's completely toxic, and I wish he could cut her loose."

"I really fucking hate her. She's been such a bitch to Elisa over the years."

Joshua holds my hand as we walk toward his car. "Probably because she realizes Caleb genuinely cares for Elisa, and she's jealous because he really doesn't give a fuck about her."

"I used to feel a little sorry for her about that until I remembered she's cheating on her husband and she's a complete cunt to my best friend. All my sympathy evaporated then. It's hard to believe she and Catarina are sisters. Cat is so compassionate, caring, and smart, yet Anais is the complete opposite."

Catarina is married to Don Greco, and Massimo and Fiero are best friends, so they are often at Maltese events, and I've gotten to know her over time. She's my hero and one of the few inspirational women within the *mafioso*. It's hard to fathom she and Anais share some of the same DNA.

"Wait up!"

Joshua and I turn around as Caleb comes running toward us.

"What's up?"

"Anais had very interesting intel." He falls into step beside us as we resume walking. "Apparently, Cruz has struck up a friendship with the new Don D'Onofrio in Florida. Been taking weekly trips there for months, and she overheard him arranging flight schedules in and out of Florida."

"Massimo and Fiero felt he was shady when they paid him a visit recently," Joshua says. "You think Cruz and Vitto are in on this?"

"It's beginning to sound like it." Caleb rubs his hands together, and he can barely contain the glee on his face. "We're starting to connect all the puzzle pieces, and when we do, they're all going down."

243

Joshua drops me off around the block from my Brooklyn apartment, shortly before four p.m. Liam is in Ireland, but after claiming ownership of me, it's not inconceivable he'd leave some goons to watch over me. We don't want him finding out I'm part of the *mafioso*. It's better he thinks I've just run in fear. He can't discover who I am because it will risk the entire operation.

"I'm sorry I can't help you to pack," he says as he kills the engine at the curb.

"You can't risk being seen. Besides, you have a meeting to attend."

"Two meetings. Caleb and I have our usual weekly meeting with Benedito and Luca before we need to be at Commission Central."

"You're busy, and that takes priority. I'm more than capable of packing up my things by myself." I lean over and kiss him, loving I get to do it whenever I feel like it.

"The moving van will pull up at the rear entrance, and the guys will use the staff elevator to move your boxes from the apartment. I have a couple of men outside your apartment already. They're your bodyguards until we get you safely back to Greenwich."

"Try not to worry, and be careful," I say, curling my hand around the door handle.

Joshua pulls me back, slamming his lips down on mine in a toe-curling kiss that warms me on the inside. "Watch your back." He slaps a small handgun into my palm. "Keep that on you at all times, and don't hesitate to use it if you need to."

I tuck it into the back of the waistband of my leggings. "Thanks, and I will."

He rubs his thumb along my lips. "Fuck, I hate leaving you." He kisses me quick.

"I'll see you tonight."

He nods. "Text me when you've finished packing, and I'll send the van over and come get you." We're going to spend a couple of nights in the city, attending to everything I need to do, before I relocate to Greenwich and go into hibernation.

"Will do. Now go before you're late to your meeting." I get out and sling my bag over my shoulder, resisting the urge to turn around and blow him a kiss.

I'm on high alert as I walk the quiet streets to the apartment, glancing all around and constantly checking my surroundings. I am close to the apartment when a vehicle comes careening up the road at speed. Tires screech, and I whip my head to the side in time to see a black van hurtling up the road toward me. I'm reaching for the gun when I'm shoved forcefully from behind. Losing my balance, I fall forward, slamming into the sidewalk. The side of my head cracks against the asphalt, and it's instant lights out.

Chapter Thirty
Joshua

"**W**hat's the update on the enemy situation?" Luca asks at the end of our regular weekly meeting.

"That's classified," Caleb says, tossing his key fob in his palm.

Benedito arches a brow. "Even from us?"

"Don't take it personally. No underboss or *consigliere* is privy to that information," I explain. We know we have leaks at the senior level, so we felt it was prudent to keep our plan under wraps for now.

"In other words," Caleb drawls, pinning our underboss Marino with a sharp look. "Stop looking so butthurt."

"It's highly irregular," Luca says. "I can't recall any time when I was acting don that such a decision was taken."

"These are highly irregular circumstances," Caleb says.

"Count yourself lucky you didn't have to deal with something of this magnitude," I tell our cousin.

"I'm getting too old for this anyway." Luca leans back in the chair, patting his rounded stomach. "I want to talk to you about formalizing a plan for Giulio to take over as *consigliere* so I can retire."

"Giulio?" My tone conveys my surprise. "He's a successful Wall Street trader, and he's barely got one foot in our world. Why on earth would you propose Giulio over your other sons?"

"He's the smartest, and he's one of your closest friends. There is an established relationship there."

"He won't want it," Caleb says.

"It's not a choice," Luca replies. "And he will do it if I ask it of him. He has always known he might be called upon."

This is where The Commission's reluctance to impose stricter rules falls short for some men. Our new laws state no one *should* be forced into initiation and servitude, but we can't legislate for their fathers. The board is loath to step in and over-rule any father, so all we can do is tell them we don't expect succession even if we value it.

Caleb and I exchange a look. Giulio has never expressed such desires to either of us.

"We have to park that for now, Luca. The priority is dealing with this threat. Then we can discuss succession."

"I just wanted to put it on your radar."

"We're aware and not opposed to it." I speak on behalf of my brother as I know he won't object. Giulio is a good guy. Whip-smart and focused. It won't take him long to get up to speed, should he decide he wants to do this. Though I don't care what Luca thinks. I won't force any man into a position they don't want. We need someone who is all in. There can be no half measure.

"We've got to go." Caleb rises to his feet.

"Was there anything else?" I ask, pocketing my cell and standing.

Both men shake their heads, and the four of us exit the conference room together.

It's eerily quiet walking the hallways of the Accardi Company as we make our way toward the underground parking lot. We're only operating a skeleton staff today with most employees still on vacation leave for the holidays. It's one of the changes Caleb and I made when we took over the business. Mom said family time is sacred and facilitating vacation time would endear loyalty within the employee base. So we increased the number of vacation days, staggering it in accordance with length of service, and made it so the business can operate at a basic level, at key times during the year, so we don't need all hands on deck during busy holiday periods.

We make small talk in the elevator as we descend to the underground parking lot.

Our shoes slap off the asphalt, and our voices bounce off the concrete pillars as we walk toward our cars. There are barely any vehicles in the lot today, and it's also eerily quiet down here. All the fine hairs lift on the back of my neck for some inexplicable reason I know not to ignore. I reach for my gun the same time Caleb does.

"Get down," Marino shouts, shoving me to the ground and covering my body as a bullet whizzes over us.

"No, Caleb!" Luca roars as I push our underboss off me and spin around with my gun raised, scanning the area for the threat. I turn around in time to watch Luca take three bullets to the chest that were meant for Caleb.

Caleb emits an ear-shattering roar as he holds our cousin upright when he loses control of his body. I fire at the two assailants hovering by a pillar in the corner while I pull out my cell and send an SOS message. Benedito is moaning on the ground at my feet. Shots are fired back as I drag Marino behind a car, and Caleb places our seriously injured cousin on the ground beside him.

"Watch him," Caleb barks at Marino before dashing to his

car. Our underboss is clutching his shoulder with blood trickling through his fingers, but I doubt it's serious.

"I called it in. Help is on the way," I say, straightening up and firing in the direction of the two men, but they're no longer there. "They're getting away!" I yell.

"Not on our fucking watch." Caleb hands me a rifle and nods.

"Keep him alive," I tell Marino, hating to leave Luca bleeding out on the ground, but we can't let the men who did this get away.

I ditch my jacket and take off running with my twin after the men. We jump down to the lower level when we hear a car starting up. "Take the left. I'll take the right," Caleb yells, and I duck behind a pillar on the right as he does the same on the left. The car is approaching at speed, and the guy in the passenger seat is firing out the side window at us.

I take aim at the windshield as Caleb shoots out the front left tire and then the right. The car spins out of control, crashing into a side wall with a deafening screech. The scrunched hood pops open, obstructing our view as we approach. Steam billows from the open hood, and glass crunches underfoot as we approach cautiously with our guns raised.

"Don't move!" Caleb calls out when the driver's side door pops open, training his weapon on the guy behind the wheel. "Fuck!" my brother yells racing to the man slumped half in and half out of the car. "Fuck, fuck, fuck." Caleb slams the butt of his rifle down repeatedly on the top of the car as I round my side, still keeping my gun poised and ready even though I suspect it's too late.

I lower my weapon when I see the two dead men in the car, froth bubbling in their mouth and a cherry-red color on their skin.

"Cyanide pills," Caleb surmises, and I nod, pulling out my cell and placing another text for a cleanup. We search the men's pockets, grabbing their wallets and cell phones. Then we search the car, but there's nothing of use.

"Come on. We need to check on Luca."

We run back upstairs, but we're too late.

"He's gone," Marino says, cradling Luca's head in his lap. "I tried CPR, but it didn't work. He died in my arms."

Caleb drops to his knees, a muscle popping in his jaw. "He died protecting me."

"He died with honor," I say. "He'd be happy about that." I clamp a hand on my twin's shoulder as we stare at the dead body of our *consigliere*, our cousin, our family. He didn't deserve to go out like this.

Caleb's cell rings, and he snaps out of it, standing and answering in a clipped voice. His jaw pulls tight with anger at whatever he's hearing. "Is he okay?" Caleb looks at me. "We were targeted too. No, no, fuck, don't tell Mom. We're both fine." He looks to the ceiling, rolling his neck from side to side. "We'll take the necessary precautions, I promise." He clears his throat. "Luca didn't make it. He took the bullets meant for me. The stubborn fucker wasn't wearing a vest, and I am." He barks out a bitter laugh. "He died for nothing."

"How's the shoulder?" I ask Marino as he places Luca down on the ground. I grab my jacket off the hood of the car and drape it over my cousin's face and upper body.

"It's not deep, and I don't think the bullet embedded."

"Get it checked out," I say as a medical team van appears in my peripheral vision, heading toward us. Thank fuck Mom wasn't on duty today. She shouldn't have to see this. She will be upset. She was fond of Luca.

"What happened?" I ask when Caleb hangs up his phone.

"Rowan was targeted too." My eyes pop wide in shock, and

I'm opening my mouth to ask a question when he answers it. "He's fine. Not even a scratch. His bodyguards shielded him. One of them died at the scene, and the other is in emergency surgery but expected to pull through. It happened at the high school, and it's a major shit show with cops and the media involved."

Marino scowls. "This reeks of amateur hour. Who the fuck did this and why?"

The next couple of hours are spent holed up in HQ making plans. Ben is livid, threatening to annihilate every fucking made man until he finds out who tried to murder his son and his nephews. It's been decided all the kids under eighteen will be homeschooled for now, and unless it's essential, the women are being asked to stay at home with beefed-up security details. None of us can do what we need to do if we're worrying about our loved ones.

"Rowan is initiating," Ben says just as I pull out my cell to call Gia and check in with her.

"I thought he was undecided," Cristian says.

"He was, but today proved he is safer in than out."

In the olden days, no kid of a *mafioso* had a choice. Especially not a kid of a don. But Ben gave his children choices and made it clear that any kids growing up within the Mazzone *famiglia* should be given a choice. He left it up to the individual families to decide. Eighty percent of all kids born into our communities join the fold, and they are there by choice, not through fear or force. It means less numbers joining the ranks, but they are more committed.

Rowan is Ben's legitimate heir, but he didn't want to initiate at thirteen, and he's been very much on the fence ever since. He has spoken to Caleb and me at length about it, but neither of us wanted to influence him. We grew up expecting this to be our destiny because it's what our father wanted, but we wanted it too. I like being a made man, and my conscience is clear.

"It's sad he's being forced to make the decision before he was fully ready, but it's a smart move. I often think it's more dangerous to have one foot in and one foot out," I say, and it reminds me of what Luca said at the end of our meeting today. "We need to talk to Giulio, and we need to go see the family."

Caleb nods.

I look up the table at Massimo. "Can we take a break? I want to call Gia too."

"Let's recess for twenty minutes," he agrees.

"I'll call Giulio. You call Gia," my twin says, and we walk out of the room and into one of the side rooms to make our calls.

I frown when I call Gia on her personal cell and her burner cell and both go to voicemail. I try again, attempting to convince myself she's in the shower or listening to music while she's packing, and she hasn't checked her phones. I call again, over and over, but they keep going straight to voicemail. Apprehension lingering in the wings swamps my system, and I'm in instant panic mode.

Something is wrong.

I feel it in my gut.

I hit the button for the surveillance team and try to summon patience while I wait for someone to answer. "Pick up the fucking phone!" I snap, and Caleb lifts his head, his brow puckering as he stares at me. I'm pacing the floor and trying to get a grip on my emotions, but I'm struggling.

"Boss. Hey," someone says, finally picking up my call.

"Where is she?" I bark. "Where is Gia?"

"Uh, she's at home, boss. In her apartment."

"Then why isn't she answering her cell phones? Check again."

I hear the tap-tapping of keys as he calls up the system. Caleb is talking in hushed tones over the phone with Giulio while keeping a concerned eye on me.

"She's at the Brooklyn apartment, sir. I sent the screenshot to your cell."

"Check her cell phones. Where do they place her?"

He taps away again. "Same, sir. They put her at the same location."

"Okay." Maybe I am overreacting and she's showering. "Keep me posted if she records or if anything changes with her location." I hang up and call one of the men I have stationed outside her apartment. He answers immediately. At least someone is on the ball.

"Don Accardi."

"Knock on the door and ask Ms. Bianchi to answer her phone."

Stunned silence greets me for a couple seconds. "Um, she's not at home, sir."

"What do you mean she's not at home? I dropped her off around the block hours ago."

"She hasn't been here. No one has in the six hours we've been outside her door."

What the actual fuck is going on? "Bust the door open and check."

I grab fistfuls of my hair as I pace the floor, trying and failing not to panic. A loud crash filters through the line, followed by stomping feet.

"She's not here, sir. We've checked every room."

"Call me if she shows up," I say and hang up.

"Fuck." I swipe all the bottles of sparkling water on the desk to the floor in a fit of rage.

Caleb ends his call and comes to me. He grips my shoulder. "What is it?"

"Gia is missing, but her cellphones and her tracker shows she's at home. What the fuck are we missing, Caleb? What the fuck is going on, and how am I going to find her?"

"Calm down." He squeezes my shoulder. "You're no use to Gia like this. Lock down your emotions. Shut them off, and go into professional mode. We'll find her. It's got to be Liam. We'll start there."

The door opens, and Massimo and Ben burst into the room. They glance at the shattered glass and wet carpet before turning to look at us.

"Gia is missing," Caleb tells them.

"I dropped her off hours ago, but she never made it to the apartment. She hasn't activated the recording device, and her tracker and cell phones show her location as the apartment," I explain, working hard to do as Caleb suggests because it's good advice.

"Fuck." Massimo covers his mouth.

"They found a way to mess with the trackers," Ben says, reaching the same conclusion as me.

"That's why they removed them from the dead bodies. They reverse engineered our chips," I say. "That's how their men are hiding in plain sight. They are fixing their locations as they move freely around, doing who the hell knows what, and we're none the wiser."

"This has Liam's fingerprints all over it. He must have gotten intel she's one of us," Cristian says, listening out in the hallway with Fiero.

"Or he's discovered she's your woman," Massimo says.

"We need to find her, but how?"

"Let's go back inside and brainstorm. There has to be another way we can trace her location."

The mood is heavy as we head back into the conference room. We've all just claimed our seats when my cell rings with a call from the surveillance team. I put it on speaker phone. "Do you have news?"

"The recording device has been activated," the man says, his voice spiking with clear terror. "She used the codeword, boss. She's in serious trouble, and she needs our help."

Chapter Thirty-One
Gia

"Wakey, wakey, whore." A stinging pain rips across one cheek and then the other as I slowly come to. Stabbing pain pounds in my skull, and my arms ache. I yelp as ice-cold water is thrown over my head, drops clinging to my lashes as I open my eyes. All the blood drains from my face when I stare into a pair of familiar cold blue eyes.

I am royally screwed, so I figure I have nothing to lose by faking confusion.

Glancing down, I see I'm strapped to a chair with my ankles bound to the legs and my wrists tied behind the back. I can't even activate my earrings or reach my watch to press the panic button. "Baby, what's going on?"

My eyes dart left and right, scanning the large derelict warehouse. A few crates are stacked high against the far wall, and a bunch of fold-up chairs are propped against an old laminate-covered table that's seen better days. Piles of old newspapers and empty bottles and beer cans roll along the debris-strewn ground. Overhead lights provide scant illumination, but I see enough to know I'm in serious danger.

I might not make it out of this alive.

Shoving those thoughts aside because they won't help me survive, I focus on keeping calm and alert.

Another slap to the face whips my head around. "What's going on is you lied to me, Emma. Or should I call you *Gia* now? You lying, treacherous cunt!" His eyes flare with anger as he grabs my crotch through my leggings and squeezes tight. Behind him, a few chuckles ring out, and I stare straight ahead, noticing the same group of men from the basement that night with three others I recognize from the bar.

"I don't know what you're talking about! You're mistaking me for someone else! Why are you doing this, Liam?"

"Don't. Fucking. Lie." He slams his fist into my stomach, and I struggle to breathe, gasping when I can't suck enough air into my lungs.

"You drugged me, you fucking cunt!" Spittle flies from his lips as he yanks my head back. He thrusts a few blurry images in my face—still shots of me rummaging through his apartment —and I know the game is definitely up. "You think you could snoop, and I wouldn't know?"

"You got cameras installed at your place." I checked for cameras and didn't find any, but it's the only logical explanation. Rolling my shoulders, I wince as pain radiates from the top of my arm up over my shoulder. My left arm throbs like a bitch, and I glance briefly at it, forcing panic back down my throat when it threatens to erupt. The arm of my sweater is gone, and dried blood clings to my skin from the wound on top where they hacked out my tracking chip.

"Got them installed a few days before you came over that last time because I already had my suspicions. Mazzone isn't the only one capable of getting his hands on high-tech proto-types. These cameras have an anti-detection layer, so your pitiful attempt to locate them failed."

The gloves are off now, and I let my anger take control. "Then I guess you already know I loathe you. You're scum of the earth, Liam McDermott, and your puny cock never once turned me on. You're the defective one, and you're going to get what's coming to you."

"Fucking whore," he yells, coming at me with venom spewing from his lips and his eyes. He goes to town on my face, punching and slapping me, and I regret my reckless outburst even if it felt so good to say it.

"I thought you wanted to have your fun with her first and record it to send to him," someone says, and the words get through to him. Liam stops whaling on my face, looking at me with derision.

"How I ever thought you were perfect is beyond me. Everything about you is fake." He grabs my chest and squeezes. "Except your tits. I might have to take these as a souvenir." He lets go of my breasts to rub my hair between his fingers. "Was this for me? Was it your idea or that asshole Accardi's?"

I attempt to glare at him through my good eye. The other is swollen and sore, and I can only half see out of it. Blood drips from my nose, over my mouth and chin. "Fuck. You."

"Oh, you'll get your wish, sweetheart. I promise we'll get to the fun part soon."

Bile travels up my throat, but I shut my emotions down and concentrate on loosening the rope binding my hands without making discernible movements. Whoever tied it didn't tie it very tight.

"You're going to die, Gia." He spits my name out like it's poison. "No one tricks me and lives to tell the tale. When I'm

Siobhan Davis

done with you, I'm going to rip your heart from your chest and send it to Don Accardi in a box with a big shiny bow."

"It will only sign your death warrant. You and everyone you care about," I say, continuing to unknot the rope at my hands. It's coming away easily, and I'll be free soon.

"Keeping her alive surely makes more sense," the same brave idiot says from the back. He's one of the men from the bar. "You can use her to barter with Accardi. She's more valuable alive than dead."

Liam is suitably incensed, and he turns to face the man who surely has a death wish. "Name, soldier," he barks.

Briefly, I wonder if he is one of O'Hara's spies. Did he bind my hands and wrists and purposely leave them loose?

"Hennessy, sir." The man straightens up as Liam approaches.

All eyes swing toward the oncoming confrontation, and I slip my hands free, holding the rope between my palms until I'm ready to let go of it. I wrap one hand around my wrist to press the alert button on my watch, but it's missing. I look down at my neck, cursing when I notice my necklace is gone too. I can't risk touching my ears to see if my earrings are still intact, but I fucking pray they are because it's the only slim chance I have of getting out of this alive.

"Well, Hennessy, who the fuck gave you the impression you could tell me what to do?" Liam squares off with him.

"It was only a suggestion, sir. I've heard Accardi is serious about her. She's good leverage is all."

"But is that all?" Liam tips his head to the side, inspecting the man like he's a science experiment. The remaining men form a line behind Liam, facing Hennessy. "Are you loyal to me or my brother?"

Hennessy's eyes drill into me with silent warning, and I'm sure now he's trying to help me.

260

"You, sir. My father was one of your father's most senior *capos*. I was at your house for dinner several times when we were younger. We even played Monopoly together a time or two."

"Is there a point to this fascinating stroll down Memory Lane?" Liam drawls.

Yes. He's distracting you so I can get free! None of the men are watching me, so I take a calculated risk and free my hands, tossing the rope off to one side as I get to work on removing the bindings around my ankles.

"Just that I have known you since we were boys, and it's an honor to watch you grow into this role and an honor to serve you. You deserve to be in charge, not O'Hara. It's your legacy. Your birthright."

"Is that so, soldier?" Liam pushes right up into his face. "Phone."

"What?" Hennessy blinks.

"Hand over your phone."

"Why?"

Liam punches him in the face, and the man drops to his knees just as I've unwound the last rope. "Because I said so, fuckface."

I look frantically around for a way out other than the front of the building, rejoicing when I spot a small side door a few feet behind me. I wonder if Hennessy positioned the chair here so I could escape?

"Here ya go," Hennessy says, throwing the cell at Liam. In the same instant, he slides a gun across the floor toward me and pulls out another gun he points at Liam. "Run, Gia," he yells as all hell breaks loose.

I don't need to be told twice.

I dart forward and swipe the gun before ducking down as bullets whizz over my head.

"I want her alive!" Liam yells as gunfire rings out in the warehouse.

I don't stop to look, racing toward the door and fleeing into the darkness outside.

I'm slammed back against the wall of the warehouse by a snarling man with a bald head and a straggly beard. "Where'd you think you're going?"

"Home," I snarl, bringing my knee up and burying it between his legs. He goes down like a sack of potatoes, but it won't hold him for long. "Sorry not sorry," I say as I lift my gun and fire. "Fuck, ow," I hiss, only now noticing the prick stuck me with a needle just before I put a bullet in his skull. I yank it out, paling at the clear liquid that is almost gone. That cannot be good, and I need to get out of here.

I take off running, fleeing toward the lights in the far distance. It's pitch-black with no streetlamps guiding my way, but I recognize the boardwalk ahead of me, confirming I'm back in Atlantic City. Reaching up, I touch my ears, almost crying in relief when I feel my earrings. I press down on them and repeat my codeword. "Dancer, dancer, dancer. I'm in Atlantic City, on the northern end, but I'm heading toward the boardwalk."

A shot flies by my side, and I scream, pushing my limbs harder. My breath oozes out in panicked spurts at the sound of approaching footfalls. There is nothing but grass all around me and the ocean on my left as I run. There is no one to run to for help and nowhere to hide. Although it's dark, I'm still exposed and outnumbered. Maybe my best bet is the ocean. I'm a good swimmer, and maybe they won't be inclined to chase after me if I'm in the water. So, I detour left and head in that direction.

"It was Liam," I say, keeping my voice low. Liam doesn't seem to be aware of the audio device, and I want to keep it that way. I glance briefly over my shoulder, spotting several shadows advancing on me, and I know I can't outrun them, so I turn around and fire off a few shots, buying myself a little more time to reach the water and to explain. "He knows who I am, and he knows who I am to Joshua. He's planning to kill me. One of O'Hara's men helped me to escape, and he paid with his life. I might not make it." I stumble a little as my legs turn to Jell-O. "I was injected with something. I don't feel too hot," I add as nausea churns in my gut. "Tell my family and Joshua I love them."

Tremors wash over me, and I sway on my feet as they threaten to go out from under me. I push my failing body forward, stumbling and almost tripping over my feet as my vision blurs and my limbs give out. Footsteps approach as I collapse on the ground, only a few feet from the water. My body shakes as nausea swims up my throat and drowsiness consumes me. I attempt to drag my body forward on the ground toward the ocean, but it refuses to cooperate. "I love you, Joshua," I whisper as the shadows approach. "You make me really happy."

"Fucking bitch!" Liam kicks me in the ribs, and a sleepy cry flees from my lips.

"Boss, they know where we are," someone says as I fight to stay with it. "Hennessy texted our location. We've got to assume they're on their way."

"Joshua," I mumble.

Liam emits a furious rage-filled shout as men surround me. They're all a blur, and I can't see properly.

"Guess we're going with Plan B," he says in a calculated voice as he leans down and begins ripping my clothes away.

I will my limbs to cooperate as I try to slap him away, but my body is hijacked under whatever drug is infiltrating my bloodstream.

"Fuck. I just came in my pants looking at those tits."

Laughter surrounds me, and I'm drifting in and out as

hands grope me everywhere. I open my mouth to tell them to stop, but my mouth won't cooperate now, and I'm silently screaming as my legs are pried open and pain shoots through me. I'm barely conscious as someone pounds into me and fingers dig into my flesh.

I drift in and out of consciousness.

"You promised us a turn," an angry man says.

"Plans change," Liam hisses. "But if anyone wants to risk getting caught for some mediocre pussy, go for it."

"I've got a better idea," someone says, and I hear the telltale sound of a zipper lowering. Laughter ensues as warm liquid flows over my body.

I barely feel it when they kick and punch me, but I push through the barrier, screaming and screaming when intense pain bears down on my arm.

Then I black out.

I wake with a jolt as freezing-cold tentacles poke at my flesh. My entire body is shaking, and my teeth are chattering. My eyelids refuse to open. For a few seconds, I don't remember anything, and then it all comes back to me. My eyes pop open as the most excruciating pain flays me everywhere. I throw up, retching as my battered body is bathed in ice-cold water. I blink my eyes repeatedly, trying to adjust to the darkness, to get some clue on my whereabouts, when another wave of freezing water laps at my chest.

"Fuck." The word comes out garbled, but at least my tongue appears to be working again. I'm shivering and in incredible pain. It's hard to remain conscious, but I push through because I know this is life or death. I have no clue how much time has passed since I blacked out and no way of knowing if Joshua has come and can't find me.

My gaze roams over the darkness before me, making out wooden boards and a few scant lights in the distance, bobbing on the water. It takes great effort to lift my head from the cold stone I'm lying on, but I do it after several tries. The rest of my body is still numb, and my hands and legs are bound so tight they're restricting blood flow. I can't move from this ledge, not even when I see the wave coming for me this time.

I brace myself, closing my eyes and whimpering as the wave crashes into me.

This is bad. So bad.

"Joshua." I pray my words are decipherable. "Under board-walk. Ledge. Tide."

I repeat the same words over and over as I'm battered by the rising tide and shivering all over. Drowsiness comes to claim me again, and I fight it, but it's too much. I'm just drifting away when I hear my name being called from above. "Joshua," I croak. My words sound clearer even with the noticeable trembling, confirming the drug is working its way out of my system. "I'm under the boardwalk. On a ledge, and the tide is coming in. I don't have long."

"Gia!" The sound of his voice is like music to my ears. He's getting closer.

"Joshua!" I try to shout, but I have no power in my voice. "I can hear him. He's close," I tell whoever is listening. I'm assuming they are talking to Joshua.

"Gia, where are you? Scream, honey. As loud as you can."

I summon whatever strength I have left and scream as loud as I can.

"Over here," someone says.

I cower as bright light rains down on me from above. "She's

here!" someone with an unfamiliar voice says, and inside I'm crying tears of joy.

"Gia. I'm here." He leans over the edge, peering at me with equal measures of concern and relief in his eyes.

"Joshua." Tears leak down my face.

"Hold tight. I'm coming to get you."

Chapter Thirty-Two
Joshua

"How is she? Does she need to be at the hospital? What can I do?" I ask Mom when she finally emerges from my bedroom where she's been attending to Gia for the past hour with a nurse and another doctor.

"Breathe, Joshua." Mom pulls me into a hug. "Gia is sleeping now, and she's in good hands. We'll take very good care of her. Try not to worry too much."

"Mom," I croak, clinging to her like I used to when I was a little kid. "Will she be okay?"

She holds my face in her hands. "Gia is strong. She'll get through this, but she's going to need time to heal." Tears well in her eyes. "She has scars on the inside as well as the outside."

"I'm going to gut that motherfucker until even his own mother won't recognize him." Pain slays me all over as I recall being in the helicopter en route to A.C. and hearing that sick fuck force himself on her while his men cheered him on.

"Good. He deserves to die a slow and painful death for what he did to her." Her voice cracks as she removes her medical hat and puts her motherly one on. "Has Caleb found him yet?"

My brother took a large team, and they're searching for Liam as we speak. I wanted to go with him, but I need to be here for Gia. Caleb will find him and keep him for us to deal with. Though I'm not sure if Gia will want to see the prick again. Either way, it'll be her decision to make.

I shake my head. "No. They ransacked his apartment and the bar, but he wasn't there. He appears to have ditched his cell, and O'Hara has no clue where he could have gone. He's in the wind, but he can't have gotten too far. Philip called the entire IT team in from their holiday break, and they're combing through camera footage in the area. He'll surface, and when he does, we'll grab him."

"You should be checked out. Your brother too." Worry fills her eyes. We called Leo shortly after leaving Commission Central, asking him to tell Mom what had gone down so she and my stepdad could visit Luca's family and relay the bad news. Giulio knew something was up after Caleb's call, and we couldn't leave him hanging.

"I'm fine, Mom. Not a scratch. Benedito and Luca took the fall."

"Poor Luca. Poor Maria. She's inconsolable. All the kids are too."

"I'll bet."

"Does it bring back bad memories for you?" She caresses my cheek.

"Not really. I'm more concerned about Gia. She's all I can think about right now."

"I'm worried about her too. She begged me not to call her mom yet. She doesn't want her family to see her like this. I didn't want to agree, but I had to because she was stressing herself out and causing herself more pain. But it doesn't sit right with me. Frankie is my best friend, and she'll be beside herself with worry when she finds out."

"Gia won't go long without telling her family, and Frankie will be reassured to know you've been taking care of her."

"I'm going to stay over for a couple of nights if that's okay?"

"Of course. I'm hoping Gia will want to stay here where I can properly protect her, but she might want to go home."

"I'll go wherever she goes. No one else is taking care of my future daughter-in-law."

I don't contest it or confirm it, but Mom smiles all the same. "How much of it does she remember?" I ask, taking Mom's hands in mine.

"She was still quite disorientated, so it's hard to tell yet. I hope for her sake she doesn't remember much."

I nod in agreement.

"We've taken a blood sample to test for drugs, but my guess is she was given GHB."

I squeeze my eyes closed and count to ten as pain lashes me from all angles again.

"You love her."

My eyes open. "I haven't told her." I wanted to when she said those three little words, but I couldn't. "It's my biggest regret."

"You will have time to tell her." Mom squeezes my hand. "She's going to need all our love and support to overcome this."

"Whatever she needs, she's got it." I wet my dry lips as my stomach rumbles, reminding me I haven't eaten since lunch and it's now after three a.m. "How bad are her injuries?"

"She had mild hypothermia when we found her, but her body temperature has returned to normal now, thank God. She has two broken ribs, a concussion, lacerations, cuts, and grazes to her entire body. And..." Tears flood her eyes again. "There's some internal tearing."

I want to pound that motherfucker until he stops breathing, then bring him back to life, and do it all over again.

"I failed her," I croak. "I promised to keep her safe, and I failed to protect her."

"No, absolutely not." Mom vigorously shakes her head. "You are not doing that. This is *not* your fault, Joshua. The only person responsible is that soon-to-be-dead Irish prick. It's not Gia's fault, and it's not yours." She squeezes my cheeks, forcing my gaze to hers. "She's alive because of the protections you put in place that enabled you to find her in time, and it could have been a lot worse. Gia is alive, Joshua, and she will heal and get over this. That's what you need to concentrate on. Not beating yourself up for failures that are not yours."

"It's easier said than done."

"It's as easy as you let it be. Push those thoughts from your mind, and focus on loving Gia and helping her recover."

"I saw what he did to her arm." I grind my teeth to the molars, like I did when I lifted her off that ledge and saw his name carved into her left arm. It was a bloody mess, and it's going to scar.

"He will rot in hell for that." She cups one cheek. "She can opt for a skin graft and plastic surgery to have it removed."

"Is she in a lot of pain?"

"She was, but we've given her morphine, and to answer your earlier question, we can care for her here better than at a hospital. It's safer too."

"Thanks, Mom." I bundle her into my arms and press a kiss to the top of her head. "Thanks for being here."

"You know I already consider Gia a daughter. I wouldn't have let anyone else take care of her."

"How is Rowan doing? And did his bodyguard make it?"

"He is shaken but unharmed, and his bodyguard made it through surgery. He'll pull through."

"Good, I'm glad." My stomach rumbles loudly.

"Come." Mom loops her arm through mine. "I'll make you a grilled cheese and hot chocolate like old times."

"I'm not five anymore, Mom."

"I'm well aware, but indulge me. Today's been a trying day."

We make grilled cheese sandwiches side by side, and Caleb shows up at the perfect moment just as we've plated a mountain of sandwiches and a jug of hot chocolate. We sit around my table, talking in low tones, as we eat and drink, and it reminds me of the past. When Mom would be waiting up after we got back from some bloody mission or a late-night party with sandwiches, apple cake, and hot chocolate.

"All we're missing is your apple cake," Caleb says, confirming our twin bond is still alive and kicking.

"I'll give you a list for the grocery store tomorrow, and I'll bake a cake for you."

"You're the best." He leans over and hugs her. "It's late. You should grab some sleep."

"I'll just clean up here and check with the night nurse."

"Go. We'll clean up," I say, kissing her cheek.

"You can sleep beside her if you like. It would be good for you to be there when she wakes."

"I was planning to."

"The nurse will be in and out to check her vitals during the night, so I suggest you don't sleep nude."

"Gross," Caleb mutters, like he's some innocent altar boy.

Mom giggles. "Night, my loves."

"Night, Mom." We take turns hugging her, gathering up the plates and cups when she walks off to check on Gia before turning in.

"Update me," I say as Caleb and I wash and dry dishes side

by side. We could put them in the dishwasher, but I find it therapeutic washing dishes sometimes.

"There's no sign of him. It's like the prick vanished into thin air."

"It's possible he was collected by a chopper and he's on a private jet halfway around the world by now."

"I don't care how long it takes, but we're finding that motherfucker and making him pay."

"He hurt her, Caleb. He really hurt her." I pass him a wet plate.

"I saw the state she was in. He's a monster." He dries the plate and puts it away.

"I should never have left her side, or I should have sent someone to her place to pack up her stuff. I should never have taken her back to the city. I—"

"Stop, brother. Stop." He takes the last plate from my hand and dries it, putting it away as I drain the sink. "There is no point looking at all the what-ifs or should-haves. You can't turn back the clock, and torturing yourself isn't going to do anyone any good. Focus on caring for Gia and helping us to bury these assholes who dare to take potshots at us, our cousin, and your girl. Store all that frustration to use on our enemy." He dries his hands and pulls me into a hug. "Let's hit the gym tomorrow at some stage."

"I'm not leaving her side. Ever again."

"That might be awkward when she needs to shit."

"Jesus. Do you always have to lower the tone?"

"Just keeping it real, broski." He flashes me a grin that quickly fades. "Let me know what I can do to help, and it's yours."

"I might need you to attend the weekly board meetings at the company for the next while unless I can call in."

"I don't see how you can't work remotely from here for as

long as you need to. And if you want me to attend an in-person meeting, I'm there."

"I spoke with Massimo on my way home. He's ready to take the fight to the Barone and whomever is pulling their strings. He wants us to devise a plan to draw them out, and we'll attack. He's sent some men to Florida to spy on D'Onofrio, and he's proposing we accelerate adding the new board members so we have more manpower to bolster our ranks."

"Good. I'm done talking about this. We have enough information now to go on the offensive." He yawns and rubs at his eyes. "There's a meeting tomorrow to draw up plans. You can pass, and I'll fill you in later or else call in. Massimo said it was your choice."

"I'll let you know tomorrow."

"Get some sleep. You look beat."

"Thanks, Caleb. For having my back tonight and for going after him when I couldn't."

"You'd do the same for me."

"In a heartbeat."

"Look after your woman. We'll talk in the morning."

The nurse is coming out of my bedroom when I approach. "She's still sleeping, but all her vitals look good, Don Accardi."

"Thank you, Lucille, and please call me Joshua."

"She's a fighter. Try not to worry. Good night, Joshua." The older woman pats my arm as she moves out to the living room.

I slip into my room and stare at my love, hating to see her so battered and bruised. Lighting is low with only one table lamp turned on, but I can see still the damage that bastard inflicted. Her face is swollen and almost unrecognizable. One eye is almost completely shut. And there is heavy bruising and grazed skin on her right temple and cheek. Her lips are cracked, and fingertip marks are evident around her throat. A large bandage covers the mess he left of her arm, and I imagine her ribs are strapped up under the blue nightdress Mom dressed her in. I just want to cocoon her in my arms and wrap her in cotton wool so no one can hurt her ever again.

I grab a quick shower and dry off in the en suite bathroom before pulling on cotton pajama pants and a white T-shirt.

I ease under the covers beside Gia very slowly and quietly so I don't wake her. Although I want to pull her into my body and hold her close, I resist, knowing it could wake her and she's in pain. She also has a drip in one arm, hooked up to a machine. Turning on my side, I look at her, my heart so full of love it feels like it might burst.

I almost lost her tonight, and it put so much into perspective.

I need to tell her I love her so she never doubts it.

And as soon as the time is right, I'm proposing.

We may not have been a couple for long, but when you know, you know.

Gia is the one, and some day, soon if I have my way, she will be my wife.

Chapter Thirty-Three
Gia

I wake a few times during the night when the nurse comes to top up my medication, but I'm barely conscious. It's only when I fully wake the next morning I become aware of Joshua sleeping beside me. His hand is extended toward me in slumber, but he's too far away, and I need his arms around me.

It hurts when I move, and I have to be careful with the drip in my arm, but I scoot sideways on the bed, ignoring my pain in a bid to get closer to him. His eyes pop open with the movement of the bed. "Hey," I whisper in a hoarse voice, setting my hand on his T-shirt- clad chest. My vision is blurry in my swollen eye, but I can see him clearly with my other.

"Gia." Emotion swims in his eyes. "I thought I'd lost you."

"Can't get rid of me that easily," I tease.

"Don't joke. You nearly died last night, Gia. If I hadn't made it in time, I—"

I press my fingers over his lips to stop him. "But you did. You saved me, Joshua. We're both alive, and that's what we should focus on." My eyes narrow as the events of last night

275

replay in my head. "Please tell me you got him. Please tell me he's in your bunker waiting for me to torture and kill him?"

"I wish I could, but he's in the wind. Caleb took a team, and they combed the area for hours, but just like the night they stole the drug shipment, it's as if he's vanished into thin air."

"What about O'Hara's man? Did you find his body."

He nods. "He was at the warehouse, riddled with bullets. Diarmuid took possession of his body last night, and they'll give him *a good send-off*. His words."

"I want to attend his funeral. He died so I could escape."

"We'll both go. I'll get the details." His gaze rakes over me. "How much pain are you in?"

I attempt to shrug, wincing as pain shuttles through me. "A fair bit," I truthfully admit because Joshua won't accept anything less. "It might be time for more pain medication."

"I'll get the nurse."

"Don't go." I hold on to his arm. "I have a button."

"Don't move." Sitting up, he reaches over me to press it.

"Come back here. I need you to hold me."

"I don't want to hurt you."

"You won't. You never could."

Very gently, he repositions us so I'm cradled against his chest and his arms are around me. He's careful not to squeeze too tight. "I thought I'd never see you or my family again."

"I had access to the audio feed. I heard everything you said. You were so fucking brave, honey. So strong." He dots kisses into my hair as the nurse enters the room.

We stop talking while she asks me some questions, checks my injuries, and then tops up my medication. I ask her not to give me too much as I want to stay awake.

I peek up at Joshua and spot the forlorn expression on his face. "What's that look for?"

He presses his lips against mine in a barely there kiss. "I'm so sorry, Gia. I promised I'd protect you. I swore nothing was going to happen to you on my watch, and it did."

"It's not your fault. I shouldn't have believed Liam when he told me he was in Ireland until January. We were both a little too careless, but it's ultimately not either of our faults. He was always going to get me, babe. What's important is he failed."

"O'Hara has already rounded up those who were working with his brother. Well, those who are still here. We have to assume Liam left with a crew and they've gone to their allies. The board is going over there to interrogate them with Diarmuid shortly. Hopefully, we'll get some useful intel."

"You're leaving?" I hate how pathetic I sound.

He shakes his head. "I'm going nowhere, honey. I'm staying right by your side, whether that's here or at your parents' place or Mom and Leo's. I've already arranged it so I can work remotely for the time being. I'm not leaving you until Liam is caught and our enemies are defeated. I won't risk you again. I can't." He presses a soft kiss to my lips again before peering deep into my eyes. "I love you, Gia. I love you so much. Almost losing you put everything into perspective. You almost died without knowing that, and it was unbearable."

"I knew, Joshua." I press a kiss to the underside of his jaw. "But I appreciate hearing it." I can't keep the smile off my face even if it hurts to do it. "Not sure it's easy to love me when I look like something Frankenstein cooked up!" I quip, attempting to lighten the mood. Or maybe it's the medication flowing through my veins that is responsible for the sense of contentment I currently feel. Which is probably a weird thing to say after the ordeal I've endured, but that's how I'm feeling right now.

"You're still your beautiful self." He places his hand carefully on my chest. "It's your soul, your strength, your spirit, I'm most drawn to. Your stunning face and sexy body are the cherry on top of the cake, but it's who you are to your core that I'm drawn to. You soften all my hard edges and make me want to be better for you."

"So romantic," I whisper with tears in my eyes. "I can't believe the man of my dreams was right under my nose all this time and I never realized it."

"Man of your dreams, huh?" A cocky smile creeps over his face. "It's only fair when you're the woman of my dreams."

A throat clearing bursts our bubble, and we turn our heads as one, discovering Joshua's mom standing at the end of my bed with tears in her eyes. "I did knock. Several times," Nat says. "I just wanted to see how you were feeling. I didn't mean to eavesdrop."

"It's okay, Nat, and I'm fine. I'm in pain but I'll heal." I tilt my head to look up at Josh. "Help me to sit up?"

Nat rushes forward, and mother and son prop me up against a mountain of pillows until I'm comfortable. My ribs ache like a bitch as I'm sure they will for some time.

"Do you feel up to eating something? I had Caleb run to the store for me earlier, and I made some chicken noodle soup."

"That explains the delicious smells." I smile at Joshua's mom. "I'd love some soup. I'm hungry."

Nat leaves to prepare our food, and I snuggle into Josh's side. "I'd like to stay here with you."

"Good." He nuzzles his nose in my hair. "We have beefed up security, and a team of thirty men are guarding the front of the building, the parking lot, the lobby downstairs, and the stairs and the lobby outside. Ben is sending a team to install panic buttons in every room and a new security system downstairs in the building and on every floor. He owns the building," he adds when he sees my perplexed expression.

"I'm putting guns in every room, so there is easy access should anyone breach the security measures. We should stay inside while you're healing, and when you're ready to go outside, we'll have a team of ten men with us, traveling in our car and in security vehicles. No one is getting near any of us again. O'Hara thinks Liam is overseas, and he doubts he will try anything now we have taken his men and decimated his support at home, but we're not taking chances."

I straighten up, ignoring the pain the motion produces. "What do you mean, no one is getting near *us* again. Did something happen I'm not aware of?"

He nods, and his tongue darts out, wetting his lips. "Before I tell you, I'm fine, so don't worry."

"Well, that isn't reassuring in the slightest. Tell me what happened." I listen with mounting horror as he tells me about the attack on him and Caleb and Rowan. "Are you okay? Did you get checked out?" My eyes roam his face and his body for injuries.

"I'm fine. Not even a scratch, and Caleb is fine too. Luca and Benedito took the fall."

"It's so sad about Luca. How is Giulio?"

"I haven't spoken with him but Caleb has. He's devastated, and he wants revenge. He resigned from his Wall Street job this morning, and he's being sworn in today as our new *consigliere*."

"Everything is happening so fast."

"We're playing catch-up, and we're on a deadline now. We're not letting these pricks run rings around us any longer. We're going to take the fight to them and bring it all to the surface."

"Was Liam responsible for the hits too?"

"You were kidnapped about an hour before the timed attacks on us and Rowan, and we think it was orchestrated by two different parties. The attacks were planned but sloppy and amateurish. A skilled marksman would have taken us out with less mess and publicity. I had an early-morning con call with The Commission, and we think the Barone went rogue. Ben and Leo are itching for blood, and Massimo had to threaten them to force them to back down."

"I don't blame them. If someone tried to murder my kids, I'd be itching to spill blood too."

"We all want revenge, but we can't act without a strategic plan. We intend to use this situation to draw our enemies out. It'll take a few weeks to pull it all together, but then it's going down, and we will emerge victorious. We approved four new dons to join the board this morning, and those appointments will be official this week."

"Will they provide men?"

"It's part of the terms. Don Greco has also sent spies to Florida and Vegas to find out if they are traitors, and we're bringing the full IT team in to review the tracker reports now we know Liam and his allies found a way to reverse engineer them."

"I'd like in on that. I can work remotely from here."

"You need time to heal, Gia."

"And I will, but when I feel up to it, I want to be involved. I was always invested in this mission as my duty, but I have a personal need to see these pricks taken down now."

"Okay. As long as the medical team in charge of your care signs off on it. I don't want you jeopardizing your recovery."

"Deal."

He stares lovingly at me before his expression sobers. "You're handling this incredibly well, but you've been through a traumatic event. You don't need to put a brave face on for me. I'm here for you if you want to talk about it or you want to break down or whatever it is you need."

"I know that, and I'll need you, but I'm not letting Liam break me. I'm stronger than that."

"You are," Natalia says, entering the room with a tray. "But I'd still recommend therapy."

Joshua takes the tray from his mother, holding it on his lap.

"I had psychological training as part of my induction. Kidnapping and assault are expected when you're a female informant. I've been trained to accept it, and I know how to compartmentalize."

"It's one thing to be trained and quite another to handle it in real life," Nat says, her face awash with compassion.

I know that personally. I was pretty upset after Liam forced me to blow him in front of his men, but this is different. I'm angry and hellbent on getting revenge. "I will attend a few therapy sessions. I'm not opposed to it. I'm just saying you don't need to be overly worried. I know I can handle this. Like I said, I won't give Liam that power over me. If I fall apart, he wins, and I refuse to allow that to happen. It helps that I don't remember much. I know some women might find that harder to deal with, but it makes it easier for me."

I think that's the big difference between what happened in the basement of the Irish bar and what he did to me last night. Not being aware means I can separate my feelings and not let it impact me as much. Plus, the former was all about power and control, but last night, he lost that. He acted recklessly and out of malice. Liam only has power if I give it to him and I refuse to do it. I won't be a victim. I'm a survivor and an avenger, and when I personally end him, I'll be the one with all the power and control.

"I'm in awe of you, Gia," Nat says. "You are a truly remarkable young woman."

"Thank you."

Joshua lifts a spoonful of soup to my mouth, and I open for him.

"I'll leave so you have privacy," Nat says, "but I'd just like to say one more thing." She sits at the end of the bed. "You asked me last night not to call your mother, and I have respected your wishes, but I'm asking you to reconsider. She's your mother, Gia, and she loves you. It will hurt her if you shut her out of this. If this was me, I would want to know. I would want to be there for my daughter."

"I don't want my family to see me like this. They will just worry."

"They will worry anyway," she says.

"I'm not sure how long we can contain the news," Joshua adds, lifting another spoonful of the delicious soup to my lips. "You know how gossipy made men are."

"They shouldn't hear it from anyone else," Natalia says.

"Okay. You're right. I only wanted to protect them, but they should know. Can you call them?"

"Of course." She leans in to kiss my cheek. "I'm so glad you're okay, Gia. You gave us all a terrible fright."

"Joshua told me what happened to Rowan. How is he doing?"

"He is shaken up but coping. It's the fathers I'm more concerned with. Ben and Leo want to burn the world down right now."

"I don't blame them. I'm sorry about Luca. He didn't deserve to die like that."

"No, he didn't. But it's an honor to die protecting your don, and his family will draw some comfort from that."

Chapter Thirty-Four
Gia

My family and Elisa show up later that day, all freaking out and crying, as I predicted, but they calm down when they see I'm holding it together. Nat reassures Mom my injuries will heal, and it helps to assuage her concerns.

The few days immediately after the kidnapping are a bit of a blur. I sleep a lot, thanks to regular doses of pain medication, and multiple tests are performed to ensure there are no lingering side effects of the GHB I was given. I breathe a sigh of relief when tests prove I didn't contract any STIs from that prick, and though I have an IUD implanted, I asked Nat to conduct a pregnancy test to ensure no accidents have happened. Thankfully, it came back negative too.

We attend Hennessy's and Luca's funerals, protected by groups of heavily armed *soldati*, and they go off without issue. I spend some time with Hennessy's family at the wake, explaining how their son willingly gave his life to protect mine and it's a debt I can never repay. I tell them to call me if I can ever do anything for them.

O'Hara has cleaned house, and his operation is running smoothly now all the traitors have been rooted out and dealt with. We got some good intel from the interrogations that took place before their deaths. We know now the big boss is an Italian, but no one knows his name. It was a closely guarded secret, and only the higher-ups know.

Confusion is ripe in our circles as we try to figure out how Italy is involved in this. In the past, our connections were with Sicily, not the larger mainland. When Serena Salerno eliminated Stefan DeLuca years ago, we thought the family line died with him. All intel points to that, but a team has been sent to Sicily to check it out.

However, if this is someone from the mainland, we are at a complete loss. Italy is a pretty big country with a population of fifty-eight million. We can't just blindly send teams of men to the mainland, and we can't decimate our ranks here because war is coming, and we need every available man.

Tension is running high in The Big Apple, but the streets are ours again. The foreign supplies coming into the city have dried up. It's no surprise considering Liam is still MIA. We're not stupid. We know it's the calm before the storm, but the newly enhanced board of The Commission is pulling out all the stops to put an end to this once and for all.

Weeks pass and I'm healing, inside and out. My face is back to normal, my concussion is gone, and while my ribs still hurt, they don't hurt as badly.

Joshua has stayed true to his word, barely leaving my side. He has taken such good care of me. Cooking my meals so I'm eating healthily. Ensuring I take my medication on time. Bathing and showering me. Applying ointment to my myriad of injuries. Watching movies with me and teaching me to play chess on the onyx chessboard I bought him for his birthday. At night, he holds me tight, helping to chase any potential night-mares away.

I am so in love with him, and I know he is it for me—the man I will marry and have a family with. The man I will grow old with. Neither of us has said it out loud, but I can tell we're on the same page. I am really happy, and I'm loving living here with him. We work well together, our strengths and differences complementing one another.

On days when Joshua has to attend a critical meeting at the company or Commission Central, he has his mom or Elisa come and stay with me and he doubles the security detail.

I'm part of the team working to ferret out the rats in our organization. Going through the chip-tracking reports for the past few months for thousands of men is painstaking work, but it's proving fruitful.

Ben's IT team identified a pattern that pinpoints those using reverse-engineered chips, and we are slowly compiling a list of men who are traitors. We can't move on them yet, not without alerting our enemy we are onto them. Some of my colleagues from the informant team are tailing a few of these men in the hopes of identi-fying the key figure or figures at the senior level within the *mafioso* who are aiding the enemy. So far, we're not making any headway, but we presume this person, or persons, is aware we are closing in and they are not doing anything to jeopardize their position.

But they will slip. They will make a mistake. And when they do, we will swoop in and do our own spring cleaning.

Today is my first day venturing outside, and I'm loving the feel of the brisk February air on my face as I walk hand in hand with Joshua toward the plastic surgeon's office where I have an appointment. Ten men surround us, and we're garnering our fair share of curious gazes. Joshua is a recognizable face around the city, but I'm a stranger to most.

"I can take a skin graft from your inner thigh and use it to repair the damaged skin on your arm," the doctor says after examining me. "You should heal in two weeks, but it will take a year to two years for the skin to fully settle. It's likely you will have some small permanent scarring, but it will be minimal and a drastic improvement." The look on his face when he saw the rudimentary name etched on my arm was priceless.

"I want to do it."

I'm eager to get that prick's name and his mark off my arm so it's not a permanent reminder of that night. I've been doing well, and I won't let this hold me back. I have attended a few therapy sessions, mostly to appease Mom, Nat, Elisa, and Joshua, but it has helped to talk it all through with a professional. I have successfully compartmentalized the ordeal and blocked it from my mind.

Joshua is another matter.

He's so gentle with me, like I'm this fragile thing he'll break. Apart from kissing and a few heavy make out sessions, he hasn't taken it any further, and I'm seriously sexually frustrated at this point. I had too many physical injuries at first to even think about sex, but now I'm mostly healed I'm keen to reset our relationship and reclaim my sexuality.

"How soon can you fit her in for the procedure?" Joshua asks, firmly holding my hand on top of the table.

"I have an opening in ten days. That is the earliest I can do it."

"Please book me in."

"I'd be happy to, Ms. Bianchi."

I wet my lips and shoot a quick look at Joshua before I ask my next question. I wasn't sure if I was going to ask it today, but now I'm here, I figure why not? "I saw on your website that you perform cosmetic procedures too, and I wanted to inquire into a breast reduction. Is that something you could do for me?"

Joshua's surprise is barely discernible because he's mastered hiding his emotions, but I see it. I probably should have mentioned it to him, but it's my body. My decision.

"I don't perform the procedures myself. One of my colleagues does, but I can refer you to him. John is here today. I can check if he has time to talk to you now?"

"Yes. That would be great, thanks."

"Excuse me for a few moments," Dr. Miller says, getting up and exiting the room.

Joshua turns to face me. "I didn't realize you were considering this."

"Is it a problem?" I'm immediately on the defensive.

"Of course not. I'm just surprised because you never mentioned it."

"I've thought of it for years. I hate my breasts. They're too big."

"That is subjective." He smiles, before raising my hand to his mouth and kissing my knuckles. "I love them, but it's your body and your choice."

My shoulders loosen in relief. "Will it upset you if they're smaller?"

He shakes his head. "I love you for more than your rack, honey. I wouldn't want them too small, but I'll live with it. You do whatever you need to."

"I love you." I lean in and kiss him passionately. "I should have talked to you instead of springing it on you. I'm sorry."

"It's okay." He tucks strands of my blonde hair behind my ears. Originally, I was just going to let the dye fade, but after what happened, I wanted rid of it and that entire persona. Alexander came over one afternoon in January to return me to my natural glory, and though I liked my red hair, I'm happy to be back to myself. "We're talking about it now."

"I get a lot of back strain, and it hurts when I run. I'm not going to go really small. I like having boobs, but I want them more manageable and less noticeable. I developed early, and it drew a lot of unwanted male attention. I'd like to walk into a room and not have everyone staring at my tits."

"Then you should definitely do it," Joshua says just as Dr. Miller returns to the room with his colleague.

"Hey, sexy," I say, pouncing on Joshua the instant he walks through the door later that night. He had a meeting to attend after the appointment this afternoon, and I haven't seen him since he dropped me off, escorting me all the way to the penthouse because he rarely lets me out of his sight. I yank him forward by his tie and plant my eager mouth on his. His arms swoop around me, and he dips me back a little as we kiss like we're never getting to do it again.

"Not that I'm complaining, but what did I do to deserve this?" he asks, his voice drenched with lust when we finally part for air.

"You exist and you're mine." I drop a slew of drugging kisses along his neckline as my hand dives between our bodies to grip his hard-on through his pants. "I love you, Joshua. I love you more than I thought I could ever love a man." I squeeze his cock as I peer into his beautiful blue eyes. "Thank you for taking such good care of me. Thank you for loving me good."

"It's hardly been a chore. I love taking care of you, and loving you is as easy as breathing. Thank you for restoring my faith in love."

"I need you." I drop to my knees in front of him and reach for his zipper, ignoring the slight pain in my ribs.

"What are you doing?"

"Making one of your fantasies come true," I confirm,

lowering his zipper and freeing his cock from his pants and his boxers.

"You're still healing."

I look up at him, holding his magnificent, throbbing cock in my hand. "Are you seriously complaining right now?"

"Jesus, Gia," he pants, his dick jerking as I slowly stroke it. "I want your mouth on me so freaking badly I'd sell my soul for a blowjob. But not at the expense of your health."

"I barely feel a twinge from my ribs now, and I'm healed everywhere else." I drill him with a pointed look as I slowly stroke his dick. "I love you for being careful with me, but it ends now, baby. I need you to fuck me and to stop treating me like some fragile doll. So, we're doing this, and we're doing it now."

"Fuck, I really fucking love you." His eyes glisten with emotion. "Are you sure?"

"Yes, now shut up and fuck my mouth."

Chapter Thirty-Five
Gia

"I have to ask you again," Joshua says when we're finally naked in bed and about to fuck for the first time in six weeks. "Are you sure you're ready?"

"Yes." I crawl over his body, positioning my bare pussy over his cock. I only finished blowing him in the hall ten minutes ago, but he's rock hard and raring to go again. I love my man's stamina. He can go all night, and he never gets tired. "I need this to heal, Joshua. I need your touch to replace the lingering remnants of his. I need you to reclaim my body and push him permanently away. I need this to feel like me again. To feel like a woman."

"You're all woman to me, Gia, and I always desire you." His hands glide carefully up my body to play with my tits. "That won't ever change."

"Good." I grin. "I'm going to fuck you now."

He shoots me a dark look loaded with promise, and delicious tremors skate over my skin. "I'm at your mercy, honey. Do whatever you want. Take what you need."

Lying on my stomach, I kiss my way down his body,

sucking his balls into my mouth and trailing my lips up and down his velvety-soft cock. Joshua shaves, and I love a well-groomed man; it makes oral sex so much easier without hairs sticking to my tongue or the inside of my mouth.

Precum leaks from the tip as I climb over him again, positioning myself on top of his dick. Using my hand, I guide his length into me. Our eyes remain locked as I slowly sink onto him, one glorious inch at a time. When I'm fully seated, I hold still, staring at my love as I relish the feel of him jerking inside me.

"Shit, condom." Joshua reaches for the drawer of his nightstand.

"I'm good to go without if you are. You know I have an IUD, and I'm clean."

"I'm clean too."

I snort out a laugh, and he lifts a brow. "You made your fuck buddies sign contracts and get tested monthly. You think I didn't know you tested yourself too?" I brush my lips against his. "You would never risk my health. I know you, Joshua Gino Accardi. I know what makes you tick."

"Are you planning on riding me tonight or next week?"

I tweak his nipple. "Where's that legendary patience of yours disappeared to?"

"Six weeks of jerking off has drained my patience reservoir. I'm desperate for you, honey. I need this as much as you do."

I lift my hips, dragging my pussy up along his hard shaft before slamming back down. Then I rotate my hips and grind on his cock, moving in sync with him as he thrusts up inside me. We both moan as I ride him, holding on to his hips to steady myself as we rock against one another. Joshua's hands caress my body. Fondling my tits. Tweaking my taut nipples. Dipping over the curve of my hip and my ass. Toying with my clit.

When the twinge in my ribs gets too much, we switch positions, and I slide under his powerful body as he drives back inside me in one confident thrust. "Any pain?" he asks, lifting my right leg and wrapping it around his waist.

"I'm good."

He hovers over me, kissing me deeply as he makes love to me with tender care. My orgasm is building, climbing higher and higher, and he reads my body, picking up his pace, and pumping inside me as we both chase that high. My walls clench around him, and he rubs my clit with his fingers as he rams inside me with renewed urgency. "Fuck, fuck, Gia," he hisses, his eyes briefly closing as he shoves inside me so deep it feels like he's touching my womb.

"I'm going to come," I scream, digging my fingers into his shoulders as I buck up with the building tension.

"Come for me, honey. Right now, Gia." He pinches my clit, and I detonate, screaming and writhing as the most indescribably blissful orgasm rips through me, filling every inch of my body with wondrous joy.

Joshua is grunting and repeating my name as he comes, and I mentally imprint his O-face for eternity.

After, Joshua kisses me quickly before pulling out and running to the bathroom. He returns with a warm cloth and cleans me up before crawling back under the silk sheets and reeling me into his arms.

We lie there in heavenly contentment with my face pressed to his chest and his heartbeat thrumming steadily against my ear.

"I want this with you forever, Gia." He runs his fingers through my hair. "I didn't like hearing the doctor call you Ms. Bianchi earlier. I want you to be my wife someday."

I lift my head, piercing him with eyes swimming in emotion. "I want that too."

"Good." His tender kiss is toe-curling. "You can expect a proposal soon. Once we get through the next few months."

I prop up on one elbow and sweep my fingers over his cheeks. "You don't need to prewarn me, babe. I will say yes. Nothing will change my mind. I have never felt this way about anyone. It's just you, Joshua. It will always just be you."

He holds my face in his hands like I'm treasure. "I told you before I'd been in love previously, but I was wrong. I never felt this with her, Gia. What I had with Bettina was some form of puppy love, but it wasn't real or true, and it wouldn't have lasted. I know that now. I have never loved anyone the way I love you. You're it for me too." He reaches up to kiss me. "You're my forever."

"I love you so much. More than I can describe." I kiss his gorgeous lips before laying my head back down on his chest.

His arm tightens around my back. "I want to bottle this happiness and never lose it."

I trace his chiseled chest with one finger. "I wish we could stay here in our little bubble and never leave. All I need is you, and I'm content."

It's the truth, but we both know we can't ignore reality for much longer.

"Are you sure you want a place on my team?" Caleb asks as we work side by side on our laptops in Joshua's home office. My love is attending an important meeting at the Accardi Company today, so his twin is keeping me company.

"Yes. It's where my strengths lie."

It's been two months since the kidnapping, and I'm fully healed and back working out at the gym and training with my team at Commission Central. Every *soldato* and *capo* in the city is undergoing refresher training ahead of the impending battle. The four new dons have brought one thousand men to the city in the past few weeks, and all are living in apartment buildings owned by Caltimore Holdings that solely house *mafioso*.

I had to postpone my skin graft and breast reduction surgeries because they would have forced me to sit out the upcoming battle, and there's no way in hell I'm missing that.

Everyone is gearing up for the clash with our enemies. The plan is highly confidential, and I'm not even privy to every part. The Commission has purposely kept it that way so nothing leaks they don't want leaked. They have made it known they are going after the Barone for the attacks on the twins and Rowan Mazzone, and they have released the date, time, and location in Jersey to draw all our enemies to the battle. It's a gamble because they may sense a trap and not show up if they aren't ready to invoke their plan, or they could turn up with more men and firepower than us, and we will lose a lot of good men.

No one knows who this Italian boss is or how many men he has on his side.

It's risky, but we're taking the fight to the enemy when it suits us. It's better than waiting for them to strike and being caught off guard.

"I thought you'd want to be by Joshua's side. You two are practically joined at the hip these days."

"Aw, jealous?" I lift my head from my laptop and swivel in my chair so I'm facing him. "Afraid I'll take him from you?"

He rolls his eyes. "Nothing will ever come between my twin and I. You'd do well to remember that."

"I wouldn't want to get in the way of your twin bond. He loves you, and he loves me. There is room for both of us. And being on your team is best for Joshua. If I'm with him, he'll be distracted worrying about me, and distractions cost lives."

"I appreciate it."

"I'm not doing it for you."

"I'm aware. I know you hate me."

"I don't hate you, Caleb. I hate what you've done to my friend. There's a difference."

"It's better this way. Elisa is safer away from me. Look how you were targeted. I wouldn't want that for Lili."

I believe he's sincere. I believe he cares about her. But he's hurt her so much. Though it wasn't intentional, I'm still finding it hard to forgive him. I tolerate him for Joshua's sake, and to be fair, he's done a lot for us since everything went down after Christmas. I've got to give him some credit.

"I was always going to be a target as an informant, but you're right, being Joshua's girl gave that douche added incentive to come after me."

"He didn't realize you've got bigger balls than most men and you're not easy to take down."

"Straight fucking fire."

"You impressed me," he says, setting down his pen. "I know it can't have been easy in the aftermath of everything, but you just got on with it. You've proven you're worthy of my brother. You have my blessing."

I flip up my middle finger. "We don't need your blessing. Your ego is showing again."

"You think my brother would marry you if I didn't approve?" He quirks a brow.

Picking up a nut from the bowl, I fling it at his head. "Yes, he would." My voice resonates with confidence because I know it's the truth. Joshua loves his brother. He would die for him, but he wouldn't walk away from me if Caleb didn't approve. I know that with my whole heart.

"You're perfect for him. Don't fuck it up."

I fling another nut at his head, and this time, he's ready for me, jerking his head to the side and opening his mouth so it pops inside. He flashes me a grin.

"Show-off."

He cracks up laughing just as his cell vibrates with an incoming call. He picks it up. "What?" He listens for a few minutes before sighing heavily. "No, don't inform him. He's busy. Let her up. I'll handle it." He hangs up and stands.

"What's going on?"

He pats my head like I'm five. "Nothing to concern your pretty face about."

I scowl at him. "Don't patronize me."

"I have a bit of a nuisance issue to handle, but it's better you let me handle it." He drills me with a sharp look. "Stay here. You have a report to submit, so *submit it.*"

I shove both middle fingers up at his retreating back, waiting until he is out of sight before I pull up the camera feed on my phone. Joshua gave me access to everything so I'm never blindsided again.

On the screen, Caleb is standing in the open doorway of the penthouse, chatting with one of the *soldati* as he waits for whatever or whomever this nuisance is. I tap a pen on the desk as I watch the elevator doors sliding open, sitting bolt upright when I see who emerges.

"What the actual fuck? Are you kidding me?" I glare at the screen where Sorella Caprese is pushing against Caleb, trying to get in through the door.

Fuck this shit. Fuck waiting here. Joshua ended things with her months ago. How dare she show up here. She's not even supposed to know where he lives! *Her fucking sister!* Joshua told me Viola Caprese was his new temp PA. She must have given her older sister her boss's address. A firing offense if I have any say.

I storm out of the office and stomp down the hallway, across the living room, and out into the entrance hallway.

"You!" Sorella jabs her finger in my direction as Caleb tries to restrain her. She's bucking and snarling and writhing like a crazy person. "I know what you're doing, and if you think you're taking him from me, you're fucking delusional!"

"Of course, you didn't listen," Caleb grumbles, glaring at me as he struggles with the witch. The shoulder of her black belted trench coat comes loose, sliding down one side, show-casing the top of a red lace corset.

I stalk right up to them, and it's taking enormous willpower not to throttle the bitch. "You dare to show up here dressed in your underwear in some ploy to tempt *my man*? The only delusional one here is you. Joshua doesn't want you. He's with me, and you're embarrassing yourself. Leave or I'll make you."

In a lightning-fast move, she pulls a gun out from the pocket of her coat and points it at me.

I glare at the two *soldati* at the front door. "Did no one check her for weapons?"

"Heads will roll for this," Caleb promises, easily wresting the gun from Sorella. He hands it to one of the men. "Starting with your sister's. Nice way to get Viola fired."

"It's not her fault. I blackmailed her into giving me the address. She shouldn't be punished." She smirks as Caleb restrains her by the upper arms. "Joshua can take it out on me. He loves punishing me. He can do whatever he wants to my body. I'll let him do anything, like always." She drags a deroga-tory gaze up and down my body, scoffing at my slides, yoga pants, and oversized sweater. My hair is up in a messy bun, and I have no makeup on my face. "What the hell does he even see in you? You're a mess, and I doubt you keep him satisfied in any aspect of his life."

There was a time I felt inferior next to her. She's always done up to the nines and immaculately dressed. But not anymore. Joshua loves me for the person I am under the exterior. He had ample opportunity when he was fucking this bitch to make her his girlfriend, but he didn't because he doesn't have feelings for her. I remember that so I don't accidentally-on-purpose murder her.

"Gia satisfies my brother in a way you never did. Jealousy is not a good look on you, Sorella," Caleb says. "Crazy psycho doesn't suit you either."

"Oh, I don't know," I say, lounging against the wall. "It has a certain appeal. You should call her father and have her committed. She did just pull a gun on Don Accardi's fiancée."

"Valid point," Caleb says, eyeballing the elevator as it opens again.

"You lying whore! You're not wearing a ring. As if he'd ever lower himself to marry you."

I might not have a ring yet, but it's only a matter of time.

Joshua exits the elevator with four armed men, and I breathe a sigh of relief.

"I *am* going to marry Gia," Joshua says, standing behind the commotion in our doorway. "And you are way out of line coming here, Sorella."

Caleb doesn't look surprised, confirming his twin must have spoken to him about it.

"Joshua! Joshua!" She attempts to turn in Caleb's arms, but he's holding her too tightly. Joshua and the men step back as Caleb moves her outside to the lobby, freeing up the doorway.

Joshua rushes inside, hauling me against his chest, as Sorella screams and shouts. "Are you okay?" he asks.

"I'm fine, though she did pull a gun on me."

"Did she now?" His cold icy stare throws me back in time to months ago when I was on the receiving end of such looks. Keeping his arms snugly around me, he turns us to face his ex-fuck-buddy at the door. "I made myself very clear in December when I told you our arrangement was over."

"You don't mean it!" Tears stream down her face. "I love you, and I know you love me!"

"I don't. I have never loved you. I love Gia. She's going to be my wife."

"Why her and not me!? What does she have that I don't?" she shrieks, bucking against the soldiers who are now holding her. Caleb looks bored, slouched against the doorway with his ankles crossed, staring at the ceiling. "Look at her, and look at me!" Somehow, she manages to rip her coat open, displaying the fitted lace corset, matching panties, and stockings she is wearing. "How can you want that hot mess and not this?"

Joshua looks ready to rip her to shreds. "Insult the woman I love again, and I'll put a bullet in your head. Gia is worth a million of you. She's my equal in every way. You were just a hole to fuck when I had an itch that needed scratching."

Gawd, he's so cold. I should be enjoying this, and there is a part of me that is, but there is something so tragically pathetic about Sorella that makes another part of me pity her.

She's crying now, big wracking sobs that come straight from her heart. I think she might genuinely be in love with him.

"Take her away," he commands his men. "I will be calling your sister to tell her she's fired and calling your father to explain what you've done here today. I'll be demanding he sends both of you overseas."

"No, please, Joshua. No. Don't do that. I don't want to leave the US. I'm sorry. I'm sorry."

"You're lucky he's not calling for your death," Caleb says,

pushing off the wall. "My brother is doing you a kindness. You should thank him."

"Joshua, please. She has poisoned you, tricked you into thinking you love her. She's not good enough for you. Please, baby, she can't give you the things I can. Remember all the good times we had, baby. Please remember."

"You pulled a gun on my future wife. There's no coming back from that. I don't trust you around Gia, and I will do whatever is necessary to ensure she's protected. You are nothing to me, and she is everything."

Ouch. That has got to hurt.

Sorella's tears dry up, and she glares at me. "You might think you've won, bitch, but I'll have the last laugh. Wait and see!" she shrieks as she's dragged kicking and screaming into the elevator.

"My ears hurt," Caleb says, slapping his brother on the shoulder as the elevator doors close and the screeching stops. "Thank fuck. I was two seconds from blowing her head off just to shut her up."

"Are you okay?" Joshua asks me again, ignoring his brother.

"I'm fine. I kinda feel sorry for her. I think she loves you and she's really lost it."

"I don't care about her." He pulls us farther into the hallway as Caleb closes the front door. "All I care about is you."

"I'm okay, but I'm all riled up now." I drive my hand down the front of his pants. "I want to bounce on your cock."

"And that's my cue to leave." Caleb's eyes light up in mischief. "Unless you want a two-for-one special?" He smirks, totally winding his brother up. "Want to fuck twins?"

"Out!" we holler in unison, pointing at the front door.

"You two are no fun." He blows me a kiss before spinning around, chuckling as he exits through the front door.

Chapter Thirty-Six
Gia

"Have you got your vest on?" Joshua asks me for the umpteenth time as we get out of his Land Rover at the large warehouse in Queens where everyone is meeting.

"Yes." I bite my tongue so I don't sass him. I know he's only worried. I loop my arm through his. "Please don't worry about me. I'll be fine. You're the one who is directly in the line of fire, so if anyone should be worrying, it's *me*."

"Hey." Leo walks up to us. "You kids good?"

Joshua rolls his eyes. "I stopped being a kid a long time ago, Leo."

"You'll always be a kid to me."

"Are Mom and the others safe?" he asks as I scan the men surrounding the area and walking in and out of the warehouse. Philip did something to the satellite signal here and the location near the construction site in Atlantic City where it's all going down in a few hours so no one can watch or pull up any reports afterward. There will be casualties on both sides tonight, and we need to keep the authorities out of this.

I spot a handful of other women walking into the high-roofed building, but we are in the extreme minority. Most of the wives and kids are holed up in bunkers and panic rooms in case this should go wrong.

I don't think it will. The planning is exemplary.

Joshua and Caleb brought me into their confidence last night, and I'm astounded at what has been pulled together in a couple of months. It's no wonder I haven't seen much of him in the past couple of weeks.

"Everyone is tucked away in the basement panic room at Ben's house," Leo says, reclaiming my attention. "Your mother, Marco, and Elisa are there too."

My youngest brother threw a hissy fit he couldn't come today. He's thirteen and already initiated, but it's too dangerous, and he doesn't have enough experience in the field, so Papa put his foot down. Mom said Marco was stomping around the house like a stereotypical teen for the past week. I'm betting he sulks the entire time he has to stay hidden on Ben's estate, but I'm glad they are safe. It's three less people to worry about. "They said to tell you not to take unnecessary risks."

"I'm not the one they should be worrying about," I say as I spy my father and two brothers coming this way.

"I heard the ambush went like clockwork," Leo says as my family strolls up.

Dad pulls me into a bracing hug before handing me off to Antonio and Cosimo. I hug my brothers close.

"We had twelve casualties during the op, but we captured ninety-nine men," Joshua says. "They are chained and locked in our bunker, under armed guard, and we have security cameras all over the area in case anything should go down."

I worked with a team for weeks to track down every traitor among the *mafioso*. Strangely, there were no rats within the Maltese *famiglia*, but we identified rats in the other four families. We waited until today to go after them in a carefully planned attack. A group of Accardi traitors were purposely left out of the ambush because we need them as part of the plan tonight.

"What about the plant in Cali?" My dad asks.

"Juan Pablo has every available man working on security tonight in case they attack."

"Are the Irish here?" Antonio asks.

Joshua shakes his head. "We'll meet them in A.C." He glances around. "We should head inside. It's not safe to talk out here."

We walk inside just as the meeting is called to order. Joshua holds my hand as we advance toward the raised section at the back of the room. "Stay where I can see you," he says when we reach the top, leaning down to kiss me in front of the packed room. I feel eyeballs glued to the back of my head, and I scowl at my boyfriend. Joshua swats my ass and winks before jumping up onto the stage to join his twin. My father glares at him from his position beside Fiero, and Cosimo chuckles. "Joshua must have a death wish."

"Doesn't he know his don status means fuck all when Dad has his fatherly hat on?" Antonio adds.

"He's fearless and confident. He doesn't need to worry about Papa."

"You're so fucking smitten. It's disgusting," Cosimo says, his lips pulling into a grimace.

"I think it's great. I love seeing you happy," Antonio says. "Did you hear what happened to Sorella?" he whispers in my ear.

"No, and I don't want to know. Stop talking," I add. "They're calling for quiet."

The board of The Commission stands on the makeshift podium with their underbosses and *consiglieri*. It's only the five existing board members before us. The decision was taken, at the last minute, not to announce the four new members even though they have been sworn in. It gives us an element of surprise we might need later. Dad, Leo, and Alesso are fully informed, because they are trusted implicitly, but none of the other underbosses or *consiglieri* were notified.

Don Greco welcomes everyone and quickly outlines the plan. "You will split into your designated groups and follow your *capo* to your assigned transportation. If anyone is in need of additional weapons or a vest, spare supplies are in the cordoned-off area at the back." He points toward the corner on the left where a temporary tent is erected. "When on location, you will be given direct instructions. Do not deviate from the plan. Follow your *capo*'s instructions to the letter."

Don Mazzone speaks next. "We are well prepared, but expect our enemy to be well prepared too. They know we are coming, and this will be bloody. Not everyone will make it home after tonight."

A solemn hush descends over the crowd.

"We protect our own," Joshua says, his voice projecting confidently across the room. "The medical team is on standby, reinforced with additional resources and a centralized facility." Nat explained how they have been working over the past year to transform one of the Caltimore Holdings buildings into a private hospital, purely for *mafioso*. They will open their doors for the first time tonight. "If you are injured, find a safe space to hide until we come for you."

"For those who die with honor tonight, know we will take care of your families," Caleb says. "They will be cared for and protected."

It's Fiero's turn next. Don Maltese clears his throat. "Earlier today, we rounded up one hundred and eleven men who were traitors working with our enemy from within our *famiglie.*"

Hushed whispering ripples across the room. "These traitors will be dealt with accordingly," Cristian says. "A few may have slipped through the cracks." I watch the tall man with balding hair on the stage for any signs of a reaction, but he gives nothing away. He's good. I'll give him that. "Watch your backs."

The meeting disperses quickly as everyone moves to their assigned team. I hug my brothers tight, silently praying both of them come home safely. "Be careful," I tell them, cupping Cosimo's face. "Especially you. Don't take unnecessary risks."

"I'll see you in a few hours. You can count on it." Cosimo gives me another quick hug before walking off.

"I'll make sure he's safe," Antonio says. "Dad put him on my team so I could look out for him."

"Don't forget to look out for you too." I yank him into a fierce hug as Joshua approaches from behind his shoulder. "Love you, bro."

"Love you too. Happy shooting." He nods at my boyfriend before racing after our younger brother.

"No reckless shit," Joshua says, tugging on the end of my ponytail.

"Right back at ya."

"I'm not the reckless one." He arches a brow.

"You're getting all the fun," Caleb grumbles, materializing alongside us.

I roll my eyes. Trust Caleb to call the impending bloodbath *fun.*

"It's your fault for being so skilled with a rifle." Joshua claps his brother on the back.

"Ready to head out?" Caleb asks me, and I nod.

"Keep her safe, little brother."

Caleb flips him the bird as he pulls me under his arm. "Don't worry. I've got your woman covered."

I shove my elbow into his side. "Don't be gross, and stop freaking him out when he's going into battle."

I fling my arms around Joshua's neck and stretch up on my booted feet. "I love you." I slam my lips against his, and he kisses me back with the same desperation I feel. "Be careful out there, and come home to me."

"Always." He kisses me one final time before we part.

"You should give me your coordinates," Marino says to Caleb as we move to walk off. "I should know where you are in case anything should go wrong."

"It's classified," Caleb says through gritted teeth.

Their underboss laughs. "You've got to be joking. I'm your second-in-command, and I have a right to know."

Caleb's nostrils flare as he steps up to the older man. I yank him back as Joshua steps in to smooth things over. "It's nothing personal, Benedito." Joshua lowers his voice on purpose. "You know we have a mole within the top level we weren't able to identify."

"You better not be suggesting it's me." His hands ball at his side as I squeeze Caleb's arm in warning.

"Of course not." Joshua's expression is sincere as he eyeballs the traitor. "If it was up to us, we'd tell you, but Don Greco would bust our balls for disrespecting his orders, and we can't afford that. We still have a lot to prove to our peers."

"He wouldn't have to know."

"I don't even know where we're going, and I'm a part of the team," I say. "It's smart to keep the intel contained. Surely you concede that point?"

He shoots me a withering glare before offering me a tight smile. He turns to Joshua. "Can I at least have my cell and my weapons back?"

"Afraid I can't do that."

Anger ripples across his face. "This is such bullshit! How am I expected to do my job blindfolded with my hands effectively tied behind my back?" he hisses.

"I know. We're not pleased about it either, but these are the rules."

Marino looks like he wants to keep arguing, but he realizes it's futile. "Very well. I'll meet you at the rendezvous point," he says, turning to walk off.

"You're coming with me. President's orders." Joshua shrugs apologetically, and I'm proud of him. He deserves an Oscar for this performance.

Marino looks like he wants to throttle Joshua with his bare hands, and I'm grateful they are going in a van with trusted armed *soldati* so he can't pull something en route. The Commission used their contacts to hire a ton of military trucks for tonight, and it truly feels like we are going to war.

"Let's go." I tug on Caleb's arm to pull him away.

"Stay safe, broski," he calls out as I drag him away.

"I love you," I mouth at Joshua, swallowing back nerves as we walk in opposite directions.

Chapter Thirty-Seven
Joshua

W e pile out of the back of the truck two blocks from the construction site where Caleb and I took Rizzo and his men down last year. Our meeting point with the Barone scum is just around the corner, only a mile from the warehouse where Gia was held prisoner in December. It's a vast grassy piece of land adjacent to the ocean. Completely open and exposed with no place to hide. However, it is dark, which offers us advantages as well as our enemy.

Ben, Cristian, and I are holding the fort here while Massimo, Fiero, and Caleb are in position a mile away.

"I think this is a bad plan, Joshua," the thorn in my side says as we join hundreds of our men heading in the same direction.

"It's Don Accardi, and you don't get to question the choices The Commission makes, Marino." He's getting on my very last nerve, and I have wanted to kill him every minute of the past two hours. Caleb and I have wanted to slaughter him in cold blood from the moment we had concrete evidence of his betrayal. Fucking backstabbing *bastardo*.

"It just seems ill-conceived meeting out in the open like this. They could fire on us from above."

Already taken care of, asshole.

"And risking all members of The Commission is downright crazy," he adds. I hope it means he isn't aware of the four members we have added to the board or the fact they are waiting in the wings to strike should we need them.

"We're here now, and raising objections is futile. It's going down like this whether you like it or not."

"At least give me a weapon. I'm a sitting duck otherwise."

"I will when the time is right." I turn to eyeball him, schooling my features into a neutral expression. "Don't worry, I wouldn't leave you defenseless." Swallowing bile, I keep the charade up, almost choking on my words as I say, "You've been extremely loyal to our family for years, Benedito. I haven't forgotten, and I'm genuinely sorry it has to be like this. But it'll be over in a few hours, and things will return to normal."

He ducks his face to hide a sly smile, but I see it. I have to shove my hands into my pockets to avoid killing him on the spot.

"I'm in position," Ben says into my earpiece. All our trusted men were given them for communication.

"We're ready and waiting," O'Hara says. "We have counted fifty men waiting with Calabro."

"Any sign of McDermott?" Caleb asks because he knows I can't risk speaking in front of the traitor.

"Negative," our stepdad says. "The drones haven't picked up any activity, either on the ground or in the air."

All the hairs on the back of my neck lift. This can't be right. The Barone couldn't be this stupid to turn up alone. Could they?

"Maybe the Barone were iced out after the failed assassination attempts," Massimo says, vocalizing my thoughts.

"It's shady as fuck," Fiero says. "Be careful."

"I really disapprove of using a child to force their hand," Marino says as we approach the grassy piece of land where we're meeting our enemy.

"We're speaking their language," I snap. "Or have you forgotten they tried to assassinate Rowan Mazzone?"

"He's not a child."

"He's still in school." I drill him with a look.

"Rizzo's child is only ten," he says, slipping up without realizing it. "I thought we were better than this. We shouldn't be sinking to their levels."

"He hasn't been harmed, and we needed something to force them to come here tonight."

It didn't sit right with any of us to kidnap Rizzo's boy, but he's the sole remaining Barone heir, and we knew they would show up to reclaim him. We couldn't think of any other way to draw them out that would ensure they didn't open fire immediately. The boy was well looked after by one of the *mafioso* wives. He dined on McDonald's and Chick-fil-A and spent his days watching Marvel movies and playing Xbox with our *soldati*. No one has harmed a hair on his head.

I walk over to Ben and Cristian and their crew while the bulk of our men hang back on the road per the instructions relayed on the journey here. Ben is bending down, whispering in Lorenzo Rizzo's ear. Leo shares a look with me as Marino glances over his shoulder, no doubt mouthing words to his men. I nod at my stepdad.

"Let's do this," Cristian says as Calabro steps forward with his underboss and *consigliere*. Armed men trail them a few steps behind.

I jerk my head at the crew gathered directly behind me, gesturing them forward with a jerk of my head.

"I need a weapon," Marino hisses in my ear as we advance

toward the welcoming party.

I slam a handgun in his palm and level him with a warning look.

We stop in the middle of the field, facing off with our enemy.

"Lorenzo. You good?" Calabro asks, eyeballing the little boy.

"I had the best time, Uncle. I got to—"

"Zip it," Calabro snaps. "Hand him over, Mazzone."

Ben glares at Calabro. "Not until you hand over the men responsible for the attempted assassination on my son. That was the deal."

Calabro smirks, lifting a hand and snapping his fingers. Two men are pushed forward from the back and shoved to their knees in the middle of both groups.

"Check them for weapons," Ben instructs, and a few of the Mazzone *soldati* move forward.

The man standing to Ben's side, with his arm in a sling, subtly shakes his head, confirming what we already knew would happen. These goons are not the men who fired at Rowan and killed one of his bodyguards. I'm sure Ben is itching to rip into Calabro for attempting to trick us, but we need to play this scene to the bitter end. We'll get the pricks who targeted his son one way or the other.

Weapons are raised as both sides point guns at each other. You could cut the tension with a knife. I have one eye on the prick at my side and one on the confrontation in front of me.

"They're clean, Don Mazzone."

"Bring them here," Ben says through gritted teeth.

Calabro steps forward and lifts a hand. "Bring the boy to me first."

"That's not how negotiations go, and we're not stupid," Ben says. "You release the men to us, and we'll give you the boy."

"We're not stupid either," Calabro says. "We know you'll kill him once you get what you want."

"You know jack shit," Cristian says. "Unlike you, we don't kill kids."

Calabro points his gun at Cristian's face. "Then give me one good reason why I shouldn't just kill you all now."

"Because Lorenzo will get hit in the ensuing gunfire, and we know you don't want your only surviving heir to die, or you wouldn't be here," I calmly say. I don't mention the fact they appear totally outnumbered because I'm sure that isn't the case. I don't know where their backup resources are hiding—which is a problem in itself—but I'm sure they're out there someplace.

"Don't be an ass," Cristian says. "Hand us the men. We'll give you the boy, and we can all go home," he lies.

Calabro sends a fleeting look to the man on my left, and I feel Marino bristling beside me. We all pretend not to notice. My fingers curl around my gun as I quietly unlock the safety.

"Take them," Calabro snaps, and our men drag the men over to our side.

The two poor scapegoats stare at us with fear in their eyes, knowing what's coming next. Although they are innocent, they need to die to set things in motion.

Ben steps forward and shoots the guy in the leather jacket in the skull before turning to his buddy and shooting him too.

Lorenzo starts crying, and I hurt for the little guy. I wish we didn't have to do that in front of him.

Ben whispers to the little guy, and he runs off toward his uncle, stumbling and crying. Calabro grabs the kid and hands him off to another man, and they take off running to the far right.

"Put the gun down, Joshua." Marino has his gun pressed to my temple as every single man on both sides now raises their weapons.

"What the hell are you doing?" I continue to play a part, staring at my underboss with fake shock.

Marino gestures behind me to his men, calling them forward. "What you don't have the balls to do. Drop it, Accardi." I toss the gun away behind me so he can't reach it. He scowls, but it's quickly replaced with a smug grin I long to wipe off his conniving face. Racing footfalls approach and Accardi *soldati* line up beside our underboss, pointing their weapons at us.

Our other men, the ones visible from this vantage point, back on the road, race toward us with weapons out and primed, no doubt thoroughly confused because we couldn't let them know about this part of the plan.

"Stop or I'll shoot him," Marino hollers, turning us around to face the advancing men.

"McDermott is approaching from oceanside," Caleb says in my ear. "I have a clean shot."

I subtly shake my head. That kill belongs to Gia, and we can't give away the ace up our sleeve. Not yet. We need to draw the remaining men out first.

"Your leadership is weak," Marino shouts to the men as they slow down in front of us. "The Accardi twins don't run their *famiglia*, I do." He puffs out his chest as he presses the muzzle deeper. "I am the one who calls the shots, not them."

"Fucking delusional prick," Caleb hisses in my ear.

"These men know where their loyalties lie," he says, gesturing to the group at his side.

"Yeah, they do, jackass." Caleb chuckles, and I work hard to smother a smirk.

"Join us. Join the winning side before it's too late. By morning, we will have a brand-new Commission, a new president, and competent new leaders will restore order to our great city.

Don't find yourself on the losing side because that is guaranteed death."

Calabro laughs, lowering his weapon as he saunters toward us like he hasn't got a care in the world. "You're outmaneuvered," he says as McDermott arrives with a few hundred men.

"Hand the prick to me," Liam says, stalking toward me.

"Your brother is out there somewhere," Marino warns, keeping a grip on my arm as he turns us around, keeping me tucked to his front like a shield, with his men at the rear.

"Get ready, brother," Caleb whispers in my ear.

I subtly slide the knife out from my sleeve, maneuvering it into position.

"Three, two, one. Go!"

I lunge at Liam just as he reaches me, slashing at his hand, and he drops his weapon automatically, yelping with pain. I slam the knife down into his thigh, careful to avoid the artery because Gia deserves torture time with the raping bastard. He crumples to the ground as Marino pulls the trigger. Men swarm past me, forming a shield around us as fighting breaks out and gunshots are traded.

O'Hara charges forward from the left with a team of one hundred, and they quickly join the melee. I grin as I turn around and shove Marino back at *his men*. "The chamber's empty, and you're a lying, cheating piece of shit who deserves to die with no honor."

"Shoot him!" Marino yells at his men, and I nod at Capo DiNardo.

The men grab his arms and restrain Marino as shots whizz over our heads and the sounds of battle surround us.

"What the hell are you doing?" Marino roars, panic splayed across his weathered face.

"We had a better offer," DiNardo says as I walk up and slowly drive my knife straight through my underboss's heart.

"You don't know what you've done," he garbles. Blood pours down his chest and bubbles in his mouth.

"Burn in hell where you belong, Benedito," I say, slashing his throat repeatedly. Blood sprays over my face and my clothes as I loom over the man who betrayed our *famiglia*, our *soldati*, and The Commission. His body jerks for a couple of seconds before he dies. "Toss him and join the fight," I tell the men who have returned to the fold.

We built dossiers on all of them, and we're holding their loved ones over their heads to force them to toe the line. What they don't know is when this is all over, they'll be slaughtered for breaking *omerta*.

No one betrays my family and lives to see another day.

Men stream onto the grass from all sides, and we've got the upper numbers. Grabbing two handguns from my hips, I enter the battle, popping off shots as we decimate the enemy, but something doesn't feel right. It's too easy, and this mysterious Italian hasn't shown his face.

"Incoming!" Caleb yells. "Fuck, they're coming from the sewers."

I shoot a guy in the face before I whip around, spotting men literally pouring out of holes in the road behind us.

"Jesus fucking Christ!" Fiero yells. "Look oceanside. More men are coming."

"It's a fucking submarine!" Massimo shouts. "They have a fucking submarine."

Hordes of men charge at us from the ocean and the road, and we're going to be submerged if we don't call in our reserve forces now. Don Greco is on the verge of giving that order when a voice booms out over a loudspeaker and blaring lights bear down on all of us, blinding everyone. The gunfire stops as everyone struggles to see over the blinding light thrust at us from the ocean.

"Tell your men to put their weapons down, Massimo. I know you're out there calling the shots. Give the order, or they'll all be slaughtered."

"What the actual fuck?" Leo says, and I follow his line of sight to where a man is being carried toward us on a high-backed chair by four tall, strong men, like he's a fucking king.

Someone stumbles into me from behind, and I whip around with my gun raised. Our men are being pushed back by the swarms of men who have emerged from the sewers. Noxious smells waft in the air as I spot a familiar face walking toward me. We didn't have proof of his betrayal, but I'm not surprised to see him. I wondered when he'd surface.

"Accardi." Cruz DiPietro smirks as he points a gun at my face while I point mine at his chest.

We're surrounded on two sides, and even though there's a current ceasefire, everyone is tense and on alert. Weapons are poised in every direction.

"Don't," I say in warning to Caleb. If he shoots Cruz, his men will retaliate, and we're currently outnumbered.

"Don't what? Shoot you?" Cruz laughs.

"What the fuck are you doing, Cruz?" Cristian calls out.

He glowers at his younger brother. "Taking back what's mine."

"Tell your men now, Massimo," a man with a loudspeaker says as he approaches us. "They must lower their weapons, or we'll slaughter them all."

The lights shining from the submarine are lowered enough to see without being blinded.

"No fucking way." Shock is splayed across Leo's face as he clearly recognizes the man with the loudspeaker.

The man being carried on the chair is set down in front of us, and he's old as dirt. The few strands of hair left on his head are flimsy and gray. Dark beady eyes radiate with smug supremacy as he stares at Ben and Leo, his deeply lined face moving as his narrow lips pull into a smile.

"This can't be happening," Fiero says in my ear.

"You died," Ben says, looking every bit as shocked as Leo. "Both of you died at the warehouse bombing years ago."

"Come now, Bennett," the old dude says, his voice stronger than his frail appearance. "Surely you don't believe in ghosts?" A wheezy chuckle rips from his lips.

"Who are you?" I ask because I'm struggling to place these men.

"Show respect for Don Maximo Greco," the man with the loudspeaker says.

"What?" Cristian looks as confused as me.

That creep died years ago, didn't he?

"Are you deaf, boy?" loudspeaker guy says. He's older too though not as old as the prick on the chair who looks like he could kick the bucket at any moment. I wouldn't shed any tears if he did. This guy looks like he's late forties or maybe early fifties, and he looks familiar.

Suddenly it clicks.

I wrack my brain to remember his name. We were fourteen when the warehouse bombing happened, killing most of the dons in the US along with some of their men and a few heirs.

"You're Primo Greco," I say as his name comes to me. "You're Massimo's older brother."

He nods. "I'm the rightful heir and your new president. All men will swear an oath to me or die."

The story continues in *Cruel King of New York*.
Available now.

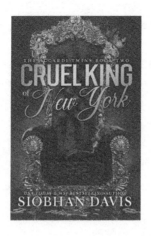

The boy I grew up loving is now the made man who broke my heart.

I had one primary goal in life: to marry Don Caleb Accardi, give him lots of babies, and live happily ever after.

Until he shattered my fantasy and destroyed my belief in love.

His playboy status isn't the issue. I learned to live with his womanizing while patiently waiting on the sideline for him to truly notice me.

But he never has. Not the way I want him to.

One promise. That's all I asked of him, and he couldn't even keep it.

Something inside me dies when I learn the truth, and I reach my breaking point.

This is the last time he hurts me.

I'm not saving myself for him anymore.

So, I cut him out of my life and begin dating.

Caleb sure doesn't like that, and a switch has flipped in his brain.

Now, he wants me. And he's pulling out all the stops to win back my heart.

Too bad it's too late—for him and for me.

Because Caleb has powerful enemies who are aware he loves me, and now I'm fair game.

Available now in ebook, paperback, alternate paperback and audio.

About the Author

Siobhan Davis™ is a *USA Today, Wall Street Journal,* and Amazon Top 5 bestselling romance author. **Siobhan** writes emotionally intense stories with swoon-worthy romance, complex characters, and tons of unexpected plot twists and turns that will have you flipping the pages beyond bedtime! She has sold over 2 million books, and her titles are translated into several languages.

Prior to becoming a full-time writer, Siobhan forged a successful corporate career in human resource management.

She lives in the Garden County of Ireland with her husband and two sons.

You can connect with Siobhan in the following ways:

Website: www.siobhandavis.com
Facebook: AuthorSiobhanDavis
Instagram: @siobhandavisauthor
Tiktok: @siobhandavisauthor
Email: siobhan@siobhandavis.com

Books By Siobhan Davis

NEW ADULT ROMANCE
The One I Want Duet
Kennedy Boys Series
Rydeville Elite Series
All of Me Series
Forever Love Duet

NEW ADULT ROMANCE STAND-ALONES
Inseparable
Incognito
Still Falling for You
Holding on to Forever
Always Meant to Be
Tell It to My Heart

REVERSE HAREM
Sainthood Series
Dirty Crazy Bad Duet
Surviving Amber Springs (stand-alone)
Alinthia Series ^

DARK MAFIA ROMANCE
Mazzone Mafia Series
Vengeance of a Mafia Queen (stand-alone)
The Accardi Twins
Taking What's Mine*

YA SCI-FI & PARANORMAL ROMANCE
Saven Series
True Calling Series ^

---

*Coming 2024
^Currently unpublished but will be republished in due course.

www.siobhandavis.com

Made in the USA
Monee, IL
05 July 2024

61235276R00204